KEROUAC'S GHOST

ROBERT DAVIES

By the same author:
Calypso Warrior
Canada's Undeclared War

Cataloguing in publication data (Canada)

McGoogan, Kenneth, 1947-

 Kerouac's Ghost : a novel

 Previously published as: Visions of Kerouac.

 ISBN 1-895854-54-7

 I. Title

PS8575.G65V58 1996   C813'.54   C96-940801-3
PS9575.G65V58 1996
PR9199.3.M4242V58 1996

Our ever-evolving catalog is available
on the World Wide Web at:
http://www.rdppub.com

Ken McGoogan

Kerouac's Ghost

Robert Davies Publishing

MONTREAL–TORONTO–PARIS

Robert Davies Publishing,
311-4999 Saint-Catherine Street West
Westmount, Quebec, Canada H3Z 1T3.

This book may be ordered in Canada from
General Distribution Services
☎ 1-800-387-0141 / 1-800-387- 0172
📠 1-416-445-5967;

in the U.S.A., from General Distribution Services,
Suite 202, 85 River Rock Drive, Buffalo, NY 14287

☎ 1-800-805-1083

or call the publisher, toll-free throughout North America:
☎ 1-800-481-2440, 📠 1-888-RDAVIES

e-mail: rdppub@vir.com

Visit our Internet website: http://rdppub.com

The publisher takes this opportunity
to thank the Canada Council and the
Ministère de la Culture du Québec (Sodec)
for their continuing support of publishing.

"Walking on water wasn't built in a day."

Jack Kerouac

1.

Yes, I was Jack Kerouac, returned from the dead, my memories and feelings intact. Yet somehow I'd changed. Earlier that day I'd awoken disoriented, found myself standing on a two-lane highway surrounded by spectacular mountain peaks, my rucksack beside me in the dirt. What was I doing here? I'd no sooner formulated the question than it was magically answered: I had a mission to accomplish involving young Frankie McCracken, who was working as a fire lookout on Mount Jubilation.

For the past hour and a half I'd been climbing that mountain, switching back and forth through a forest of evergreens, and pondering how when you die you're transformed—especially your mind. Death is The Great Transmogrifier. You come out the other side but you're not the same person, not exactly. The body is the least of it. My memories persisted but my rhythms had changed, the way I thought and used language. Also certain attitudes, though I didn't know why.

This was in August of 1970, ten months after I'd finished drinking myself to death. The air grew thin while I talked to myself, the white-barked pines less bushy. Now painted rocks lined the trail—surely a sign I was approaching the lookout. I kept climbing, thought I heard a voice and then, yes, someone up ahead was strumming a guitar and singing. Thirty yards more and I could make out the words: *Don't know why there's no sun up in the sky, stormy weather. / Since my gal and I ain't together / it's raining all the time.*

Sounded like Frank Sinatra—the early Sinatra, but with an added sense of desolation. And that's when the first rush hit me, triggered by the singing, and I realized that in transformation I'd lost plenty, but also I'd gained. Images and scenes flooded me, incidents and episodes out of Frankie McCracken's past, and I hiked the last stretch of trail in time to the music: *Life is bare, gloom and misery everywhere, stormy weather.*

I rounded a final corner, emerged from the evergreens and stood staring up at a wooden fire tower straight out of the nineteen forties. An octagonal office, all eight windows open, perched thirty feet above me on four gigantic telephone poles. Still I couldn't see Frankie, hidden inside, but as he hit the bridge his voice made me shiver: *When she went away the blues walked in and met me / If she stays away that old rocking chair gonna get me.*

I strode towards the tower, still lugging my pack, and found myself joining in: *All I do is pray / The Lord above will let me / Walk in the sun once more.*

Frankie didn't miss a beat. He stepped over to the window on my side and looked down, still strumming. Now the visions came thick and fast, revealed vistas of experience, but we finished the song as a duet: *Can't go on, everything I had is gone, stormy weather / Since my gal and I ain't together / Keeps raining all the time, the time / Keeps raining all the time.*

We held that last note.

"Stormy weather?" I waved my hand at the sunshine, the cloudless sky, and broke into another Sinatra standard: *Blue skies smiling at me / Nothing but blue skies do I see.*

"I don't believe it!" Frankie slapped the window ledge. "A fellow Sinatra fan?"

I dropped my pack on the ground, wiped my brow with my forearm, then stood savoring the picture-postcard panorama: green trees, blue sky, jagged mountain peaks and, far below, a turquoise river winding through a shadowed valley.

Frankie called, "Come on up and check the view from here."

I climbed the wooden ladder that ran up one side of the tower to a platform. Frankie opened a trap door and I went up a second, shorter ladder into his office.

Here, besides the guitar, an old Harmony Sovereign leaning against one wall, he had a hardback chair, a wastebasket full of crumpled paper and a fold-out table that held a typewriter, a dictionary and a typewritten manuscript. Everything from the waist up was open windows. I looked out: "This is incredible."

"Here, try these." He handed me binoculars. "Put the cord around your neck."

Frankie was half a head taller than me, and slimmer, but we had the same coal-black hair, the same blue eyes, and we were both struck by the physical resemblance. My unexpected arrival at this, the most isolated fire lookout in the Rockies, had excited Frankie, and I was almost swept away by the torrent of images out of his past.

I peered through the binoculars, focusing with difficulty, but he babbled oblivious: "Directly opposite, that's Mount Murchison. Local Indians used to think it was the tallest mountain in the world. There's the highway—that necklace in the forest. And see where the Saskatchewan River meets the Howse? That's Saskatchewan River Crossing. The early fur traders used to travel through that pass. But, hey, you must be thirsty."

Frankie handed me a thermos of water.

I said thanks and took a swig. "How high are we, anyway?"

"Seven thousand feet."

"And the mountains around us?"

"Most are ten-thousand-six or ten-seven. The one we're on, Jubilation, is ten-nine."

"Mountain goats, look!" I peered again through the glasses. "This reminds me of my own days as a fire lookout."

"You worked as a lookout?"

"Down in Washington. The Cascades. I was on Desolation Peak."

"No kidding! That's where Kerouac worked. When were you there?"

"Let's see. Must have been 1956."

"Wow! You don't look that old! I forget when Kerouac was there, exactly, but it was in the mid-fifties. Ever run into him? Jack Kerouac?"

"Maybe I should introduce myself." I let the binoculars fall to my chest and held out my hand. "My name's Jack Kerouac."

"Hey, that's not bad." Frankie laughed and took my hand. "Jack? I'm Friedrich Nietzsche."

"No, you're not. You're Frankie McCracken."

"Ha! This gets better and better! Come to think of it, you do resemble the King of the Beats. But haven't you heard? Kerouac died last October."

"Drank myself to death," I said, turning again to stare through the binoculars. "Not to worry, though. As you can see, I'm still on the road."

"Uncle!" Frankie clutched his head and did a spinning dance. "Uncle! Uncle!"

2.

If it's not otherwise memorable, a first time is a first time and is seldom forgotten. So it is even after you've given up the ghost, or become one, and for the resurrected me, Mount Jubilation was a first. As I hiked up the trail to the lookout, images and scenes whirling at me out of Frankie McCracken's past, I realized I'd plunged into a kaleidoscope of personal history—that day's second magical twist.

I've already mentioned the first, which began with me waking, disoriented, on a two-lane highway surrounded by mountain peaks. I was still blinking, wondering what I was doing there, when a top-down cinnamon-red Lincoln-Continental convertible roared around the bend and squealed to a halt. Behind the wheel sat an ethereal blonde in a white bikini. A cosmic joke, this initial bit of voodoo, because a famous editor had made me cut just such an incident: "It's unbelievable, Jack. Doesn't matter if it happened."

Grinning madly, chortling even, I swung my rucksack into the back seat and hopped over the door into the front. Like the original, this dynamite blonde was maybe twenty-two years old, but she spoke English with a French accent—a lovely twist. She said her name was Camille and, with a wave of her hand, identified the mountains around us: *Les Rocheuses*. We tooled west along the Trans-Canada and then north up Highway 93, the Banff-Jasper Highway, with me oohing and aahing at the scenery and the crisp, clean air, at the elk and horned sheep roaming wild.

Camille told me I was on my way to visit a young guy working as a fire lookout on Mount Jubilation, halfway between Banff and Jasper. "Frankie McCracken's a long-time fan. He's in his early twenties, your basic rucksack warrior. He spent a year in San Francisco, watched the Haight-Ashbury go bad. Hails from Montreal."

"He's French?"

"Half and half—*comme toi*. She pronounced it "tway," *à la Québécoise*. "His father's half-French and his mother partly Acadian. *Sa langue maternelle, c'est l'anglais*. But he grew up in a French town: Sainte-Thérèse-sur-le-lac?"

"I remember now!" A fragment came back. "This is the guy I've bet on!"

"Frankie's your kick at the can, Jack." She pulled over onto the shoulder. "Today's August thirty-first. You've got three days."

Camille let me out at a sign saying "Jubilation Lookout, 4.5 miles," then waved and zoomed off up the highway, gone from me forever. I shouldered my pack and followed a rutted road into the pine-smelling forest. Soon I came to a wooden bridge, where I leaned over the railing and watched an angry river twist and roar through a steep-walled canyon.

For the next hour I hiked through a forest of fir, spruce and lodgepole pine, enjoying the feeling of

13

being alive, even the buzz of the black flies and the stink of bear droppings. The trail grew steeper, switched back and forth, and as I climbed I talked to myself about The Great Transmogrifier. Then I heard Frankie singing—and that's when the rushes began. More magic.

By evening I'd learned to distinguish sequences of experience and patterns of meaning, but initially, in the flashing bombardment, I could discern only scenes and occasional episodes. I remember focusing on Frankie at age nineteen. He'd long since moved into Montreal, into the heart of downtown, but here he was sitting in the kitchen of his parents' house in the nearby town of Sainte-Thérèse, performing in a familiar duet.

"It's time you settled down, young man," his mother said. "Got yourself a steady job."

"Why would I want to do that? I'm having the time of my life."

"You should get a job, move back home and start helping out with the bills."

"Mother, your bills aren't my problem."

"Not your problem! Maurice, you're his father! You tell him!"

His father was making for the back door, hammer and nails in hand. "You can't tell these guys anything, Maggie. He'll find out."

"Damn right I will."

His father went out the door into the yard.

"Anyway, mother, I'm going to Mexico."

"Mexico?" His mother said. "What are you talking about, Mexico?" She'd finished washing the dishes and poured the dishwater down the sink, careful not to splash any on her flowered housedress. "Frankie, you're nineteen years old. Have you gone mad?"

14

He tilted his chair back on two legs, folded his arms across his chest and sighed loudly. No use. His mother continued: "Collecting unemployment insurance. A big hulking brute like you." She made a clicking sound with her tongue. "It's a disgrace."

"I'm going to be a writer, mother. I need experience."

Frankie had just spent several weeks in southern Ontario, priming and hanging tobacco. He'd saved five hundred dollars—a small fortune—and didn't intend to fritter it away.

"Well, I don't understand it." His mother took a dish cloth out from behind the stove and began drying dishes. "Mexico? You could get experience right here in Sainte-Thérèse if you put your mind to it."

"What do you want me to do?" Frankie snapped his chair upright. "Go back to delivering *Gazettes*?"

"You had a good job at that personnel agency. Why don't you go back to something like that?"

"I don't want a job, that's why." Frankie stood up so he could tower over her. "I'm going to be famous. Famous, understand?"

"Oh, Frankie, you're talking foolishness. Your father wanted to be an actor, a movie star. Look what happened to him."

"He didn't have my talent."

"You don't think so? Well, mister, if you're so talented, what have you accomplished?"

"What have I accomplished?" Astonished, Frankie appealed to the ceiling. "Eighteen years old, I was interviewing people for jobs. Youngest vocational counsellor in the history of the agency. What have I accomplished?" He paced back and forth, waving his arms, between the kitchen and the front room. "I've

been around, woman, that's what. I've lived in
Toronto. I've lived in New York City."

"Yes, for three weeks."

"Greenwich Village? Frankie McCracken lived
there! I've picked tobacco in southern Ontario, hitchhiked to Winnipeg and back. I've visited Boston and
Chicago."

"Oh, for the love of God."

"What have I accomplished? I've read the great
books, mother! Miller, Dostoevsky, Nietszche! Don't
try to tell me. I've read Kerouac! All things are lawful
to the superman. All things possible."

"You've done nothing for the past six months
but gallivant around the country or sit on your back-
side in that dirty little room."

"I've been writing, remember? Writing!"

"So what have you published?"

"That isn't the point, mother." Stung, Frankie
brought his face close to hers and opened his eyes
wide. "Don't you know anything?"

"You're going off half-cocked, that's all I know.
When you could be staying home here and helping
out with the bills."

"Bills?" Frankie grabbed his jean jacket from the
back of a chair. "I just lent you twenty-five bucks. What
do you want, blood?"

Two steps and he was out the door.

"A no-good drunken bum!" Dish-cloth in hand,
red-faced, his mother followed him to the top of the
stairs. "That's what you're turning into. A good-for-
nothing alcoholic, just like your father!"

"That's right!" Frankie stormed out the pebbled
driveway, yelling over his shoulder: "I'm going to be
just like my father! Just like him, I tell you!"

16

3.

Have I mentioned the rushes? Trying to make sense of shifting images while they tumbled around in a three-dimensional kaleidoscope? Here was Frankie McCracken in Chicago, nineteen years old, lugging a giant duffle bag through late-night empty streets. There he was in a rubber wetsuit, jacket and trousers both, riding a tractor into a tobacco field in southern Ontario. Now here was Frankie in New York City, trying to pacify an angry ex-footballer with a peanut butter sandwich. And oops! there he was as a boy, lying in bed in the tiny Quebec town of Sainte-Thérèse, listening for the long, lonely whistle of the train from Montreal, and waiting for his father.

All through the afternoon and evening they kept coming, these visions, and I thought I was getting the knack of it, of processing and functioning both, when Frankie brought me back to Mount Jubilation with a fair-enough question: "How'd you know my name anyway?"

He'd waited until bed time. We were in the one-room cabin. I was rooting around in my rucksack for a flashlight, getting ready to take my sleeping bag outside, and Frankie was using the flickering light of the kerosene lamp to make finger shadows on the wall.

That afternoon, before quitting the tower, I'd said something about sleeping under the stars, how sublime it would be at this elevation.

"You've got a sleeping bag?" Frankie said. "You're welcome to spend the night."

Later he'd given me the grand tour—showed me the weather instruments, the wood-chopping block, the path to the stream where he fetched water. Then the tool shed and the outhouse, tilted crazily into the mountain, and finally this cabin in the trees.

The cabin, like the out-buildings, had been painted regulation maroon. Around it someone had built a fence of trimmed white logs—probably the same lunatic who'd lined the nearby paths with painted stones. Inside the cabin: a gas burner, a wood stove, a sagging bunk and a built-in table with a moveable bench. Also a doorless cupboard, a wide shelf arrayed with canned goods and, instead of a sink, an old dishpan. Two-by-four girts ran horizontally between studs and served as shelves, mostly for books.

We'd tucked into dinner, baked beans and carrots and rice, and washed it down with apple cider. Then, as I made coffee, I noticed that Frankie was sinking into a depression—he was remembering Camille—so I started reminiscing about my sixty-three days on Desolation Peak: "For a while I thought I'd found the perfect arrangement. Two months of each year I'd be an exemplary Buddhist, a Mahayana fire lookout chopping wood, writing haiku and praying for all living creatures. The rest of the time I'd live cheaply in Mexico."

"You don't expect prompting?"

"The loneliness wore me down. And Hozomeen! Mount Hozomeen looming in my window."
Frankie snorted and shook his head: "You've
got this Kerouac rap down pat, haven't you?"
I grinned at him.

As we did the dishes, I felt Frankie sinking again
and said, "You're lucky to have a separate fire tower.
Some other place to go. On Desolation the lookout
was all one building—just a cabin with windows."

"This has advantages," he agreed, "but what
about lightning storms? To mark strikes, I have go
outside and climb up into that sucker. All you had to
do was roll out of bed."

"Fair enough, but how's it go?" I swung into a
take-off on Stormy Weather: *Way up high, there is
lightning in the sky, stormy weather.*

Maybe you had to be there, but Frankie laughed
and we began comparing notes on Old Blue Eyes. I
told him how on Desolation I'd stand at the edge of
the cliff and shout Sinatra standards into the wind: *I'll
Never Smile Again, They Say It's Wonderful, All or
Nothing At All.*

Between songs, I said it was unusual, someone
his age—"what? twenty-three?"—relishing Sinatra.
Turned out Frankie owed the man his first name: "My
father's a Sinatra nut. Caught his act in Montreal."

"Back in the forties? I saw him then myself, at
Carnegie Hall—me and two thousand screaming fe-
males. Sinatra wore a white suit, sang *Mighty Like a Rose.*

Frankie made eyes at the ceiling, because how
could someone my age have caught Old Blue Eyes in
his prime? But he said: "Nobody could sing like the
early Sinatra. That magic voice. And clarity?"

"His enunciation was exquisite. And what about
his phrasing? The way he'd sing a song, not according
to its melodic structure, but the fall of the words."

19

"Learned that from Bing, my father said."

The dishes done, Frankie picked up his guitar. Somewhere along the line he'd mastered not only bar chords but diminished sevenths and augmented fifths and soon we were crooning Sinatra hits: *Imagination, Without A Song, Everything Happens To Me*. Finally we did such a rousing rendition of *Stardust* that we dissolved into laughter and Frankie set aside his guitar knowing we'd never get higher.

By now it was ten o'clock, bed-time, and I stood up and stretched. I untied my sleeping bag and rooted for the flashlight and that's when Frankie, idly making finger shadows by lantern-light, asked casually, "How'd you know my name, anyway?"

I said, "Frankie, I know everything about you."

"Stop putting me on. Who are you?"

"I told you. I'm Jack Kerouac."

"Okay, Kerouac, who's Dean Moriarty?"

"The hero of *On The Road*. In real life, my best old buddy, Neal Cassady."

"Japhy Ryder?"

"Gary Snyder. Come on, Frankie, you can do better than that."

"Which Kerouac novel was about life on the fire lookout? Or, no. That's too easy. Which one focused on Kerouac's French-Canadian boyhood in Maine?"

"Nice try, Frankie. I didn't grow up in Maine, but in Lowell, Massachussetts. Stinktown on the Merrimack, my father called it. *Dr. Sax? Visions of Gerard? Maggie Cassidy?* I treated my boyhood in all of them. *The Town and The City*, too, except there I buried the French-Canadian side. And I wrote about my days on Desolation in three different books."

"All right, so you know Kerouac's work. Proves nothing."

20

"I've got nothing to prove." I located my flashlight and waved it triumphantly. "Knew it was here somewhere."

I stood up to go.

"One more glass!" Without waiting for an answer, Frankie poured us each another tumbler of cider. "Okay, let's pretend you're Kerouac," he said, then shifted smoothly into *joual*, that slangy Quebecois French only natives and their descendents understand: "*Qu'est-ce tu fais icitte?*"

That's when I realized whose rhythms I was borrowing. I hadn't known because I'd taken the French in my mind for granted. Why not? All my life I'd dreamed and heard prophecies in that language. "*Tu ne lâches pas, toi!*" I said. "You don't let go! You invited me."

Frankie laughed but persisted in French: "What do you take me for? An idiot? I never invited you."

"*Mais oui, tu l'as fais!*" I rattled on in *joual* for the sheer joy of it: "Sure, you did! Remember last January, the day you climbed Tunnel Mountain? Discovered the cabin on top, all boarded up for the winter? You were peeking in the windows when you realized it was a fire lookout. The kind of place Old Kerouac had written about in *Desolation Angels*."

Now I had his attention.

"Back in town you ran into a fellow dish-washer from the Banff Springs Hotel. He told you some government types were coming to town next day, that they'd be interviewing people for summer jobs in the park—and fire lookout was one of them. Later, at home in your two-room cabin, you waved your hands in the air and did a dance: 'Kerouac! Kerouac! Be with me now!' *C'etait bien un invitation, non?*"

Frankie reverted to English: "Where'd you learn all this?"

I followed him into his native tongue. "I don't fully understand it myself. Somehow we're linked outside Time. I get flashes."

"What are you doing here?"

"Frankie, you need help."

"Help? With what?"

"How's *Funeral Song* coming?" His stalled novel.

"That's nothing." He waved dismissively. "You saw the manuscript on the table in the tower."

"You think so? And what about Camille?"

"That's it!" Frankie slapped his forehead. "You've been talking to Camille! She's the only one who knew about that little dance and 'Kerouac! Kerouac! Be with me now.'" He laughed and shook his head. "For a moment there you had me going. How is Camille, anyway?"

"She's faring better than you—though I've never met her in the flesh."

"Why don't we cut the crap?"

Secretly, I relished his resistance, but I said, "Frankie, lighten up." I emptied my glass, put on my jacket and picked up my sleeping bag and flashlight. "Come see the stars."

Frankie knocked back the last of his cider.

We went out the door, stepped off the porch and strolled to the middle of the white-fenced yard. The night air was cool, the sky alive with stars.

"That's Cygnus, directly above us," I said. "The Northern Cross. God, what a night. There's Hercules. And Draco, the serpent. Look! A shooting star."

"Really a meteorite. Should I make a wish?"

The star rocketed across Cygnus and disappeared.

"Remember when you were twelve years old, Frankie? And your least favorite chore was bringing the rent money to Madame Francoeur?"

22

For a few seconds, Frankie was silent. Then he said, "Yeah?"

"Somebody robbed you—stole the rent money. That night you stood in your back yard in Sainte-Thérèse, looking up at the star-spangled night. You swore on a shooting star that you'd repay your mother—every last penny, remember?"

Frankie stood staring up at the sky. Finally he said, "I never told anybody that. Not even Camille."

I put on my best W. C. Fields' voice: "Right you are, my boy."

Back in my own voice, I said, "Sleep tight."

Then spun on my heel and walked out the gate.

4.

There's no city like the first city, and for Frankie McCracken at seventeen, eighteen, even nineteen years old, that first city was Montreal. He said goodbye to the town he'd grown up in, to Sainte-Thérèse-sur-le-lac, in the fall of 1964, and spent the next two years falling in love with Montreal. Three times he left and went on the road—dry runs, though he didn't realize it, for his San Francisco Vision Quest—but never for more than weeks at a stretch, and returning always to stock-pile more memories.

For Frankie McCracken at seventeen, eighteen, even nineteen years old, Montreal became a whirl of images and associations, of red-brick apartment buildings and odd-smelling rooming houses, of fast food in cheap restaurants, movies in theatres both uptown and down, English and French, and live music in folk clubs and *boîtes à chanson* and down-and-dirty bars like the Black Bottom and the Esquire Showbar, this last going strong until three in the morning, so he'd turn up after midnight if he found himself alone and the crew-cut bouncer would wave him past the line-up for tables and he'd perch on a stool at the bar, knock back a Molson's and lose himself in the frenzied magic of rhythm and blues.

Montreal's where it began, Frankie's conscious obsession with me and my work. So I discovered on Mount Jubilation by seizing the moment. December, 1965. Suddenly here's Frankie in a downtown bookstore, the long-gone Mansfield Bookmart, leafing through a paperback copy of *On The Road*. He's decked out in a blue-pinstripe suit, a white shirt and tie, his overcoat open—a Young Turk with something to prove. He's six feet tall, also dark and intense. Yes, and handsome, too: slim and fit and not yet nineteen. In high school he'd been an athlete.

Myself he knew only by reputation, as King of the Beats: a wild-man writer in the tradition of Jack London and Thomas Wolfe, two of his father's old favorites. The connection made him uneasy, but recently he'd resolved to bury the past, let bygones be bygones, and so he took out his wallet and brought my novel to the counter.

Nine o'clock that night, intending to read for twenty minutes, half an hour, Frankie again picked up *On The Road*. The novel hit him like the fulfillment of some half-forgotten prophecy. He didn't put it down until two in the morning, when he finished it. Impossible, then, to sleep.

Frankie swung out of bed, pulled on blue jeans and bulky sweater, overshoes and duffle coat, then plunged into the winter night. The cold didn't bother him, though he could see his breath as he strode the empty, snow-banked streets, waving his arms and talking to himself—the mad ones, yes! He ended up at Ben's Delicatessen, where he downed a lean smoked-meat sandwich on rye, dill pickle on the side. And decided he was due for a holiday.

Frankie was working at a personnel agency as a "vocational counsellor," really a glorified salesclerk, and hadn't yet made his monthly quota of "placements." Even so, he phoned in sick next morning and spent the day scouring bookstores for my novels. *The Dharma Bums* and *The Subterraneans*, *Big Sur* and *Dr. Sax* and even *The Town and The City* — Frankie found them. As Christmas came and went, slowed only by seasonal revelry, Frankie raced through them. Early in the new year, when *Desolation Angels* appeared in hardcover, he celebrated his nineteenth birthday by staying home from the agency and reading about life on a fire lookout.

What was it about me and my work that attracted Frankie? Certainly my poor-boy biases and French-Canadian cadences rang familiar—my *pauvre Emil* this and *tiens, Ti Jean* that. Above all, though, Frankie relished my yea-saying exuberance, my wild shouting joy at being alive. Six months before, he'd discovered Henry Miller and followed him back to his heroes, to the Four Horsemen of his Apocalypse, among them Dostoevsky and Nietzsche. From there Frankie had stumbled into Sartre and Camus, into Kierkegaard and Heidegger and Walter Kaufmann, and can you imagine trying to make your way through this maze of God-is-deadness without guidance?

At the risk of sounding immodest, I report what arrived in a rush on Mount Jubilation. Somehow, my work shook Frankie awake. It showed him that he'd got lost in a labyrinth designed by middle-aged Europeans, reminded him that he was young and North American. In my celebration of experience, Frankie found a thread he hadn't realized he was seeking. Experience! That was it! To become a writer he needed first-hand experience.

This revelation put Frankie on the road—the archetypal, rutted and winding road that, in his case, wound through Chicago and New York and Psychedelic San Francisco, twisted and turned through the valley of death and rebirth and eventually spiraled off to apocalypse. But this won't do. I'm getting ahead of the story as it came to me on Jubilation.

A few months after he fell in love with my work, and while still socking away funds for his Great Escape, Frankie got fired from his job at the personnel agency. He'd met an attractive ex-job-seeker, an erstwhile agency client, at a down-and-dirty bar and imagined—such was his naivete—that she'd appreciate his ferreting out her old application form to discover her height and weight and where she'd gone to high school.

The firing plunged him penniless into his new life, though psychologically he was overdue. No thought of looking for a new job. Instead, with a ne'er-do-well friend named Duggins, a fellow would-be writer, Frankie hitchhiked to Toronto. Covered the distance, three hundred and forty-odd miles, in three rides, nothing to it, and went to visit Dixon, an old basketball buddy.

A couple of years before, Dixon had dropped out of high school and moved to Toronto to live with his sister. But she had an inconvenient boyfriend and recently he'd answered an advertisement to share a one-bedroom apartment with an "older guy" named Charles, who was all of twenty-eight. The place was on Jameson Avenue in the west end, on the fourteenth floor of a highrise. Hardwood floors, fridge and stove, a small balcony—it was perfect. Dixon said the newcomers could crash as long as they helped out with the rent. Party time.

Two weeks into this arrangement, tired of the juvenile carousing, Charles moved out, just disap-

peared one afternoon, taking his furniture with him.
An old record player and a couple of Bob Dylan
albums belonged to Dixon, and those he left behind.
Also a few dog-eared paperbacks.

Who cared? The hide-a-bed they missed, and the
table and chairs, because now they had no place to sit
except on the floor. The only real problem, though,
was the rent. Dixon was struggling to pay off a new
sports car, a Triumph TR-3, while working as a stock-
control clerk. To get the job he'd lied, claimed he'd
graduated from high school. Lately his boss had been
asking to see written proof. Dixon insisted that he'd
sent for the records.

Every morning he'd crawl out of his sleeping
bag and stumble around the apartment getting
dressed in the dark. Duggins would open one eye and
complain: "Jesus, Dixon! Show some consideration."

Duggins kept promising to borrow salvation
money from his father, a management consultant who
lived there in T.O. But he never got around to doing
it. In the secret pocket of his houndstooth jacket, he'd
stashed fifteen dollars and figured nobody knew. Instead of spending it, though, he mooched.

As for Frankie, before leaving Montreal he'd
applied for unemployment insurance. These were the
sixties, after all: boom times would last forever and the
world owed writers a living. A friend who'd sublet his
bachelor pad had promised to forward all cheques,
but as yet he'd sent nothing.

Frankie decided Canada Manpower was the
answer, get some temporary work. The hard part was
reaching the Manpower centre before six in the morning, when the dispatcher doled out jobs. Duggins kept
promising to join him in the crush, but never managed
to emerge from his sleeping bag.

28

One day Frankie loaded cartons of tomatoes onto trucks. Another he spent out front of a factory using a pike-like tool to pick up paper, cardboard and banana peels. Then he emptied a warehouse of automobile parts—bumpers and steering wheels and boxes full of seat belts—and almost crippled himself. Frankie decided that maybe Duggins had the right approach. Let Dixon head off to work. He'd stay on the floor in his sleeping bag.

Trouble was, cooped up, penniless, in a fourteenth-floor apartment, Frankie and Duggins began developing their own vocabulary, a private language of macho posturing. The trick was to be as patronizing and disdainful as possible, and the key phrase was Do It Or Back Down. They started with large assertions—with Duggins declaring that soon he'd be drinking rum in Jamaica, mon, or Frankie boasting that, before he was twenty, he'd publish The Great North American Novel.

Gradually, they worked their way down to smaller issues, until finally one of them would say, "I'm going to make a peanut-butter sandwich," or, "I think I'll take a shower," and instantly the other would challenge him: "Go ahead, talker. Do it or back down."

Then, if you didn't do it, whatever It was, you were a coward, a craven milksop, a whey-faced poltroon, or perhaps a spineless sniveller whose entire balled-up courage would look like BB-shot rolling down a four-lane highway.

Probably you had to be there.

Dixon caught the virus, of course, and all three young men began pushing it, this Do-It-Or-Back-Down Game. One evening, as they sat leaning against various walls in the living room, eating spaghetti drenched with ketchup, Dixon said, "This tastes awful."

Duggins said, "You'll eat it, talker, and like it."

29

Dixon looked up in mock astonishment. He was the strongest of them, a muscular six-three, though Duggins was heavier. "Duggins, I don't like your attitude."

"Now wait a minute, guys," Frankie said. "This is the only food in the house."

This Duggins ignored: "What are you going to do about it?"

The point of no return. Everybody started to laugh. Dixon said: "I'm going to shove this plate of spaghetti into your face."

"Do it, talker. Do it or back down."

That's how the final free-for-all began. Dixon tried to make good on his threat but Duggins ducked and most of the spaghetti hit the wall. Duggins ran to the stove while Dixon, laughing despite himself, shook his finger in the air: "I'm warning you, pal."

Duggins put the remaining noodles on a plate, added ketchup, then wheeled and raced across the room. Dixon ducked. The spaghetti landed in Frankie's lap and suddenly there they were, three overgrown five-year-olds in a highrise apartment, flinging food and fighting for water taps.

Dixon was emerging as undisputed king until Duggins grabbed the broom and began swinging it like a staff, yelling, "Stand aside, varlet! Let the better man pass!"

Dixon took a few whacks in the shoulder but managed to grab the broom. The two of them crashed against the balcony door before tumbling onto the floor, wrestling and punching now in earnest.

"What's going on in there?" This from the front door, where somebody was hammering: "Hey! Open up!"

The boys froze. Frankie called, "Who is it?"

"The superintendent! Open up or I'll call the cops."

30

Nobody else made a move, so Frankie went to the door, opened it a crack and explained that they'd been practising jujitsu. That they weren't properly dressed and couldn't invite him inside. "But if we're bothering our fellow tenants, we'll stop right away."

The usual adolescent arrogance. But the red-faced super didn't want trouble. He growled that next time he'd call the cops and strode away down the hall. Frankie closed the door and leaned against it: "That's it for me, jokers. I'm pulling a Kerouac."

"Do it, talker," came the derisive chorus. "Do it or back down."

5.

Did I mention my stay on Desolation Peak? Summer, 1956? Often at night I'd sit reading by the light of an old kerosene lantern. I remember a book called *The God That Failed,* which consisted of confessions of ex-communists who had repented when they discovered the totalitarian beastliness of the system they'd worshipped. All about spies and dictators, plots and assassination attempts, people fighting for the sake of fighting, purges and failed revolutions and murders at midnight. Depressing stuff.

Yet I remember my fascination, and the marvellous strangeness of reading that in February 1922, one month before I was born, such-and-such was happening in Moscow and something else in the streets of Vienna. How could there have been a Vienna, I wondered, or even a concept of Vienna, before I was born? The One Mental Nature rolls on, of course, regardless of individual arrivals and departures, indifferent to those who fare in this Nature and are fared in by it. Step back far enough and individual human beings dwindle to Nothingness.

Me, I don't like to remain at that distance. With Neal Cassady I spent countless hours laying out Timelines and looking for connections, for echoes and reflections, signs and synchronicities. And I remember lying in bed with my real-life "Mardou Fox," my quintessential Subterranean, the two of us realizing that in 1944, when I was twenty-two and she was thirteen, we were both living in New York City, and oh, God, let's see, at Easter you were downtown, rambling around Times Square? So was I! Maybe we passed each other in the street.

You can learn a lot by comparing chronologies. And when, outside of Time, I began laying out the life of Frankie McCracken, I discovered all the requisite parallels. The Celtic and French-Canadian heritage, tinged with Iroquois. The tragic father, the indomitable mother. The ubiquitous Catholicism. Later, the travels. The descent into the maelstrom.

On Mount Jubilation, that first night under the stars, it all came flooding back. I remembered that in Frankie I'd recognized the lineaments of an eternal travelling companion, the hapless Sancho Panza of my soul. In seeking to emulate me, Frankie had sought a difficult passage, one in which to develop humility, perseverance and love. The Kerouac family motto, as it happens, is *Aimer, Travailler, Souffrir*. To love, work and suffer. See the fit?

Plunging into the flesh always entails the risk of drowning in darkness, of forgetting yourself and so wasting a life. As Frankie-to-be stared into the maelstrom of Time, preparing to plunge, he heard a thousand voices buzzing with the Ancient Counsel: "No, no, don't do it! Don't be born! Darkness will engulf you!"

Frankie realized that thematic parallels might not blaze brightly enough. Knowing how I love to compare chronologies, he seized upon the idea of planting markers—signs and omens and portents—that, should he find himself in trouble, would almost certainly catch my eye.

Date of conception would be the first signpost, and Frankie thought initially to signify my father, who died of cancer in May of 1946. That meant being born in February of 1947, or maybe early March. He'd never be able to hang on until my own birthday, March 22, but he wanted a double signpost at birth and settled on one that would identify him with my blood-brother, Neal Cassady.

I'd met Neal in December of 1946, when he'd arrived in New York from Denver, and I was still getting to know him early the following year. Having discerned this and more, Frankie decided to enter the world prematurely, on Feb. 8, 1947—the day Neal Cassady turned twenty-one.

Yet still Frankie didn't feel safe.

He analyzed the geographic options available to his parents-in-waiting and, twenty miles northwest of Montreal, discovered the village of Sainte-Thérèse-sur-le-lac. Immediately he recognized the beauty and relevance of the town's profound Frenchness—that the ambience was more than convenient.

His father was half-French, of course, and his mother descended from *les Acadiens*. Yet Frankie fretted because his parents-to-be spoke mostly English together, where mine had spoken French. He himself would be able to find both French and English friends, but his mother, he knew, would insist on raising him Protestant, no matter where she was, and also on sending him to an English school.

The absolute Frenchness of Sainte-Thérèse would minimize the chance that Frankie would grow up too comfortably English. Likewise the Roman Ca-

tholicism that permeated the place. The two-lane highway that ran through the centre of town was called
Chemin Saint-Esprit. And the streets, most of which
ran south to the lake, had names like *Avenue des
Anges*, *Avenue des Archanges* and *Avenue des Oracles*.
And look at the Roman Catholic Church! Located further west up the highway towards Saint-Nar-
cisse, Sainte-Anne de la Providence and
Saint-Redempteur, the church was easily the most
spectacular edifice in town—all stained-glass windows and manicured lawns, and with a huge
wooden cross out front. On it there hung a plaster
statue of Jesus, larger than life-size and crowned with
thorns. Perfect.

The isolation did give him pause. For nine
months of the year, Sainte-Thérèse was home to just
three hundred souls. Yet in summer, because of the
lake and the sandy beach, the town became a poor-
man's resort, its population exploding into the thousands. People would organize bingo games in the
church basement, and a loud-speaker truck would roll
up and down the streets blaring: *Attention s'il-vous-
plaît. Grand Bingo demain soir à sept heures à l'église
Sainte-Thérèse-sur-le-lac. Mille dollars de prix à gag-
ner. Demain soir à l'eglise Sainte-Thérèse-sur-le-lac.
Bingo!*

The Frenchness of it all overcame most qualms.
But what finally decided Frankie was the town's name,
which invoked my all-time favorite saint, Saint Thérèse
de Lisieux—the Little Flower of Jesus. Frankie knew
that never, not even at the height of my Buddhist
phase, did I ever stop praying to the Little Flower. He
knew that "Ste-Thérèse" would serve as a final signpost for me, and so keep him safe in the dark.

Outside of Time, having decided, Frankie nudged
Destiny. His parents-to-be, Maurice McCracken and

Margaret (Maggie) Granger, had married in Halifax in 1944—a civil ceremony with one of Maurice's Air Force buddies acting as best man. When the war ended, the young couple moved to Montreal and rented a room in a downtown flat. For weeks Maggie complained about noise and crowdedness and urged her young husband to take her out of Montreal, to show her the surrounding countryside.

Finally Maurice, an amateur film-maker, roughed out a script that called, curiously enough, for desert scenes and mirages and also a body of water. Where to shoot these scenes? As a boy, Maurice had attended a family picnic in the north-shore town of Saint-Eustache. Vaguely, he remembered a lake.

Maurice convinced his movie-making partner—Henry owned the camera—of the need to scout locations. And one Sunday morning in May of 1946, he and Maggie piled into Henry's old car and drove north out of Montreal.

They crossed the Cartierville Bridge, then followed the twisting, two-lane highway as it meandered along Rivière-des-prairies through Saint-Martin, Sainte-Dorothée and Laval-Ouest. Finally they arrived in Saint-Eustache, where Maurice asked a gas station attendant for directions. The man told them to keep driving west, to follow the highway, *Chemin Saint-Esprit*, through Coeur d'Aimée to Sainte-Thérèse-sur-le-lac. Turn left at the hotel, *La Fin du Monde*, and they'd run right into the finest beach in the world.

They followed the man's directions, and as they rolled slowly down *Avenue des Archanges*, looking out at boarded-up summer houses, Maggie noticed signs saying, "*À Louer*." And in smaller type: "For Rent." At the beach, where a breeze was blowing in off the lake, Maggie remembered Nova Scotia. This is more like it, she thought. Only the seagulls are missing—and the smell of the salt sea air.

On the way back to the car, Henry having walked on ahead, Maggie said to Maurice, "This town wouldn't be a bad place to raise children."

"This is the sticks, Maggie! We'd die out here."

"Maurice, we're dying in the city!"

That night, Frankie plunged. And when he surfaced in Darkness on the eighth day of February, 1947—eight and a half months after the death of my father, and on the day that my blood-brother, Neal Cassady, turned twenty-one—Frankie McCracken did so in a drafty, three-room house in Sainte-Thérèse-sur-le-lac. Under the protection of the Little Flower of Jesus.

6.

Abizarre string of accidents and mishaps, Frankie would call it in Winnipeg. A wildly unlikely series of setbacks, reversals and personal calamities. In this general description he included the Chicago flophouse, the North Dakota jail cell and the looming perfidy of his would-be roadbuddy—feared and suspected, entirely predictable, as yet unacknowledged.

But even a fragmentary road tale, a brief rush of travelling *à la Kerouac*, cries out for linear treatment, so take it from Toronto, where The Original Plan featured Frankie and his friends heading West, all three. Vancouver, San Francisco, Mexico City—these were certainties. South America was a strong possibility.

After the sophomoric free-for-all on the fourteenth floor, and his declared intention to go on the road, Frankie laid out a Revised Version. Dixon would drive him from Toronto to Detroit, so precluding any hassle at the American border, and there he'd start hitchhiking. He'd hit Chicago, swing north through Winnipeg and set up a new base in Vancouver. Duggins and Dixon would follow, and together the three would embark on phase two.

Money was the challenge. Still, Frankie had thirty dollars—almost enough to make the trip—and Duggins owed him forty more. He'd spent his secret stash on cigarettes and beer, but also visited his father. The man had refused to lend him a penny—"can you believe that?"—but had phoned around and found him a furniture-moving job.

On Monday, Duggins would start lifting and carrying. Wednesday, he'd receive his first pay cheque. Thursday, Frankie would reach Winnipeg—and Duggins would wire him twenty dollars. The remainder he'd send to Vancouver the following week, care of General Delivery, along with any unemployment cheques forwarded from Montreal. Frankie said: "How's it sound?"

"Do it or back down."

The expedition started well enough. Sunday morning, Frankie roped his giant black duffle into the trunk of Dixon's TR-3. At ten o'clock, jammed into bucket seats, the three pulled out. And five hours later, having lied at the border about the purpose of their visit, they rolled into Detroit City. They drove around downtown, joked about visiting a strip joint and ended up in a greasy spoon eating club sandwiches.

Late afternoon, Frankie waved goodbye and lugged his monster duffle up the ramp to Highway 94, a high-flying interstate. His head was still spinning with the sudden-ness of his solitude when two sailors pulled over in a Rambler. They'd seen his black duffle, regulation American Navy, and figured he was one of them. By the time they knew better, Frankie had settled into the back seat.

The sailors drove him to Gary, Indiana, just outside Chicago, laughing and talking together while

Frankie, entranced, watched the miles roll away: Ann Arbor, Battle Creek, Kalamazoo. Frankie piled out at a train station and caught a commuter special. He propped his giant duffle in the seat beside him and found himself rattling towards Chicago, clickety-clack, staring out at twilight America, his face against the window, *clickety-clack, clickety-clack,* thinking of Thomas Wolfe crossing the continent this way, with Kerouac hot on his heels and then, well, *clickety-clack, clickety-clack, clickety-clickety clack*: Maybe hubris was a factor in what followed?

Chicago was full of surprises. On arrival, Frankie discovered the first of them: train tracks that wound through the downtown on a trestle high above street level. This made an impression, I know, because months later, in San Francisco, Frankie dreamed a variation on this theme. Now he lugged his kitbag down wooden stairs to the sidewalk.

The Sunday night streets were almost empty. The night air was cool, maybe forty degrees Farenheit, but no problem: Frankie was wearing his red-and-black hunting jacket. Quarter past twelve. No sense wasting money on a room. Instead Frankie staggered the streets, his kitbag on his shoulder, looking for an all-night restaurant. A couple of seedy bars were open, but they would cost money.

Finally, he spotted a small bus depot enclosed by frosted windows. A place to crash? Through the door he went and surprise: fifteen or twenty down-and-outers, every one of them big and tough-looking, had already claimed the place. Most were snoring peacefully, jammed against each other, but two guys eyed him and exchanged a look.

Frankie lugged his duffle back outside and walked quickly into the night, glancing over his shoulder. Half a block away, he spotted a sign: "Rooms, 55 cents. Deluxe, 65." He climbed battered stairs to a deserted counter and pounded on a bell. A red-eyed man, unshaven, dressed in baggy trousers and an undershirt, shuffled out from behind a curtain. Frankie said he wanted a room.

"Plain or Deluxe?"

Frankie handed him a five: "Deluxe."

The man gave him change, took a key from a rack and tossed it onto the counter. He jerked his thumb at a sign on the wall behind him and quoted it without looking: "No refunds." Then he said, "Third floor," and nodded at the stairs.

Two flights up, Frankie emerged from the stairwell into a corridor covered with wire mesh. Had he made a mistake? Bent low under the weight of his duffle, he checked the big red number in the stairwell. Yes, this was the third floor, all right. Now, as his eyes adjusted to the dim yellow light, Frankie saw doors. Two rows of cubicles faced each other across the corridor. Finally it hit him. He was going deluxe in a Chicago flophouse.

Frankie made his way down the hall to his numbered cubicle and swung through the door. Found a cot, a hard-backed chair and just enough floor space for his duffle. Flimsy sheets of wall-board separated the cubicle from its neighbors. These "walls" ended six inches above the floor. Instead of a ceiling, wire mesh ran over the top of the cubicle, and through it Frankie could see rafters. He lowered his duffle onto the floor with a grunt and the guy in the next cubicle told him to keep the noise down.

The cot looked clean enough, but he threw back the covers to check. Nothing. Frankie stripped down to his T-shirt and shorts and crawled between the sheets. On the wall above the bed was a yellow 40-watt lightbulb. When he tried to turn it off the string broke, so he reached up and unscrewed the bulb, burning his fingers.

Frankie lay in the semi-dark listening to drunks snore and moan in their sleep. At the far end of the corridor somebody retched. Somebody else couldn't stop coughing. Still, this beat lugging a monster duffle around the streets of Chicago. He closed his eyes to sleep, but found himself scratching. Realized he was itchy all over. Bedbugs?

Frankie twisted the lightbulb and threw back the covers. Nothing. He turned off the light and tried to relax, but the itching resumed. Quick now, on with the light, back with the covers. Still nothing. Maybe the bedbugs were too small to see? He looked up. Maybe they fell down through the chicken-wire mesh? No, that was crazy. The guy in the next cubicle muttered something about his god-damn light.

"Just a minute, just a minute."

Frankie had paid money to sleep in this cubicle. No way he was going back outside to stagger the streets. He pulled on his jeans and tucked them into his socks. Then his sweaty workshirt. Again he lay down, this time on top of the sheets, though under the blankets. He turned off the light—and soon started itching again. His legs, his arms, even his face.

But no way Frankie was going back outside. Instead he dozed fitfully, tossing and turning and scratching until six in the morning, when finally he rolled out of bed, pulled on the rest of his clothes and emerged into the streets of Chicago. City map in hand, kitbag on shoulder, he made for the Greyhound Bus depot. There, after removing his shaving kit, face-cloth and towel, he deposited his duffle in a locker. Things were looking up.

Then, in the washroom mirror, another ugly surprise: red blotches covered his face and neck. Good

God! Had he caught some disease? Worried now, but refusing to panic, Frankie made for the downtown YMCA, strolled in nonchalant and went straight to the elevators. He got off at the ninth floor, found a communal washroom and spent twenty minutes in the shower. After drying himself and dressing, he checked his face in the mirror. Looked like the blotches were disappearing. Could it be?

At a nearby cafeteria, Frankie devoured toast and extra coffee. This time, when he checked, the blotches were gone. Who cared what it meant? Feeling good again, though tired from lack of sleep, Frankie roamed the rush-hour-crowded streets looking for Carl Sandburg's Chicago, the Hog Butcher of the world, but found only skyscrapers, glass canyons and windy waterfront. Enough! Frankie retrieved his kit-bag and caught a bus to the outskirts of town.

Now Destiny dealt Frankie a card that sent him indirectly to jail, so justifying his later use of this term "personal calamities." Its form? An occupied police car. If that car full of cops had not been parked beside the ramp onto the main highway north, probably Frankie would have reached Winnipeg within two days. There, however, the car sat—next to a sign blaring NO HITCHHIKING, and with several wide-awake policemen in it, when Frankie stepped off the city bus at the last stop.

What could he do? Frankie walked past the ramp, nonchalant, trying to make his overstuffed duffle look like a handbag. Grinning, the policemen watched. And watched. And so he got shunted onto a secondary highway. Nine hours and four rides later, he'd covered less than one hundred miles. And in Madison, Wisconsin, exhausted, he splurged on a room at the YMCA.

The next two days brought nothing but long waits and short rides. Frankie spent one night in a train shelter in St. Cloud, Minnesota, another in a field outside Grand Forks, North Dakota. Late the following morning, near a town called Drayton, a car with a flashing light screeched up beside him. A potbellied man in a brown uniform jumped out with a gun in his hand. He yelled at Frankie to put his hands on the roof, then kicked his feet apart, patted him up and down and told him to get into the car.

The man wore a badge. Frankie said, "What's this all about, sheriff?"

"Don't make me tell you again."

The sheriff drove Frankie back down the highway to a town called Grafton, where he pulled into a restaurant and left him sitting in the car behind bullet-proof glass. The back doors had no inside handles. Three little kids came out of the store to stare at him. After twenty minutes, another car, North Dakota State Police, pulled into the parking lot with its siren blaring.

Two state troopers got out—one grey-haired, almost fatherly, the other young, a crewcut blond, looked like a marine. They chatted with the sheriff, then transferred Frankie and his kitbag to their car. Drove him back, many miles, the way he'd come.

At the police station in Grand Forks, a uniformed woman took Frankie's finger prints. Then the crewcut trooper led him down a hall and showed him into a jail cell, iron bars floor to ceiling. Shut the door and locked it. Frankie asked what was going on, but the man just glared and walked away down the hall.

The jail was empty. Frankie sat on his bunk—the only furniture in the cell—and rested his chin in his hands. Until now he'd remained unshaken, secure in his innocence. He'd done nothing illegal. Nothing but hitchhike, and surely that wasn't a jailing offence? He couldn't believe it. He'd been two hours from Winnipeg and suddenly here he was in jail. He'd have to phone home. "Hi, mom. Got a map handy? Look up Grand Forks, North Dakota."

Two hours later, Frankie was still elaborating this fantasy—and remembering stories of innocent people spending years in jail—when the older trooper returned and unlocked the cell. "You got a guardian angel or what?"

The previous night, he said, a tall, dark and bearded man had robbed a convenience store. Frankie wore no beard but maybe he'd shaved. Anyway, they'd caught the thief at a laundromat in a nearby town. At the front desk Frankie signed for his belongings.

Then, as he swung his giant duffle onto his back, the crewcut trooper grinned at him: "Don't forget, kid. In this state hitchhiking's illegal."

"Okay, I'll take the bus. Tell me where to find it."

The older trooper waved his hand. "Aw, never mind. I've got to patrol the highway anyway. I'll take you to the Canadian border."

Crewcut glared at him.

This time Frankie rode in the front seat. In answer to the trooper's questions—this was 1966—he said he was on the road for the experience. The trooper didn't understand. No, he'd never heard of Jack Kerouac. But at the border he spoke with the border guards, then told Frankie to march on through: "Keep an eye out for that guardian angel."

On the Canadian side of the border, Frankie got a ride with a retired high-school teacher who kept insisting that he was one of his ex-students. "Tell the truth, now," the man said as he dropped him off in downtown Winnipeg. "You're really Jacques St. Clair, aren't you?"

"All right, you guessed it," Frankie said. "I'm Jacques St. Clair."

"I knew it!" The man drove away happy.

Frankie sat on his duffle at Portage and Main and checked his watch. Four o'clock. Still, today was Thursday and here he was in Winnipeg—right on schedule. He had eleven dollars in his jeans and Duggins was sending twenty more. Things were looking better. He found the telegraph office just around the corner. Nothing for him yet so he whipped off a telegram: "ARRIVED WINNIPEG STOP STILL ON ROAD STOP SEND TWENTY FAST STOP."

At the YMCA the desk clerk wanted $5 for a room, but admitted, under questioning, that he had a tiny one, almost a broom closet, available for $3.50. Everything was going right. Frankie took the cheaper room, showered and found a restaurant. A T-bone steak was obviously in order, but when he saw the prices Frankie settled for a simple rib with mushrooms. No sense being frivolous.

After dinner, he again checked the telegraph office, which stayed open until nine. Nothing yet—but Duggins would come through in the morning. Frankie discovered *Don't Look Back*, the Bob Dylan movie, playing at a downtown theatre. What the hell? Tomorrow he'd be getting twenty dollars—maybe even forty—and he'd be on his way. He found the movie disappointing, but later had a great sleep at the YMCA.

Next morning, early, he hit the telegraph office. No money yet, but not to worry: Duggins had solemnly promised. Frankie had planned to stay another night at the YMCA, get rested, but now he had to check out. No way he could lug that monster duffle around all day. He carted it to the Greyhound Bus depot, crammed it into a stand-up locker and deposited a quarter.

Starting to worry that Duggins might not deliver, though he refused to admit it, Frankie called Canada Manpower. Explained that a bizarre string of accidents and mishaps had stranded him in Winnipeg short of funds and getting shorter. A wildly unlikely series of setbacks, reversals and personal calamities. The woman on the other end of the line listened politely but explained that she'd filled all temporary jobs hours earlier. She said there would be no pay cheque anyway until next Friday, because here in Winnipeg, that was how things worked.

Back outside, Frankie scoured cast-away copies of both *The Free Press* and *The Winnipeg Tribune*, but neither advertised temporary jobs. He rambled the streets and repeatedly checked the telegraph office. At noon he decided that when his money arrived he'd return to the YMCA and stay one more night, even if he had to rent a more expensive room. It was three o'clock before he let himself believe that Duggins might not come through after all, and began seriously to regret his extravagance of the previous night.

At five, Frankie sat on a park bench and counted his money. Two dollars and change. Since breakfast—bacon and scrambled eggs, toast and coffee—he'd eaten only a bowl of clam chowder. Now he craved another hot chicken sandwich—his mouth watered—but settled for a hot dog. As night fell, the temperature dropped and he made for the bus depot.

From his duffle, Frankie retrieved an extra sweater. Then he stuffed the oversized kitbag back into the locker, took out a quarter and stopped: Why not save the money? Who could steal a bag this size? The bus depot closed at eleven, he'd already checked. Overnight, the bag would be safe. Frankie waited until nobody was around, then shut the locker and walked away.

Back at the telegraph office, the clerk had taken to shaking his head as Frankie stepped through the door. Come nine o'clock, when the office closed, he'd received no money. Now it was dark. He checked the bus depot one last time, made certain his duffle was safe, then headed for Union Station.

The place was empty, ominously quiet, but Frankie remembered his Grade Six geography: Winnipeg was an important railway centre. Surely the train station would stay open all night, like Central Station in Montreal? He sat down on an out-of-the-way bench and picked up an abandoned *Free Press*. He'd scarcely begun the letters to the editor when a man in a red cap arrived: "Sorry, sir. Station's closing. You'll have to leave."

"What do you mean, closing? It's not yet eleven! Winnipeg's an important railway centre!"

Across the street in yet another greasy spoon, Frankie sat on a stool and drank coffee. Duggins was no doubt sleeping soundly in Toronto. Frankie brooded about this until he noticed a sign saying the restaurant closed at one o'clock. Then he tried and failed to pick up the waitress, maybe get her to take him home, and spent the rest of the night walking the empty weeknight streets of downtown Winnipeg—Fort, Garry, Smith, Donald, Hargrove, Carlton—and ducking into hotel lobbies to get warm.

Morning became sixty-seven cents in his pocket. At nine, when it opened, Frankie checked the telegraph office. Still nothing. He tried phoning Duggins in Toronto, thinking to reverse the charges, but an operator said that number was no longer in service. No longer in service?

Over yet another coffee, Frankie weighed his options. He could proceed to Vancover as planned, maybe get lucky. Or he could turn around and make for Toronto, where presumably he still had a place to stay. That way, if the worst happened, he could keep going to Montreal and crash at his old apartment with his friend Baxter.

At the bus depot, his kitbag was gone.

Methodically, refusing to panic, Frankie checked every full-sized locker. Then, still calm, he walked around the corner to the baggage counter.

"We've got the bag, all right," a grinning handler said. "Cost you fifty cents."

Frankie tried reasoning—"look, the locker cost only a quarter, so I'll pay a quarter"—but the man just widened his grin. Frankie paid and staggered out of the depot with his duffle on his back and seven cents in his jeans.

Three days, it took him to reach Toronto. Three days and two nights of flapping his arms by the side of the highway and singing *Wabash Cannonball* to keep a trucker awake and riding bone-jarred and freezing in the back of a farmer's half-ton pick-up. Three days and two nights of cold and tired and hungry, but finally Frankie reached north Toronto and bummed a token from a newspaper vendor and rode the subway south. At King Street he transferred onto a streetcar, and seven o'clock Monday night found him lugging his monster duffle down Jameson Avenue.

Nobody was home at the apartment.

Frankie sat down in the hall to wait forever, but along came one of the clean-cut young guys who lived next door. Frankie said he'd forgotten his key and, grudgingly, the guy let him walk through his apartment to the balcony. Frankie climbed the railing and entered his former abode through the sliding back door, which hadn't locked properly since the free-for-all.

Three battered suitcases sat in a corner of the living room. Otherwise the place hadn't changed: it was short on furniture, long on spaghetti stains and piles of dirty clothes. Frankie hauled his monster duffle inside, then went to the fridge. There, on the unwashed kitchen counter, lay the telegram he'd sent Duggins. "ARRIVED WINNIPEG STOP STILL ON ROAD STOP SEND TWENTY FAST STOP."

So Duggins had no excuse. Next to the telegram lay a fat brown envelope, unstamped, addressed to Frankie "Kerouac" McCracken, c/o General Delivery, Vancouver, B.C. Inside, he found a government cheque worth fifty-four dollars. Unemployment insurance! He was rich! Also two letters—one from Baxter, who'd forwarded the cheque from Montreal, another from his mother, urging him to come home.

Also, he discovered a note from Duggins.

This Frankie read twice. Dixon had been fired, his boss having ascertained that he'd never graduated from high school. And Duggins had realized that he wasn't cut out to move furniture. The two of them were planning to sneak out of the apartment without paying the rent. "We've decided to drive to Vancouver in the TR-3, leaving mid-week. It's good that you're already there. Hope you've found us suitable accommodation. Sorry I couldn't send money to Winnipeg, but Dixon and I need every cent we've got for gas . . . ."

The fridge was almost bare. Frankie made himself two peanut-butter sandwiches, then sat down on the floor, leaned against a wall and munched away. So Duggins wasn't cut out for moving furniture. He'd talked Dixon into driving him to Vancouver. While Frankie had been walking the weeknight streets of Winnipeg, they'd been dreaming up ways to spend his money.

The sandwiches finished, Frankie sat breathing deeply. Finally he stood up, went to the closet and, yes, there it was: Duggins' houndstooth jacket. He checked the secret pocket and jackpot! fifty-seven dollars! He pocketed the four tens Duggins owed him, replaced the rest. They were even. He hoisted his duffle bag onto his back and made for the door. His hand on the handle, he stopped. Why stay even? He remembered the Chicago flophouse, the North Dakota jail cell, the Winnipeg streets at three o'clock in the morning.

Frankie dropped the duffle and returned to the closet. He retrieved the seventeen dollars and stuffed them into his jeans. Quickly now, he fetched the brown envelope Duggins had intended to send him, maybe, in Vancouver. Chuckling, and before cramming it into the secret pocket of the houndstooth jacket, Frankie scrawled a note across the front: "Going west, talker? Do it or back down."

7.

Fitst morning on Mount Jubilation, I awoke to the sounds of Frankie in the tower, windows open, trying to raise the park warden on his two-way radio. "Jubilation Lookout calling Saskatchewan River Crossing. Do you read me?"

For a moment I didn't know who, what, where, when or why I was, never mind how. I was a stranger to myself, lost, haunted and alone, and then I remembered waking to that same feeling in a fleabag hotel by some railroad tracks, my first time seriously on the road. And smiled sadly to think that now, in 1970, I'd become the ghost I imagined then—a ghost lost in the echo chamber of somebody else's life.

"Jubilation Lookout calling the Crossing."

"Crossing here. Go ahead, Jubilation."

From the tower, Frankie relayed his weather report: current temperature, minimum last night, maximum yesterday. Relative humidity twenty-seven per cent, wind west-south-west at six miles per hour, visibility excellent, barometer steady.

While Frankie made small talk with the warden, I crawled out of my sleeping bag. The air tingled, pine-scented. I stood looking out over the green valley and up at snow-capped mountain peaks etched white against the sky.

Frankie signed off and clambered down the ladder with a thick brown envelope under one arm. Together we went through the gate and into the cabin, which smelled of buckwheat pancakes.

"Had to use condensed milk," Frankie said as he shovelled them onto plates. "But look." He held up a can. "Real maple syrup. My mother sent it from Quebec."

We smothered the pancakes in syrup and washed them down with coffee, black and bad. Without any prompting, Frankie invited me to stick around for a day or two, said he'd been alone on this mountain for almost three months.

I held out my arm: "Twist it."

"Glad that's settled," Frankie said, "because last night in bed I got thinking." From a shelf he retrieved the thick brown envelope he'd carried out of the tower. "Don't know how you knew about the rent money. Guess I told Camille and forgot." He stared intently but my face gave nothing away. "Anyway, you mentioned my novel and I thought you might want to glance at it."

As I took the manuscript, a flash-flood hit me. Here was Frankie as a boy in Sainte-Thérèse, lying awake and praying that tonight his father wouldn't come home. Here he was pedaling up *Avenue des Archanges* in autumn sunshine, anxious and fearful about entering *La Fin du Monde*. And what was I to make of Frankie in rainy-night San Francisco, nineteen years old, stripped to jeans and T-shirt and wading into the storm-tossed Pacific Ocean?

I knew I'd seen it all before, and that this was A Great Remembering. Yet still I felt myself floundering, going under, fighting to breathe as waves of remembrance and revelation washed over me. One day Frankie would write about his life and mine. But the tenor of his tale was undecided. Would he come out in favor of Magic or against it? Could I rouse him?

As if on cue, a giant whitecap washed over me, a spectacular double-whammy involving Camille. It sent me reeling across the cabin, left me shaking my head, holding my eyes.

Frankie said, "You okay?"

"You're blocked and don't know why," I said, waving away his concern. "You figure anybody who knows Kerouac the way I do just might be able to help."

"Listen, if you're not feeling well—"

He reached for the manuscript but I pushed away his hand and sat down. "You've got the language skills," I said. "Terrific ear for language, a fine sense of rhythm. Also, you can be funny."

"You haven't even read the thing!"

"You do have a penchant for telling. You tell us your father loved Sinatra, for example. But you never show him sitting at the kitchen table, still in his overcoat, playing the same old records over and over again."

Slowly, without taking his eyes off me, Frankie sat down on the edge of the bed. "I see what's happened. You read the book last night. That's it! You climbed into the tower and used your flashlight. The rest is extrapolation." Frankie chuckled, almost convinced. "You had me going there. But what I'm wondering, since obviously you've read the manuscript, is whether my approach is too, I don't know—too autobiographical?"

"All fiction is autobiographical, Frankie. It's a projection of the creative mind behind it." Still at the table, I poured more coffee. "What you're seeking is a shift from literal to allegorical autobiography—a symbolic encounter with the deepest self."

As I spoke I realized again how much Death had changed me. A symbolic encounter with the deepest self? Once I would have fled howling. Now I plunged on: "Ever wonder, Frankie, why so many novelists write about growing up?"

"No—but you're going to tell me."

"It's because everything you experience while growing up, you experience for the first time. And that makes an indelible impression. Your first home run, your first day of school. Who could forget them? Your first disaster in love."

"I treat that in my novel."

"No, you don't." I patted his manuscript. "Here you treat a minor mishap in puppy love. Full-blown disaster didn't come until later—with a woman you met in an art gallery."

"I don't like where you're taking this."

"Disaster in love means being haunted by sorrow and might-have-been. I'm talking heartache, Frankie. I'm talking shame and self-loathing and aching for some impossible second chance. I'm talking Beat. I'm talking the way you feel now, Frankie, now that you've driven away Camille. Now that, for the first time, you stand to lose her forever."

Frankie went white. "Camille is none of your business!"

"All of which goes to show," I said lightly, realizing I'd pushed him too fast, "that the problem here is not autobiography but vision." Again I patted the manuscript. "Change the vision and the details will take care of themselves." I handed Frankie his unopened manuscript, knocked back the last of my coffee and stood up. "Which way to the outhouse? I've forgotten."

"Turn right out the back gate and follow the path uphill. But what do you mean: change the vision?"

Ah, youth. What powers of recovery. I assumed the voice of W. C. Fields: "Existential angst, my boy, just does not become you." Back in my own voice: "All this God-is-dead stuff, Frankie. So cold, so isolating. So false. You're back where you were when you said a first goodbye to Montreal."

"But God IS dead." He was getting used to me. "That's what shapes the novel, gives it coherence."

"Frankie, you're more driven by ideas than I was or ever wanted to be. But if you must have some heavyweight thinker in your corner, forget Friedrich Nietzsche. Check out Carl Jung. Archetypes, synchronicity, the collective unconscious. The good doctor's not bad, either, on relations between Self and Ego."

"Camille told me to read Jung. Wanted me to go back to university."

"Maybe she was right."

"Get real. I'm twenty-three years old."

"Yes, and I was twenty-six, Frankie, when I enrolled at the New School of Social Research. Already I'd drafted *The Town and The City*."

"You've got this Kerouac rap down," Frankie said as he adjusted his pillow against the wall, "but your continuity needs work. "One minute you're the quintessential bohemian, the non-conformist *par excellence*. The next you're urging me to join the fraternity crowd."

"I never acquired survival skills, Frankie. Couldn't earn a decent living until too late."

"You think I care that"—he snapped his fingers—"about earning a living? I'm an artist."

"My sentiments, exactly, when I was your age and even older. Having published my first novel, I travelled to San Francisco. I arrived expecting someone at *The Chronicle* to cry, 'Genius!' and offer me a job as a sports columnist. Found out the world doesn't work that way."

"You're urging me to sell out. But the real Jack Kerouac wouldn't spout higher education. He'd talk spontaneous prose."

"Ah, my spontaneity rap." I stood up, chuckling, and stretched. "That was a reaction to the state of the art when I arrived."

"What? The conventions of psychological realism?"

"More the celebrating of the superficial. The idea that literature is a value-free word-game and never mind the spiritual, never mind the heart."

"Kerouac said writers shouldn't revise."

"I revised like a fiend and didn't admit it. But in knocking revision, I didn't go far enough. I didn't push the idea out the other side. I'm telling you, Frankie, that RE-vision is all. Change your vision and the rest will follow—which brings us full circle."

"So can we quit this charade? You don't sound even remotely like Kerouac."

"Frankie, I've got to run. But which Kerouac don't I sound like? Kerouac at twenty-eight? At forty-five? Your problem is vision."

"There's nothing wrong with my vision!"

"*Au contraire, mon ami.*" I bolted out the door and hollered over my shoulder as I ran: "You don't believe in miracles!"

8.

Yes, there's no city like the first city, and for me that first city was New York. Seventeen, eighteen, nineteen years old, I fell in love with The Big Apple—with Times Square and Greenwich Village, with Harlem, the Bowery and the Brooklyn Bridge, with the uptown jazz clubs and the waterfront bars and the never-ending bus ride through the red-brick sprawl of the Bronx.

For me, that first city meant French films at the Apollo Theatre and wolfing down hot dogs at Times Square while digging the hustlers and the junkies and the petty thieves flogging watches; it meant leather-jacketed pimps and red-haired hookers and solitary walks *à la* Walt Whitman and Thomas Wolfe and riding the Staten Island Ferry with a childhood friend, drunk as the sun came up, to shout Byron's poetry at the Statue of Liberty.

Some of this feeling must have crept into my work because early in the summer of 1966, having recovered from his Do-It-Or-Back-Down fiasco, and eager to renew his Kerouwacky quest for experience, young Frankie McCracken rode a passenger train south out of Montreal carrying sixty dollars and a small travelling bag, never dreaming that his own New York experience could take shape and resonate as anything other than a romantic idyll.

A few days before, he'd tried to hitchhike across the American border but suspicious guards had checked his wallet and turned him back. This time he lied to a customs officer who strolled through the train and, full of self-congratulation, got out at Plattsburgh, New York, where, on a park bench, he spent the night.

Next morning, Frankie hit the highway. Rides were short but numerous and the sun was setting when a trucker dropped him at a subway stop on the northern outskirts of New York. He rode the subway south, one eye on the overhead map, rattling happily through the soot-smelling dark. Finally, at 42nd Street, he trotted up out of the subway station to Times Square.

It was far grubbier than he'd imagined, despite the bright lights and neon signs, but he bought two hotdogs and stood wolfing them down. A few hookers strolled past. A man with no legs paddled by on a platform. A red convertible pulled up, three men in it, and one hollered, "Hey, slim! You looking for a place to spend the night?"

Frankie started walking. He bought a city map at a kiosk, rented a room at the YMCA on 34th Street and slept like a dead man. Next morning, travelling bag in hand, he tumbled into the streets: New York City! He couldn't get over the scale of the place. He'd seen hundred-storey skyscrapers in Chicago, but not in this concentration.

In Greenwich Village, the only area he'd consider, Frankie checked out hotel prices. Worried, though not panicked, he entered the Greenwich Hotel, a grubby-looking place he'd originally dismissed.

The lobby was full of rheumy-eyed men and ominous signs—"No Women Allowed" and "Check Out Time 7 a.m."—but Frankie figured he'd survived worse. The desk clerk said the cheapest rooms rented for eleven dollars a week. Frankie said, "We're talking rooms, right? Walls that extend from ceiling to floor?"

The clerk raised his eyebrows, but Frankie insisted on seeing for himself and rode a rickety, old-style elevator to the sixth floor. He passed a communal washroom, three or four men in their undershirts, bent over sinks, but already he could see that the Greenwich was a step up from your average Chicago flophouse. The room itself was cupboard-size with a cot in it, but boasted floor-to-ceiling walls and even a sink. A tiny window looked out onto an air shaft. Here, day resembled night—but who cared?

During the next few days Frankie wore holes in his sneakers, bought cheap sandals and kept hiking: Grand Central Station, Madison Square Garden, Radio City Music Hall, the Port Authority Bus Terminal, Columbia University, Broadway, Fifth Avenue, the Brooklyn Bridge, the Algonquin Hotel. He spent an hour at the top of the Empire State Building and rode the ferry to Staten Island.

One night he caught Shakespeare in the Park, *A Midsummer Night's Dream*, fantastic production. But most evenings he spent in The Village shuffling from one cafe to another, half-expecting to round a corner and bump into Bob Dylan or Allen Ginsberg or even Old Kerouac himself. (He didn't know it, but at the time I was drunkenly roaring around Hyannis, Massachussetts, well on my way to oblivion.)

A freakish early heat wave hit New York. The temperature reached 102 degrees Farenheit, then 103, 104. Humidity you wouldn't believe. Night two, as Frankie lay sweating in his glorified cupboard, he remembered Lawrence Ferlinghetti's *Coney Island of the Mind*—not the poetry but the title image. And quickly dug out his subway map.

The next three days Frankie spent at Coney Island. He strolled the boardwalk, lay in the sand, took the occasional dip—the water not yet polluted beyond use—and lived on pizza and ice cream. Finally the heat wave broke and he resumed rambling around Manhattan, though now he was running short of money.

He'd listened in a bar to the agonized maunderings of a wanna-be draft dodger and bolted from a boys-only birthday party into which he'd been hailed from a third-floor window, and whose nature he'd discovered too late. But that was it for excitement.

On his last scheduled night in New York, Frankie was sprawled on a bench at the fountain in Washington Square when a pretty girl caught his eye—a black girl in a summer dress strolling around the fountain arm-in-arm with two white guys. When she passed a second time, he nodded and smiled and, to his surprise, she dragged the two men over and said, "Man, you're sending out good vibes. You high or what?"

"High? Oh, you mean on grass! Don't I wish!"

"Come walk with us." The girl extended her hand and Frankie took it. She asked his name, introduced the two men, one of them older, tough-looking, and said, "My friends call me Jeunesse."

"Jeunesse! I love it!"

She prattled on, then, as if they were alone. Hadn't she seen him at the fountain last night? Frankie told her probably, yes—that he came from Montreal, had been rambling around New York City for two weeks and spent most evenings here in The Village.

Suddenly the younger man said he had to split, that he had to work tomorrow. After waving goodbye,

Jeunesse said: "Don't be such an old grump, Sylvester. Let's get this man high."

Sylvester didn't like the idea, Frankie could tell, but Jeunesse kept pushing and finally the three of them caught a subway train heading for Central Park. As they rode Frankie told his story—young writer seeks experience in New York—and learned that Jeunesse had arrived from upstate just three days before.

She'd met Sylvester and his friend last night. They'd smoked grass together and today Jeunesse had moved a suitcase into Sylvester's apartment. She planned to stay a couple of days, just until she received some money she was expecting.

By now they'd reached Sylvester's apartment, which was on the fourth floor of a redbrick building on 119th Street. It was a spotless one-bedroom, featured a gurgling bowl full of goldfish and a shelf of books on Eastern religions. Sylvester, who looked at least thirty, worked as a hospital orderly at a place called Mount Sinai. He was studying Yoga, and lately he'd been experimenting with psychokinesis: "You know—moving things with your mind."

The three of them sat on the floor and shared a joint. Jeunesse showed Frankie how to suck in the smoke and hold his breath and laughed when he had a coughing fit. She was sitting next to him, cross-legged, their knees almost touching. Big brown eyes, full lips. The only word, he decided, was gorgeous.

When they'd finished the joint—it gave Frankie a buzz, nothing memorable—Jeunesse urged Sylvester to demonstrate mind over matter. He produced a tiny windmill he'd rigged up using paper, popsicle sticks and elastic bands. "The grass we've smoked will increase our mental power," he said. "If we work together, we should be able to make the windmill spin without touching it."

Nothing happened the first time, so Sylvester passed around a second joint and told them to focus, to get onto nature's wave-length. This time Frankie saw the windmill move.

"Amazing," he said. But he'd focused his attention on his left knee, where Jeunesse had laid her hand. Without warning, she jumped to her feet: "Let's go up on the roof and look at the lights."

"It's getting late," Sylvester said. "I work tomorrow."

But Jeunesse insisted. She led the men up five flights of stairs and through a small door onto the gravel-covered roof. She showed Frankie her favorite vantage point and they stood at the rail oohing and aahing, looking out at the lights. Then she remembered the binoculars—they'd used them last night—and asked Sylvester to fetch them. He said no way, but Jeunesse pouted and finally he capitulated.

Alone with Jeunesse, Frankie put his hands on her shoulders. She leaned back against him. He turned her around, she came into his arms. They kissed and he ran his hands lightly over her breasts. She moaned. When they came up for air, Frankie said he wanted to spend the night with her.

"Might be nice," she said. "Where you staying?"

"Jesus! I just realized! I'm at a men's hostel."

"So you couldn't sneak me in?"

"There's an all-night desk clerk. What if —"

Sylvester, puffing hard, reappeared with the binoculars. The three took turns gazing through them, oohing and aahing, then headed back downstairs. Frankie asked Sylvester if he, too, could stay the night—save himself a subway ride.

"No way, man," he said. "No visitors allowed after eleven. Already, by letting Jeunesse stay, I'm taking a chance."

Jeunesse walked Frankie downstairs. At the side of the building, they stood necking. Frankie explained that the Greenwich Hotel had a no-refunds policy on by-the-week rentals, so he couldn't switch. And that he had less than five dollars in his jeans. Maybe they could cross the street and duck into Central Park?

Jeunesse said no, let's wait. Tonight she'd sleep on Sylvester's couch. Tomorrow, her father would send money. She and Frankie would rent an apartment together.

"Yes, yes," he said. "I'll get a friend to forward my unemployment cheques."

They agreed that, next afternoon, he'd pick her up from Sylvester's. And into the night, Frankie went whistling.

Next morning, after breakfast, he checked out of the Greenwich Hotel. He rambled the streets congratulating himself for carrying such a small bag, and also for clicking with Jeunesse. Eventually, he made his way uptown. He arrived at Sylvester's precisely at two o'clock, as arranged. Jeunesse answered the door, put a finger to her lips and gestured with her thumb.

Sylvester called, "Who is it?"

Frankie whispered, "What's he doing here?"

"Phoned in sick." Jeunesse made a face, then led him into the living room. "Look who's here!"

Sylvester sat on the floor surrounded by stereo components. He grunted but didn't get up. Frankie sat down on the couch. Jeunesse looked lovelier than ever, but when she went into the kitchen to make coffee, he didn't dare follow.

He tried small talk. Sylvester responded with grunts. Jeunesse returned and said, "He's just an old grump, aren't you, Sylvester?"

Frankie asked Jeunesse if she'd heard from her father and she said no, she hadn't. Then Sylvester said,

"I'm getting hungry. Did you take those wings out of the freezer?"

"Of course."

Since breakfast, Frankie had eaten nothing but a slice of pizza. Emboldened by hunger, he said, "You're having chicken wings?"

"Sorry we can't ask you to stay," Sylvester said. "But we don't have enough to go three ways."

"No, no. I understand." A silence ensued. Finally, Frankie rose to his feet. "Guess I'll be on my way."

Jeunesse said, "I'll walk you to the door."

Sylvester, who hadn't moved from the floor, got up and came with them. At the door, Frankie said: "Sylvester, do you mind if I have a private word with Jeunesse?"

Sylvester glared but Jeunesse said, "Sylvester, please."

The man turned and stomped into the living room. Jeunesse stepped into the hall and pulled the door shut behind her.

Frankie said, "What's happening here?"

"Nothing. That's why Sylvester's so grumpy."

"What about us? You still want to get an apartment?"

"Yes, yes. But I didn't get my money. Probably I'll get it tomorrow."

"And tonight?"

"I'll be fine here."

"You sure?" Frankie tried to take Jeunesse in his arms and kiss her, but she pushed him away. "Not now. Come tomorrow morning. He'll be at work."

"What time's he leave?"

"I don't know. Come after nine. By then he'll be gone."

"You sure you're all right?"

"Don't worry." She kissed him on the cheek. "I can handle Sylvester."

"Tomorrow morning, then." Frankie started down the hall, swinging his bag, then turned: "Hey, wait. Why don't you keep this for me? Save me carting it around."

Jeunesse took his bag, kissed him again, this time on the lips, and disappeared into the apartment.

Back on the sidewalk, Frankie counted his money. Three dollars and change. He decided against another slice of pizza, opted instead for a loaf of bread and a small jar of peanut butter—more protein. Then, having nothing better to do, he walked down Broadway to Washington Square, swinging his plastic-wrapped loaf. He visited bookstores, filched a plastic knife from a hotdog stand and sat at the fountain eating peanut-butter sandwiches.

As evening fell, he figured why wait? Why not hike uptown tonight? Fifth Avenue, West 42nd, Times Square, Broadway, Central Park West—to Frankie they were all still magical. By the time he got within hailing distance of Sylvester's apartment, street lights were blazing and Frankie was exhausted. He knew better than to venture deep into Central Park, and found a bench in a well-lit area adjacent to the street.

By now, ten o'clock, nobody was a pedestrian. Frankie stretched out on the bench and closed his eyes. Cars streamed steadily past on Central Park West and he dozed off thinking about tomorrow morning—how he'd head up to Sylvester's and crawl into bed with Jeunesse. Come afternoon, she'd receive her money. Together they'd rent a room . . . .

A hand touched his thigh. Startled, Frankie opened his eyes. A giant black man stood grinning down at him: "Didn't mean to scare you."

Frankie sat up. The man wore a T-shirt that showed off his pectorals, his biceps. He looked like a football player: stood maybe six foot five, weighed roughly two-sixty. "People call me Angel." He sat down beside Frankie. "What's your name?"

"Jack." Frankie didn't know why he lied, maybe just a reflex, but he knew enough to stick to it. "My name's Jack. I'm visiting from Montreal."

"Tell me, Jack. What you looking for, out here in Central Park all by yourself?" Angel grinned broadly, showing off a gold tooth.

"Nothing. Nothing at all. Just trying to get some shut-eye."

"You like sex, Jack?"

"Women, you mean? Sure, I like women." Frankie reached under the bench, no sudden movements, and retrieved his bread and peanut butter. "Want a sandwich?"

"How you like sex with men, Jack?"

"Angel, I don't." Frankie had stuffed his plastic knife down the side of the loaf and couldn't get it out. He opened the peanut butter and, using his finger, spread some onto a slice of bread.

Angel said, "Let's you and me crawl into them bushes over there."

"Nothing personal, Angel. I just don't swing that way." Frankie took a bite of his open-faced peanut-butter sandwich, glanced at his watch. Three o'clock in the morning. Few cars on the street. "You sure you don't want a sandwich?"

"You playing games with me, boy!" Angel grabbed his left forearm. "Let's shake it!"

"Hey! Let go!" Frankie tried to shake loose, couldn't. In his right hand he had his slice of bread and peanut butter. Without thinking he swung around and shoved it into Angel's face. The big man roared and let go of his arm.

Frankie stumbled free.and made for the side-
walk but Angel brought him down with a flying tackle.
"You gwon' a get it now, Jack." Angel had him in a
headlock and was hauling him towards the bushes.
Frankie was punching and flailing at his back but the
man was a powerhouse, too big and strong.
"Let him go, Angel."
"Huh? Who say that?"
Angel stood still but didn't release the headlock.
Frankie couldn't see a thing, though he could hear
because his right ear was only partially covered.
"Let him go, Angel. I mean now."
"Who gwon' to make me? Where are you?"
Suddenly Angel said, "Hunh!" and doubled
over as if he'd been slugged in the stomach. He let go
of Frankie and fell to the ground.
"Run, Frankie!" A black-haired man in a checkered sport shirt stood over Angel. He appeared to be
holding the giant down by pressing a finger to his
temple, but Frankie's eyes hurt and he couldn't see
clearly. Angel was kicking and thrashing and yelling,
"Where are you, motherfucker? Come out and fight
like a man!"
"Frankie, scram."
The words had the force of a command. Frankie
raced out of the park. He ran hard along the sidewalk
until he got a stitch in his side, and then he trotted a
few more blocks. Finally he slowed to a fast walk, and
only then did he wonder how the stranger had known
his name.
The rest of the night Frankie spent circling
Columbia University, taking comfort in the knowledge
that it was Old Kerouac's alma mater. He regretted the
loss of his bread and peanut butter, but had no intention of going back for it. Kept himself awake by thinking of Jeunesse.

Nine o'clock in the morning, Frankie made for Sylvester's. He knocked on the door, no answer. He knocked again and Sylvester appeared—wearing only a towel.

"Sylvester? Uh, hi. How's it going?"

"You again?"

"Jeunesse around?"

"She doesn't want to see you."

"Well, I want to see her."

"She's finished with you, dig?" Sylvester reached down behind the door, tossed his travelling bag at his feet, then closed the door in his face.

Frankie knocked again, harder than before. Sylvester opened the door. "Didn't you hear me, bright boy?"

"I want to see Jeunesse."

"She doesn't want to see you."

"I want her to tell me that herself."

"She asked me to deliver the message."

"Jeunesse!" he called. "Jeunesse, are you —"

"Hey, asshole!" Jeunesse shouted from inside the apartment. "Can't you take a hint?"

Sylvester grinned and slammed the door in his face.

Back outside, on the street, Frankie unzipped his travelling bag and checked the contents. Everything was there: shaving gear, dirty socks, a dog-eared copy of his favorite among my novels (*Dr. Sax*). He zipped up the bag and counted his money: one dollar and eighty-five cents.

If he left right away, Frankie figured he could make it home to Montreal before starving to death. But first he located a telephone booth and called Mount Sinai Medical Center. He asked for the personnel department, the senior person in charge, and told the woman who came on the line to check out an

69

orderly named Sylvester who'd booked off work for the past two days.

"He's not sick," Frankie said. "He's home doing drugs."

9.

That first night on Mount Jubilation, as I lay looking up at the stars, I began comparing chronologies and realized that in April of 1956, while I was living in a shack in Berkeley, California, and writing *The Scripture of the Golden Eternity*, in which I explored the Buddhist idea that all things are One and related, a farmer in Sainte-Thérèse-sur-le-lac decided to raise money by selling three tiny houses, one of which he rented to the parents of Frankie McCracken.

In early May, when I launched into creating *Old Angel Midnight*, that wild experiment in which I berated myself for ever having dreamed I could get rich by madly scribbling, Frankie's father visited friends and relations, raised a down payment of $300—and found out it wasn't enough. The McCrackens would have to move.

Later that month, while I rambled San Francisco drinking too much Muscatel, Frankie's parents investigated houses in Sainte-Thérèse. On *Avenue des Archanges*, halfway between the highway and the lake, his mother found a summer camp selling for two thou-

71

sand dollars. The annual spring flood threatened the place, but Madame Francoeur, the owner, said forget the down payment, just pay me forty dollars a month.

And in June of that year, 1956, while I hitch-hiked north to Desolation Peak, hoping at thirty-four to have a vision that would change my life, nine-year-old Frankie McCracken helped his parents pile their belongings into a half-ton truck, three separate loads, then rode his bicycle across the highway and down *Avenue des Archanges* to the place he'd call home for eight years.

The property, fifty feet wide and one hundred deep, boasted six or eight trees, three of them fully grown: two poplars out front, one on each side of the yard, and a weeping willow at the foot of the sandy driveway. The back yard was a swamp of waist-high grass and bullrushes. In July of 1956, while on Desolation I wrestled Buddha and sang Sinatra songs into the wind, Frankie and his father attacked the grass with a scythe, then covered their handiwork with three truckloads of sand.

The house lacked a foundation. It sat, not on the usual stilts, but on horizontal beams, once telephone poles. The roof leaked, the clapboard walls needed paint and the double windows didn't fit. "At least it's ours," Frankie's mother said. "Or will be one day. We can fix it up."

The house included a kitchen and an adjoining front room, three tiny bedrooms with curtains for doors and two porches, obviously after-thoughts. The front porch was windows from the waist up, several different sizes, and winter would mean sealing it off. The back porch ran along the side of the house from the middle, where the kitchen door opened onto the steps. It was dark and enclosed and at the far end, behind a door with a latch, was the toilet—a seat with a hole in it.

By September of 1956, when I left Desolation, Frankie's father had partitioned the kitchen and, with the help of his oldest son—"Pliers? Dad, they're right in front of you!"—installed a septic tank and an indoor flush toilet.

Fourteen years later, on Mount Jubilation, I remained focused on the house as Frankie's father enlarged the front room by taking out part of a wall and boarding up the front-porch windows. He helped a local contractor raise the place and put a cement-block foundation under it. To the bathroom he added a sink. Then he replaced the hand pump in the kitchen—it required endless priming—with an electric pump that worked automatically.

In the beginning, the kitchen sink was the only sink and often it backed up. Bad news. Next to the sink stood an ice-box. In summer, once or twice a week, depending on the weather, a man came around selling blocks of ice out of the back of a truck. In winter, Frankie had to fetch ice-blocks from this man's house a mile up the highway, trundle west under the train bridge and on past the French school, the BP Station and the Roman Catholic church.

That's where Frankie went to get stove oil, as well, when the drum in the back yard ran empty, hauling a two-gallon bottle on either a wagon or a toboggan, depending on season. The oil stove was opposite the back door. Black stove pipes ran up the wall behind the stove and then across the kitchen, suspended by wires. They joined the pipes from the front room and disappeared into the ceiling above the back door. "Looks like Hell," his father admitted, "but we have to heat the place somehow."

Above the ice-box, to the right of the kitchen-sink window, open shelves displayed cereal boxes, bags of flour and sugar, cans of soup and beans—everything Frankie's mother needed, or at least all she had, to feed a family of five and then six. There were more shelves in a waist-high counter which separated the kitchen from the front room, though the same worn linoleum, red-and-green checks, ran from one end of the house to the other.

Besides the wood stove, the front room boasted a worn couch, a ratty arm chair and a rocker. A black-and-white television set picked up two channels, one French, one English. Beyond it lay the front porch where, in an old buffet and on makeshift shelves, Frankie's father stored books and records.

Of the three bedrooms, Frankie's sisters shared the only one big enough for two beds. It lay to the right as you entered through the back door, which was really at the side of the house. His parents, with their double bed, shared the next largest, off the front room. Frankie and his brother had bunkbeds, so they got the smallest bedroom, at the back corner of the house.

Frankie was almost eleven before a classmate who'd visited gave him a North American perspective on his home. The boy shook his head as Frankie joined a circle of laughing friends in the hall, a circle gone suddenly silent: "I don't understand it, Frankie. How can a guy like you come out of a place like that?"

He was twelve, the only seventh grader on the high school basketball team, before the house contributed further to his consciousness. Two mornings a week, Frankie attended basketball practices that began at 8 a.m.—one hour before classes. He would finish his Gazette route, and then, instead of returning to bed for an hour, eat breakfast and hitchhike into Coeur d'Aimée. Usually he'd get a ride right away and stand at the front door of the school flapping his arms to keep warm until the janitor arrived.

If he didn't get a ride within the first fifteen minutes, he'd start walking, hitching as he went. This particular morning, Frankie had to walk all the way to school, almost three miles, and so arrived late for practice. He changed as quickly as he could and ran down the hall to the gym, just in time for scrimmage.

Not until first period, Scripture, did he remember the rent money. That's what they called it, rent money, though really it was payments on the house. Once a month after school, Frankie had to deliver this rent money, trudging twenty minutes along the highway to Madame Francoeur's house in Saint-Eustache. He hated this chore. He didn't mind missing the school bus and having to hitchhike home. And Madame Francoeur he liked. She'd invite him inside, offer him milk and cookies.

What Frankie hated was accepting May's rent receipt in October, or last November's in July. And watching Madame Francoeur, honestly confused, flip through her records saying, "Can that be right?" And having to say, "Yes. Yes, that's right."

So always he'd put the rent money out of his mind until he had to deliver it. Remembering it suddenly that morning, first period, Frankie realized that in his rush to get to the gym for basketball practice, he'd neglected to lock his locker. He decided to check, just in case.

At the front of the room, the teacher was droning on about loaves and fishes. Under his desk, Frankie opened his wallet. The rent money was gone. The classroom began to spin. Frankie stumbled to his feet and made for the door.

His teacher, startled, jumped out of the way: "Frankie?"

"Got to call my mother!"

Out the door, along the corridor and down the stairs he ran, taking the steps two at a time. He didn't stop running until he reached the principal's office, where he banged on the door until it opened.

"Mr. Herder, I've been robbed!"

"Are you trying to break down the door?" The principal, a myopic man who stood six-foot-five, looked down at Frankie through thick glasses, his eyes huge and blue and watery. "Come in, then."

Mr. Herder closed the door and motioned Frankie into a chair, then sat down behind his desk. "Now, Frankie, what's happened."

"I've been robbed. I—"

"You mean something is missing. Don't be too anxious to accuse." He leaned forward and made a steeple with his fingers. "What's missing?"

"Forty dollars."

Mr. Herder's eyebrows went up.

"I had it in my wallet. I want to talk to my mother."

"What were you doing, carrying that much money?"

"It was rent money. I was supposed to deliver it."

"Where did you lose this rent money?"

"In the locker room." Frankie's voice quavered. "I went to basketball practice and . . . and I left it in my locker."

"Ahhhhh." Mr. Herder, satisfied, leaned back in his chair. "You forgot to lock your locker."

Frankie didn't trust himself to speak. He nodded at the floor.

"How many times do I have to tell you people? Never leave your lockers unlocked. Never, never, never."

"Mr. Herder, could I use your telephone, please?"

"So now you've lost forty dollars. "

"I want to call my mother."

"All right, go ahead." Mr. Herder got up from his desk, stepped to the window and stood looking out, his hands clasped behind his back.

"Mum? It's me, Frankie."

"Frankie? Is something wrong?"

"Mum, I've lost the rent money."

"The rent money?"

"Yes, Mum." His voice broke. "I forgot to lock my locker. When I got back from practice, the money was gone."

"Okay, Frankie. Don't cry."

"Mum, we're already late. What are we going to do?"

"Don't worry, Frankie. I'll think of something."

"I'll pay it back, Mum."

"Don't talk foolishness. And stop crying, now. Where are you calling from?"

"The principal's office. Mum, I'll pay it back."

"Stop crying, Frankie, please. Forget the rent money. It's not the end of the world."

"I'll pay it back, Mum. I'll pay it back."

10.

Flash forward seven years, to early summer, 1966, and here's Frankie McCracken in New York City, muttering to himself as he arrives at the George Washington Bridge, fuming not about rent money but Jeunesse and Sylvester and his late-night chase around Central Park, so distracted that he spends several moments standing on a ramp that spirals onto the bridge before realizing this is no good. A driver can't stop here without getting rear-ended. Besides, where's he going? To Hartford? Providence?

Frankie swung up the ramp, rounded a bend and there, in an even-worse spot, stood another hitch-hiker. Blond, early twenties, he sported a button-down shirt and a red-and-white cardigan and right away Frankie pegged him: Joe College. On his left foot he had a white cast that reached almost to his knee. He was holding a cardboard sign that said "Boston."

Frankie stopped briefly to chat, as you did in those days, but moved off saying he was going to cross the bridge and try his luck on the other side. The blond guy put his sign under his arm. "Hell, I should do that

very thing." Broad southern accent. "I've been here
over an hour. Mind if I walk with you?"
Frankie pointed at his cast: "You think you
should be walking?"
"Nothing to it." The blond guy held out his
hand. "Bubba's my handle. Bubba Dunkley, Georgia."
"Frankie McCracken, Montreal."
They shook hands and started across the bridge,
cars whizzing past and a wind blowing hard enough
that they had to yell to be heard. "What'd you do to
your foot?"
"Chipped a bone playing tennis. Ain't nothing,
really."
Besides the fancy shirt, Bubba was wearing a
pricey wristwatch and well-pressed trousers, the left
leg cut open neatly, at the seam, to allow for the cast.
He wasn't carrying any bag and Frankie said, "First
time on the road?"
"How'd you guess? It sure as hell ain't by
choice."
Swinging along in his cast, plonking it down
and then dragging it, *thonk, tshht*, Bubba explained
he'd just completed second year at the University of
Texas. When school let out, he'd flown north for a
holiday. New York was more expensive than he'd
expected, and a couple of days ago he'd had to phone
home and get his father to wire two hundred dollars.
Then last night, he'd met a woman in a bar. He
wouldn't go into details, but this morning when he
woke, both the woman and his money were gone:
"Can you beat that?"
Bubba wasn't worried because he had friends
in Boston: three airline stewardesses. They were expecting him. They would feed him steak and wine,
chauffeur him around town, show him a great old

time. He'd visited before. In fact, he'd stashed a complete wardrobe at their apartment. "What about you?"

Frankie said he'd had a good time in New York, but now he was down to his last one dollar and change and so had to get home.

"Well, at least you're not flat broke and starving," Bubba said, looking him up and down. "You know, we're about the same size. You'd look all right in one of my suits. Why don't you come to Boston? Meet the girls."

By now they'd reached the end of the bridge. Ahead lay Highway 87 to Montreal; the road to Boston, Highway 95, ran through an underpass below. Three stewardesses waiting to party? No, too good to be true.

Frankie said he was meeting friends in Montreal.

Bubba tried to change his mind, but finally, disappointed, he climbed over the guard rail, waved goodbye and disappeared down a grassy slope.

Three stewardesses waiting in Boston? No way.

Frankie crossed a median, dropped his travelling bag at his feet and stuck out his thumb. But now his heart wasn't in it. What if Bubba was telling the truth? He'd thrown away the party of a life-time. If he let Bubba disappear now, he'd never know. And that, Frankie realized, grabbing his bag, that he couldn't bear. "Bubba!" He raced back across the highway and scrambled down the slope. "Bubba, wait! I've changed my mind!"

At Frankie's urging, Bubba stood in front, his white-casted foot prominent. Within minutes, a Buick Roadmaster pulled over. The two young men piled into the front seat, Frankie first so he could do the talking. The driver was a swarthy, muscular man in his mid-forties, looked like a furniture mover. He was going all the way to Boston and had picked them up so they could chip in for gas. "That's how it works, right?"

"I've got a buck and a half," Frankie said, "but we were hoping to get something to eat."

The driver, who'd grunted that his name was Bruno, stared at him. Bubba said he'd been robbed, but he'd take Bruno's address and send him fifty dollars.

For a while Bruno drove in angry silence and Frankie thought he was going to kick them out. Bubba was boasting about how his father owned several companies—oil and gas suppliers, mostly, but also a chocolate-making outfit—and one day all this would be his. Meanwhile, if they gave him their addresses, he'd send them boxes of liqueur-filled chocolates like they'd never tasted.

"Enough bullshit!" Bruno slashed his arm through the air. "Cut the crap!"

Bubba flushed. To Frankie, he whispered, "Damn it, I'm telling the truth!"

For half an hour they drove in silence. Then Bruno pulled into a service centre. He filled his Roadmaster with gas before parking in front of the restaurant. Over his shoulder, while walking away, he said: "Fifteen minutes."

Bruno took a booth and polished off a three-decker clubhouse with salad and fries and a piece of apple pie. At the counter, Frankie and Bubba shared a plain hamburger.

Bubba went to the washroom. Bruno finished eating, paid his bill and outside, at the car, Frankie had to say: "Hey! Wait for Bubba!"

Back on the highway, he watched the speedometer. They were doing seventy-five, eighty miles per hour and Frankie was thinking, well, at least we're tooling along, when a police car came out of nowhere, just zoomed up behind them, lights flashing. Through a loudspeaker, the policeman ordered them to pull over onto the side of the highway. As Bruno got out, white with anger, Bubba said: "Hey, don't worry. I'll take care of it."

Five minutes later, Bruno plunged into the car clutching a sixty-dollar speeding ticket: "This is what I get for picking up hitchhikers."

"I'll take care of that," Bubba said. "We're in Massachussetts, right? I know a judge here, owes my father. Pull into the next gas station and I'll make a phone call."

Bruno looked over and Frankie shrugged.

Bubba insisted that he wanted to phone this judge. And next service centre, Bruno pulled in: "I don't know why I'm doing this."

"Come and listen!" Bubba said. "I want you both to listen."

Frankie and Bruno stood outside the booth while Bubba placed a collect call to Hyannis. He gave his name and somebody accepted charges. Bubba said, "I want to talk to Judge Hackett personally. No, it's a private matter."

When he spoke again, Bubba extended his father's regards and said he'd run into a small problem with a speeding ticket. Would the judge be able to take care of it? He read off the ticket number, said, "You're sure this won't be any problem?"

Goodbyes completed, Bubba emerged grinning from the phone booth and tore up the ticket with a flourish. "That takes care of that. Shall we go?"

Frankie had heard the judge's voice. Bubba was for real—and that meant three stewardess were waiting in Boston. On the way back to the car, Frankie danced a jig.

Bruno insisted on buying coffees all around.

At four o'clock they rolled into Boston. Bruno was late for an appointment. He was going downtown and where did they want to get out? Bubba said near Harvard but Bruno said that was out of his way. Frankie checked his map and suggested the Greyhound bus depot.

Bruno dropped them there and disappeared forever into the rush-hour traffic. In the depot, Bubba said, "The girls will pick us up, no problem. Carolyn's mine. The other two . . . ."

Frankie handed over his last dime, having saved it for this purpose, and sat on a bench to wait. Bubba reappeared looking confused. "There's no answer."

"Are they expecting you?"

"I've already told you: yes!"

"Maybe they're out shopping for groceries or something."

"They should be home. Their plane was due to arrive from Miami three hours ago."

"You mean they're flying in?"

"They should be here already."

"Try calling again. Maybe you dialed the wrong number. If there's still no answer, call the airline and see if the plane's delayed."

Frankie followed Bubba to the phone booth. Still no answer at the apartment, so Bubba called United Airlines. He mentioned Miami and waited. Then he said, "Grounded! What do you mean, grounded? I'm waiting for people on that plane."

Silence. Then Bubba was yelling: "That's not good enough! My name's Dunkley! Do you realize who you're talking to? I'm Bubba Dunkley, Junior! My father owns most of Georgia and half of Arkansas! I want to speak to the president of this airline! I don't give a damn about company policy! What's your name?

My father's going to hear about this! Do you understand me?"

Bubba slammed down the receiver. He stood a moment looking around, wild-eyed, then made for the front door. Frankie caught him out front, on the sidewalk, and told him to relax, take a few deep breaths. "Okay, so the stewardesses don't arrive until tomorrow. It's not the end of the world. You can phone your father now, get him to wire some money and presto! We're back in business."

"We haven't got a dime to make another call."

Out front of the bus depot, while Bubba paced and looked the other way, Frankie tried to bum a dime. Finally a bearded black man stopped to listen. Frankie said he was visiting from Montreal, and through a bizarre series of accidents—but the man waved off the rest of the story and handed over a dollar.

Back inside the depot, Bubba made a collect call to Georgia. Again Frankie stood listening.

"Accept the charges, Cassie," Bubba said. "It's me, Junior. Tell the operator you accept the charges." Suddenly, he was roaring: "Cassie, god-dammit! You accept these charges or you'll be out on your ass! You hear me, Cassie? You'll be out on your fat black ass! Listen, operator, she accepts the charges. Operator, she accepts the charges."

A conversation ensued. From Bubba's end, Frankie deduced that Bubba Dunkley, Senior had flown to Houston, some emergency business meeting. His wife was still in San Diego. Cassie was in mid-sentence—Frankie could hear her voice—when Bubba smashed down the receiver. Again he made for the front door.

Again Frankie chased him. Talked him into returning once more to the counter. They sat on stools, drank coffee and shared a donut. Bubba kept glancing around, distracted. To settle him down, Frankie told the story of Jeunesse and Sylvester and how he'd eventually evened the score with a phone call. Bubba just stared at him. Suddenly he said: "I've got to get out of here."

"Might be wiser," Frankie said, "to stay right where we are." He pointed out the window. "It's getting dark. Looks like rain. Here, at least, we'll be warm and dry. Tomorrow we'll phone the steward-esses and—"

"This place stinks!" Bubba jumped up to his feet. "I've got to walk."

"What about your foot?"

"Walking will be good for it. If I sit still all night my foot will stiffen up."

"Bubba, you're not making sense."

The darkness, the cold, the gathering storm—Frankie ran through it all again. Why not just sit in the bus depot and wait, keep phoning the stewardesses to check. Bubba moved towards the door: "You coming or not?"

Finally Frankie took their last bit of change, deposited his bag in a locker and followed his friend out the door.

Bubba said: "Which way's Harvard?"

Frankie checked his map and pointed and Bubba stomped furiously into the night, refusing to explain why the big hurry: "I don't want to talk."

Frankie didn't believe Bubba could maintain the pace he'd set, not with one foot in a cast, but after fifteen, twenty minutes, Bubba was still pounding ahead, teeth clenched, eyes fixed in front of him, ramming the base of his cast down onto the sidewalk, then swinging his foot up beside it. *Thonk, tshht, thonk, tshht.*

Tomorrow, Frankie told himself, everything would change. Stewardesses would whisk them away to hot showers, steak dinners and God knew what else.

After about an hour the sidewalk turned into a dirt-and-gravel shoulder but Bubba pounded on. Frankie paused under a street-lamp, checked the map and decided they were still heading for Harvard. He caught Bubba and strode along beside him in silence for another fifteen minutes. Then he said: "Storm's blowing up."

Bubba ignored him. Again Frankie reminded himself that only this bad-tempered lunatic knew the way to heaven. "Maybe we should head back to the bus depot."

Thonk, tshht. Thonk, tshht.

Sooner or later Frankie would have to go back for his bag. The faster they walked, the farther he'd have to return. He'd already tried slowing the pace for short stretches, but Bubba had pounded ahead. *Thonk, tshht. Thonk, tshht.* Now Frankie slowed down again, only this time he didn't bother to catch up as soon as Bubba pulled ahead. Twenty yards. Thirty yards. Fifty. Frankie let Bubba get almost out of sight. Wanted to get rid of him, did he? Frankie considered letting this happen, but thought again of the stewardesses, of how tomorrow everything would change. He stumbled into a trot and didn't stop running until he'd caught up.

Together now, Frankie and Bubba pounded silently into the night. *Thonk, tshht.* Shoulder to shoulder. *Thonk, tshht. Thonk, tshht.* His legs ached and he craved sleep but Frankie went onto automatic pilot and lost track of time. *Thonk, tshht. Thonk, tshht.*

Rain on his face. He came out of his trance. They'd long since passed the walled grounds of Harvard University, where they might have sheltered under trees. Now, as they pounded into the foggy night, Frankie could see only the lit windows of apartment buildings. What was he doing here?

As he pulled his jacket over his head, he thought of the Ghost of the Susquehanna, bound for "Canaday." Remembered that somewhere, on yet another rainy night, I myself had followed a certain ghostly old hobo seven miles in a downpour, sweating, exhausted, the old man urging me to walk faster, the two of us making desperately for a bridge to "Canaday"—a bridge that didn't exist.

"Bubba, this is crazy!" Frankie pointed across the street at a three-sided bus shelter. "Let's get out of the rain."

"I've got to keep walking," Bubba said. "Don't want my foot to seize up."

"You bloody-minded fool!"

Frankie trotted across the street to the shelter. As he dried his face on his sweater, the rain began to pound in earnest. Cars pulled over because drivers couldn't see. Frankie smiled grimly and stretched out on one of the benches. He was dropping off to sleep, his arms crossed on his chest, when Bubba erupted into the shelter. He mumbled something about not wanting to catch his death and lay down on the bench along the opposite wall.

Children woke him, chattering as they passed on their way to school. The sun was shining. Frankie rubbed his face and sat up. Bubba was already sitting. He looked grey but said he wanted to resume walking.

"You're making for the apartment," Frankie said. "Figure you'll sit outside until the stewardesses arrive. But what if they don't turn up until tomorrow?"

"Got any better ideas?"

"I'm going back to the bus depot. Wash my face. Maybe pawn my watch and get something to eat."

Bubba said he wasn't going back to the bus depot. Anyway, he was certain the stewardesses would arrive this morning. "Wait for me at the depot. We'll pick you up."

Frankie said, "Give me the girls' phone number."

"Can't do that. It's unlisted. But we'll pick you up at the bus depot. Two o'clock. You have my word."

"See you at two," Frankie said. He waved good-bye to Bubba, then stepped off the sidewalk and stuck out his thumb. He got a ride with a Harvard student, business administration, who was heading downtown. Frankie mentioned that he was starving but the student didn't take the hint. Suddenly, Frankie couldn't believe how quickly, they arrived at the bus depot.

Two nearby pawnships refused his watch, said it was worthless. He went into the depot, retrieved his bag and brushed his teeth in the men's room. That made him feel better. Out front, through sheer dog-gedness, he bummed a dollar and a half—enough for breakfast. He sat down at the counter and wolfed down bacon and eggs.

This cleared his head. Eleven o'clock. Maybe the stewardesses had arrived. They'd feed him steak and wine. Chauffeur him around town. God knew what else. All he had to do was wait until two.

Then Frankie thought: Who are you kidding? Bubba has no intention of returning for you—not if the stewardesses turn up. He wants you here in case they don't, so you can save his ass. By now Frankie was sitting on a bench. The depot was quieter than last night, far less crowded. And as he looked around, suddenly the missing piece clicked into place, and he understood why Bubba had refused to stay here last night, why instead he'd plunged into the streets: Most of the people around him were black. Bubba was a racist.

Frankie sat a moment, digesting this.

Then he called United Airlines. The flight from Miami was in the air. Frankie said he wanted to leave a message for one of the stewardesses, a woman named Carolyn. "No, I don't know her last name," he said, "but I'm a friend of a friend. Please write this down. Tell her to ask Bubba how he lost his money in New York. Tell her a friend thinks Bubba caught something. Got that? Bubba Dunkley caught some terrible disease in New York."

When the woman asked his name, Frankie said, "Kerouac—Jack Kerouac."

He spelled this for her, then rode a city bus north to the outskirts, where he climbed onto a highway and stuck out his thumb.

11.

That first morning on Mount Jubilation, I spoke of full-blown disaster in love. And found myself remembering Springtime Mary Carney, whom I fictionalized as Maggie Cassidy. Twenty, twenty-five years after saying goodbye to Mary, I'd flick on the radio, catch Frank Sinatra in mid-song and find myself transported to Carnegie Hall, a teenager forever with Mary beside me, listening to Old Blue Eyes croon *Mighty Like A Rose*. You want melancholy, Frankie? You want shame and self-loathing?

This outburst was prompted by the rush I'd taken out of his recent past—that spectacular, double-whammy flash involving Camille.

"*Frankie, ce n'etait rien.* It meant nothing."

He responded in French and they continued in that language: "Don't say another word."

"I hadn't seen him in years. We got drunk."

"No more, please! I can't bear it!"

Frankie had returned from a second furious hike to the top of Tunnel Mountain. He was pacing around the two-room cabin they'd lucked into on arrival in Banff, punching his hand with his fist.

Camille switched to English: "This is childish, Frankie. You've been carrying on for two days. Why don't we—"

"Childish! You sleep with some bozo—"

"Frankie, it had nothing to do with you and me."

"And then you have the nerve to tell me I'm childish."

"All right, it was stupid."

"How'd you find each other, anyway? Some scribbled message in a public toilet stall?"

"It was stupid, I apologize, it won't happen again."

"That's it, isn't it? 'Looking for a good time? Call Camille at the School of Fine Arts.'"

"Don't be ridiculous." Camille started to cry: "What about Barbara, Frankie? I forgave you, remember?"

Now, on Mount Jubilation, the flash crested like a wave, swept me back to Montreal and the previous autumn—the autumn of 1969. That autumn, when I was drinking myself to death in St. Petersburg, Florida, young Frankie McCracken shook off his San Francisco hangover and began really to live again.

Every Friday after teaching school, Camille would drive into Montreal to spend the weekend with him. Usually they stayed in town and rambled from Mount Royal to Rue Saint-Denis, visiting bookstores and art galleries and coffee houses. The Matter of Opinion. *Les Trois Amants.*

As winter blew in Camille drove Frankie to the Laurentians and taught him to ski, laughing until she cried when by mistake they wandered onto an expert slope. He refused to remove his skis—and paid the price. Later he laughed about it, too.

But really their mutual enchantment was rooted in parallel passions. Camille's architect father, long dead, had painted watercolors as more than a hobby. Since childhood, Camille had doodled on notepads and napkins, but lately she'd grown serious. The house she shared with two other teachers was crammed with her work, everything from delicate pen-and-ink sketches to spectacular acrylics that filled half a wall. In her passion for painting, Frankie recognized himself.

Since returning from San Francisco, he'd determined that a never-ending series of one-night stands wasn't the answer. Yet alone in his room he'd lie awake nights: "My God! This relationship with Camille is getting too serious." He'd call and suggest they cool it. Then, after moping all weekend, lonely, he'd break down and call her again. When he wasn't with Camille, he ached for her. He'd never resolved to be faithful. But that's what was happening. Was he ready for this?

So Frankie was wondering one Friday afternoon as he swung home along Sherbrooke Street from work—an office job where he wouldn't last much longer. As he approached McGill University, Frankie recognized a young woman walking half a block ahead. She was struggling with two bags of groceries. He caught up and offered to help.

Six months before, Frankie had run into Barbara at a bar and remembered her from high school—a pretty girl, athletic, but two grades younger. Now she worked as a bank teller and lived alone just one block away. He'd taken her home that first night—turned out she'd always had a crush on him—but hadn't seen her since.

Now, as they passed his street, Aylmer, Barbara said, "Why don't you show me where you live? I could use a coffee."

Frankie hesitated, glanced at his watch—Camille wasn't due for two hours—and led

Barbara up the street, telling himself nothing would happen. But no sooner had he put the groceries on the kitchen table than Barbara was in his arms, her tongue in his mouth. They tumbled onto the mattress and tore off each other's clothes. As he entered her, Frankie heard footsteps.

Having lived in the rooming house for six months, Frankie had inherited the best quarters—one and a half rooms on the ground floor at the front. Now, glancing up, he saw that he hadn't closed his blind properly, that along one edge it flapped open six inches. Through this crack, unable to breathe, he watched Camille, ninety minutes early, climb the last few stairs. Maybe she wouldn't see him? But she did. Her face registered surprise, then shock, then horror. And then, just before she turned and fled, it split open.

Frankie lost his erection. He felt sick. He asked Barbara to leave and she did—though not before cursing him out.

Camille didn't return. Next day and the day after, she refused to take his calls. Finally, mid-week, Frankie booked off work sick, caught a bus to the north shore and intercepted Camille after school. Rather than create a scene in the parking lot, she let him climb into her car and drove him back to the house.

Taking up with him had been a mistake, she said. He was disgusting—"*absolument dégoûtant.*" She never wanted to see him again. Having intended to make a dignified plea, Frankie found himself on his knees. He clung weeping to Camille's legs, said he didn't deserve her forgiveness, but nothing like this would ever happen again.

Camille relented.

They made love gently—and then like animals.

Afterwards, as he stared into Camille's eyes, Frankie realized that he was more deeply involved than he'd ever dreamed possible. Here was a woman who'd seen his worst self and still found it possible to love him.

Now, in Banff, outraged and hurt, Frankie said: "Barbara was different. You and I were just starting out."

"*Ce n'est pas vrai et tu le sais.*" Tears ran down Camille's cheeks. She contined in French: "I've said I was sorry!"

"Sorry's not good enough."

"I love you, Frankie. But I can't take any more of this."

"Better brace yourself, then, because you've got a summer of it coming."

"No, Frankie, I haven't. I'm not going onto Jubilation with you."

"*Bon! D'accord!*" Frankie grabbed his jacket and made for the door. "Go back to Montreal, Camille! Find your old flame! See if I care!"

He slammed out the door.

Three hours later, when he arrived home drunk, Frankie found the place empty. Camille had left a pen-and-ink sketch she'd done on Mount Royal. A sketch of himself sitting on the balustrade near the top, gazing out over the skyline of the city.

12.

Too many loud-hailers of
the King of the Beats disregard my French-Canadian
heritage. They forget that my first language was French,
that I heard almost no English before I was five. That
my first teachers were French-speaking nuns at paro-
chial schools. At eleven I changed schools, but spoke
English so haltingly that the teachers thought I was slow.

Put it this way. When I first began wrestling with
On The Road, and before I had my vision of The Great
Walking Saint, I conceived my hero as a bilingual
French Canadian—a Canuck. His travelling compan-
ion was to be a "pure" French Canadian called Cousin.
These two would roam America like Don Quixote and
Sancho Panza, with Cousin constantly chiding the
hero for his English foolishness. The idea was to
contrast the unrelieved gravity of the clannish French
Canadian with the romantic hopefulness of a Canuck
who had set out, like myself, to conquer the Anglo-
American world.

I abandoned this scheme as unworkable.

Yet the French Canadian in me, whom I'd ren-
dered invisible in my first novel, *The Town and The*

City, and who didn't make it into *On The Road*,
refused to lie down and die, but turned up between
the lines of everything I wrote. My naivete, my religi-
osity, even my celebration of Beat, and of beautiful
Fellaheen losers who survive from one civilization to
the next without belonging to any of them—all quin-
tessentially French Canadian.

Look at my language—my vocabulary, my coin-
ages. Listen to my rhythms. Even the way I use English
is French. *Tabernac!* French words and phrases and
even extended passages figure in six or eight of my
books. At one point I wrote an entire novel in joual—a
Dr. Sax-like fantasy about Neal Cassady and me, and
involving our fathers, W. C. Fields, a couple of sexy
blondes and a French Canadian rake.

What's it all mean? Does it matter? Only if you
care what shapes people's lives. On Mount Jubilation
I realized that, perhaps more than anything else, the
French fact made me who I am. Same with Frankie
McCracken—middle name, Maurice. I'm talking not
just racial heritage, and not just bilingualism, but the
million small turning points that make up any life.

Consider Frankie's jaunt to southern Ontario,
which followed hard on his Boston debacle. He'd
learned in a favorite bar that tobacco season was about
to begin. That tobacco pickers or "primers" could earn
twenty-five dollars a day in the fields. The work was
killing but, if you could hack it for even twenty days,
you'd end up with five hundred dollars in your
jeans—big bucks.

Frankie hitchhiked from Montreal to Tillson-
berg, Ontario—heart of Canada's tobacco country.
There he learned that farmers were hiring in Delhi,
about twelve miles east. He got a ride with a local
contractor and arrived around noon. Canada Manpower had set up a special employment office on the

main drag, a large room with a file cabinet and a waist-high counter and three rows of hard-backed chairs.

The place was empty except for a duty clerk, an older man who said primers were getting nineteen dollars a day, not twenty-five, plus room and board. Hangers were making seventeen. Frankie declined to reveal his ignorance by asking why the difference. The man said most hiring was done early in the morning, but if he sat down and waited, some farmer would probably come along. Sure enough, twenty minutes later, a husky guy in overalls, early thirties, arrived in a pickup truck. Wanted to know if Frankie had any tobacco-picking experience. "You're tall. Long legs can be a problem."

Frankie grinned reassuringly: "I've done a little priming."

"Where was that?"

"Up around Otterville?"

"Yeah? What family?" The man had an accent Frankie didn't recognize.

"Gee, I don't remember. This was a couple of years back."

The farmer looked sceptical. "Where you from?"

"Montreal."

"You speak French?"

"Yes, I do."

"You sure?"

"*Mais oui. On peux le parler si vous voulez.*"

"Save it." He turned to the duty clerk. "He'll do."

The farmer scrawled across a form, then spun on his heel and disappeared out the door, waving at Frankie to follow.

Soon they were out of town and speeding along a dirt road raising dust, nothing to be seen but fields and fields of six-foot tobacco plants, an occasional

97

farm house in the distance. In answer to Frankie's questions, the farmer said his name was Wakulich—Nick Wakulich. He and his father ran the tobacco farm together and work started tomorrow. The crew consisted of a hanger and six primers, including Frankie. He himself handled the tying and his father drove the boat. Frankie kept nodding and saying, "Mm hmmm."

The hanger and three of the primers came from New Brunswick, Nick said. "Don't speak a word of English."

"Acadians!" Frankie said. "I'm part Acadian myself."

As they arrived at the farm, he stared up at the two-storey frame house, mostly white, and thought, hey, this is going to be all right. Nick showed him around the back to a bunkhouse, really a converted chicken shed, and said, "This is where you stay."

Two guys were seated inside, playing cribbage on an overturned washtub. Nick said, "This here's Pierre and that's Alf."

Frankie said, "*Ça va les gars?*"

"*Tu parle français?*"

"*Pourquoi pas? Je viens de Sainte-Thérèse, près de Montreal, mais ma mère vient d'Acadie.*"

"*Ciboire!*"

Alf grinned shyly, but Pierre, a wiry guy with long black hair and blue eyes, jumped up and shook his hand: "*On a besoin de quelqu'un comme toi.* Welcome aboard."

Nick wasn't the only one, apparently, who'd been feeling the need of a translator.

Frankie met Old Wakulich and his wife that afternoon, and also the rest of the crew. Among them was an American named Freddie, an athletic-looking guy who wore his blond hair in a crewcut. He came from North Carolina, spoke with a drawl. Frankie had more trouble understanding Freddie even than the Wakuliches, with their Ukrainian accents, or the Acadians with their New Brunswick French.

But what stunned him was that Freddie couldn't read or write. He found out because a letter had arrived from Freddie's mother, written by the local letter-writer, and Nick had invited Freddie up to the house to hear it read. Frankie had failed to mask his astonishment—an illiterate of roughly his own age?—and when Freddie returned to the bunkhouse, he started doing cartwheels and standing back-flips: "Come on, Frankie, let's see you do this."

Pierre grinned and shook his head: "*Maintenant, c'est à toi, le grand bébé.*"

"What's he saying?" Freddie said. "What's that Frenchie saying?"

The crew ate with the family at a big round table in the farmhouse. That first night, after a supper in which potatoes and cabbage figured prominently, and his translating had prevented more than one misunderstanding, Frankie returned to the bunkhouse and played hearts with the Acadians. Freddie, meanwhile, showed off his agility by walking around the room on his hands: "Come on, Frankie. Let's see you do this! What about you, Pierre?"

Next morning, five o'clock, Frankie woke to the sound of a clanging gong and for a while didn't know where he was. Then he pulled on his clothes and followed the rest of the crew through the pitch black towards the blazing lights of the house. In the kitchen, breakfast was laid out: great bowls full of scrambled eggs and fat loaves of fresh-baked white bread, boxes of cornflakes and pitchers of fresh milk and as much coffee as you could drink.

The crew ate quickly, then returned to the
bunkhouse where the primers, Frankie among them,
pulled on the wet-suits they'd been given: rubber
boots, rubber pants, even rubber jackets. Then, as day
broke, they followed Old Wakulich's tractor out into
the fields, past rows and rows of large-leaved tobacco
plants standing six feet tall.

The previous night, privately, Frankie had confessed to Pierre that he'd never cropped tobacco.
Pierre had given him a discreet lesson, but he worked
in the kiln as hanger, so he wouldn't be out in the
fields. He told Frankie to stick near Alf and do what he
did—and now, suddenly, away they went, one primer
to a row.

Technology has since found ways to reduce the
difficulties of harvesting tobacco. But we're talking
southern Ontario in the sixties, when for primers, the
hardest part of the season came at the beginning.
That's because the ripest leaves on a tobacco plant,
the ones that have to be cropped first, are also the
lowest. Sometimes these leaves are three inches off the
ground, but more often they're buried in the dirt,
which is why they're called sand leaves.

A primer would bend low, reach in, grab a leaf
at the stem and snap it off. Then, while stepping
forward to the next plant, still stooped over, he'd
shove the leaf under his free arm and clamp it there.
When he'd gathered as many leaves as he could
carry—and this was a males-only job—he'd march to
the middle of the row and dump them into a deep,
narrow wagon called a boat. When he'd finished one
row, he'd turn around and go back down another.

By the time Frankie had finished cropping his
second row, he understood why tobacco-priming was
considered one of the all-time toughest jobs, especially for the tall. Plucking the leaves was easy enough.

But this stooping business? Good primers were built close to the ground. They had short legs and a low centre of gravity. Frankie had long legs, and this had implications.

At lunch time, the crew doffed their wet suits and sat in the sun eating sandwiches and drinking milk out of thermoses. Frankie ate quickly so he could stretch out flat on his back. He'd done hard physical labor before—worked more than one summer lugging cement blocks for a contractor—and so knew what it was to be tired and sore. But never had he felt anything like this deep, throbbing pain in his lower back.

After lunch, nobody needed wetsuits because the sun had dried the leaves. Frankie told himself he felt rested. But ten minutes into the afternoon, his back was aching worse than ever. He gritted his teeth and kept going: reach in with his right hand, grab the stem, snap off the leaf and shove it under his left arm. Advance two steps and repeat the process. By three o'clock, desperate to ease the pain in his back, Frankie was on his knees and crawling from plant to plant. This slowed him down even more, but still got the job done.

The crew knocked off at four, having filled the kiln, and headed back to the farm. After about twenty minutes, Frankie could stand up straight and walk almost normally. As he helped with the cleaning, Pierre showed him how the rest of the tobacco-farming process worked.

When the boat was full, Old Wakulich would haul it by tractor to a kiln. A dozen of these wood-frame kilns were scattered around a field half a mile from the house. They had dirt floors and were empty except for six or eight wire-covered burners which sat on the ground and dried out the tobacco leaves once they were hung. The peaked roof of each kiln was strung with parallel two-by-fours, the lowest of which were maybe twelve feet off the ground.

The hanger, Pierre, stood balanced in a door at the front of the kiln. On the ground, Nick hauled tobacco leaves out of the boat and led two older women in tying them, stem first, to a three-foot stick or lat, thirty or forty leaves to each stick. He tossed the finished lats onto a broad conveyer belt that led up to the door of the kiln. Pierre would grab the stick with both hands—it weighed a good twenty pounds—then turn and scamper along a system of planks to hang it on adjacent two-by-fours, before rushing back to snatch the next heavy stick.

By the time he was finished hanging, the roof of the kiln would be packed thick with green tobacco leaves. Next day, while the heaters dried the leaves, he'd move to another kiln. Hanging was tough physical work, no question—but it wasn't concentrated solely, and brutally, on the lower back. That's why it paid slightly less. Even so, it attracted the most senior crew members, and Frankie could see why.

Near the chicken-shed bunkhouse, Nick Wakulich had rigged up an outdoor shower stall. Frankie took his turn under the lukewarm, sun-heated water, then went and stretched out on his bunk. He got up for supper and did some translating, helping Pierre understand where the primers would work next day. But afterwards he went straight to bed. Except for Freddie, all the other primers were feeling it too—though they were short and stocky. Freddie entertained by doing cartwheels, handstands and even a standing reverse flip. "Who's gonna try it? Come on, Frankie. No? What about that Frenchie long-hair?" Freddie did an especially fancy twisting flip. "Tell your friend to beat that."

KEROUAC'S GHOST

Frankie was hoping his back would heal overnight and maybe somehow get stronger—like a muscle. That by morning he'd be able to stoop without wincing, be ready to spend another seven or eight hours doubled over, shuffling, ferreting sand leaves out of the dirt. Five o'clock came early. Frankie's back was still sore, but he was able to stand up straight. He told himself that he just might make it.

After breakfast, the crew donned their wetsuits, followed the tractor out into the fields and plunged into the tobacco. By seven-thirty Frankie was into a squat and scuttling, his back worse than ever. By nine he was on his knees, crawling from plant to plant. The other primers roared up and down the rows and Frankie fell further and further behind. Alf, the fastest primer except for Freddie, would turn when he reached the end of his row and help out.

Frankie felt ashamed. Maybe he should quit? Just stand up, throw down his gloves and walk out of the field. But how could he do that? This was his trip-to-Mexico money. No way he was quitting. Frankie gritted his teeth and kept going. A few minutes later, he heard the tractor cut out. He looked up and saw Old Wakulich striding down the row towards him. So this was it. They were going to fire him. Frankie struggled to his feet and stood up as straight as he could.

Only then did he see that behind Old Wakulich came Pierre, bouncing along on the balls of his feet, waving to his friends.

"You got guts," Old Wakulich told Frankie. "But now Pierre crop. You hang."

Frankie said, "Pierre?"

"*Pas de problème.* I can use the extra money."

Turned out Pierre was a lightning-fast primer. While Frankie and Old Wakulich watched, Pierre fin-

103

ished cropping his first row a good three yards ahead of Freddie. The other primers were left far behind. Freddie cried: "Let's try that again!"

Old Wakulich told Frankie to hop onto the tractor and drove him back to the kilns. Frankie knew that hanging tobacco wouldn't be easy. But he also knew he could do it. Nothing could stop him now. By the time the tobacco season was done, he'd have five hundred dollars in his jeans. Thanks to the fact that he could speak French, Frankie was on his way to Mexico.

13.

General Delivery,
San Francisco,
California,
Nov. 26, 1966.

Dear family!

Ahoy from San Francisco! Real palm trees every-
where I look! Yes, I'm in California! Arrived with-
out incident. A young guy picked me up in Sault
Ste. Marie and drove me all the way to Vernon,
B.C. I visited an old friend in Penticton, hitch-
hiked to Vancouver and caught a bus to Seattle.
From there I rode a freight train all the way to
San Francisco.

Everything's under control. I'm staying in the
Haight-Ashbury district—sort of a friendly Greenwich Village. Have met some really far-out people, one a major American poet, another who is
putting together a literary magazine. I really dig

it here. Maybe San Francisco will turn out to be my real home.

Malheureusement, I'm running low on funds. I've paid next week's rent, but after that, well, thank God there are plenty of crash pads around. Even so it looks as if sooner or later I'll have to find a job. What a thought!

But we've got a few problems to address:

1. That $14 you sent the Montreal Library in overdue fines? Please deduct that from the $25 I lent you. And don't give them another penny. I'm sending them a letter.

2. Two or three long-distance phone calls totalling $8 or $9 will soon appear on your phone bill. Please deduct that, too, from what I lent you.

3. I hope that by now my last unemployment cheque has arrived. If it has, please forward it c/o General Delivery. If it hasn't I wonder, Mum, whether you'd mind calling the commission. Tell them to send the cheque immediately. That money is mine. I was in Montreal and capable of working. Don't let them intimidate you. I need that money.

4. Any responses to manuscripts I mailed out? Hell, maybe I've published another story and don't even know it. Which reminds me. Look in my box of papers. In it you'll find a story called A Piece of Wandering Orgasm. A carbon copy. I need this sent down right away. Please don't read it. Just send it. If any of my other manuscripts have come back, I would appreciate having them forwarded too.

Not much else to report. How is everyone? I just realized that by now you must have snow. In a funny way I miss it—though not the cold. Two nights ago I was galloping naked in the Pacific Ocean.

I'm looking forward to hearing all your news, and also to getting the stuff I mentioned. Please send your letter Air Mail Special Delivery. Good luck and health to all. Janey, keep yourself pure. Eddie and Maureen, stay out of trouble. Mum, you too, and Dad, well, I guess it's too late for you, Dad.

Waiting with bated breath,
Frankie

14.

With the sometimes exception of New York City, San Francisco was always my favorite metropolis—though God knows it, too, could be a city of blues and broken dreams. My best time in San Francisco was 1952, when I arrived as a published author dreaming of landing a newspaper job, of becoming Kerouac of *The Chronicle*, man about town, but then I couldn't get myself hired even as a railroad brakeman and ended up working as a baggage handler and yard clerk.

Still, that period in San Francisco, early 1952, was probably the happiest of my life. I lived with Neal and Carolyn Cassady and their two kids on Russian Hill, in a tiny brown house with a false-brick front and a peaked roof. Had my own room in the attic where I'd wake in the morning to the clang, clang, clang of the Hyde Street cablecar and know I was in San Francisco, I'd arrived, and that's where I wrote *Visions of Cody*, and also, while entertaining the kids, an early cartoon version of *Dr. Sax*.

With Neal's blessing, Carolyn and I made love in that attic room, and we lay together listening to the pitter-pat of rain on the roof, and sometimes we'd go walking together, swinging up Hyde Street past barbershops and laundromats and beauty parlours, and then down the hill on Union towards City Lights Bookstore and Vesuvio's Bar, or maybe we'd wend our way slowly through Chinatown.

Just off Kearney at St. Francis Park we found a Chinese restaurant that served great hot bowls of wanton soup for thirty-five cents, or fried rice for a quarter, and also smoked fish, curried chicken, fabulous duck cakes and other steaming wonders, and after gorging ourselves we'd sit on a bench in the park and watch people go by, myself never dreaming that fifteen years later, young Frankie McCracken would sit often in that exact same spot to eat his bagged lunch and ponder his vocation.

But I'm getting ahead of our story.

Frankie was now at his most arrogant and selfish, his most callous. In his first letter home, he bent the truth. Yes, he'd hitchhiked from Montreal to Vancouver, six days on the road, without serious incident. Travelled most of the way with a guy in his early twenties who had just returned from Australia and wanted someone to split the cost of gas.

Yes, from Vancouver, Frankie travelled south by bus. At the American border he told the customs officer that he'd be visiting a friend, staying three or four days. He was ready with a Seattle address he'd gleaned from a phone book, but the officer waved him through. Ten o'clock at night, he arrived in Seattle.

And that's where the omissions began.

At the bus depot, Frankie remembered my habitual railroading. He played a hunch—asked the ticket clerk if he knew where to hop a freight to California. The clerk sent him to the baggage room, where an old black handler told him that a freight left

109

for Sacramento every second night. Tonight was a go, and if he hurried he could probably catch it. He gave precise directions to the yards, said the bulls didn't care if he rode and might even give him directions. But riding rail at this time of year could be cold: "You be travelling through mountains. You ready for that?"

Half an hour later, Frankie located the only open boxcar on the southbound train. He swung his knapsack and guitar into it and clambered after them. Surprise! Three tough-looking hoboes, men in their forties, had already found their way into the boxcar and sat huddled on the floor at one end, sharing a bottle out of a brown paper bag. They'd covered their legs with newspapers and old blankets. They stared at him in silence.

Frankie got the message. He dumped his gear at the other end of the car and sat down against the wall. Ten minutes later the freight pulled out. He unrolled his sleeping bag and crawled into it. Old Kerouac was right, he thought as he drifted off. This was the only way to travel.

Frankie awoke into freezing cold darkness. He burrowed deeper into his sleeping bag and cursed himself for having bought such a cheapie. What was that? Snow? Snow was blowing into the boxcar. Frankie spotted a vertical strip of relative light. Decided it had to be the door, standing slightly open. He crawled out of his sleeping bag and made his way towards it. The train was clattering and swinging along far too quickly. The hoboes were lost in darkness at the other end of the car, but Frankie could hear one of them stamping his feet and flapping his arms. The man yelled: "Don't close that door. We'll be locked inside."

Sounded scary enough to be true. Frankie stamped his feet and flapped his arms and then crawled back into his bag. He rode through the night hugging himself against the cold. Finally, a pale day dawned. No more snow, but a biting cold wind whipped into the boxcar. Frankie needed to relieve himself. He waited until the train was clacking along slowly, then got up and went to the door. He'd seen one of the bums do this trick and stood hanging onto a leather strap that could be used to pull the door shut.

He was zipping his fly when a sound made him look over his shoulder. One of the bums was rushing at him. "What the—" Frankie ducked and the bum bounced off his shoulder and spun out the open door, howling. Now a second hobo came at him, brandishing a broom stick. The train lurched around a corner and threw the man off balance, and Frankie drove at him with his head down. The bum staggered backwards and fell and Frankie grabbed the broom stick.

Too late he remembered the third hobo. He turned as a blow caught him on the side of the head and sent him spinning into a thick fog. Suddenly all was silence. The fog cleared and Frankie found himself watching a backwards-movie of the last two moments, a replay in reverse. He saw the first bum come spinning over his shoulder into the boxcar. Backwards he walked to his sleeping bag and disappeared into it. He saw himself sleeping.

A familiar voice said: "Hold it right there." The backwards movie stopped. The voice said: "Okay, let's try that again."

Again Frankie awoke and needed to relieve himself. But this time he remembered a bad dream, a nightmare about fighting the three hoboes. He decided to wait. Twenty minutes later, the train slowed and shuddered to a halt on the outskirts of a large town. Frankie had no idea where he was, but he grabbed his rucksack, waved goodbye to the hoboes and tumbled out of the boxcar.

He carried his gear up the road, his legs stiff and cold, his whole body aching. In the centre of town he found a cafe and ordered toast and coffee. A local newspaper told him he was in Eugene, Oregon. Frankie checked his map. Enough with the freights, already. He was going back on the road.

15.

Fire hazard is at its peak between noon and two o'clock, so Frankie left the tower just long enough to eat some alphabet soup, a peanut-butter sandwich and half a dozen chocolate-chip cookies. He brought his coffee back into the tower. From below I could hear him clacking away at the typewriter, making notes about this lunatic visitor who wouldn't quit pretending he was Jack Kerouac. I chuckled, stretched out on a blanket in the sun and lost myself in the echo chamber of his life.

At three Frankie shook me awake. The sky had clouded over and we were going to fetch water. Frankie had a four-gallon steel carrier, an ancient back-pack contraption. On the front porch, while shrugging it on, he waved away my offer of help. "Empty, it weighs nothing," he said. "Coming back, we can maybe take turns."

Out the back gate, we swung left and marched south along the side of the mountain. An overgrown path branched off and wound away into the trees. It led to an older stream, Frankie said, long since dried up. The stream we wanted was half a mile farther. He had to visit every second or third day, but preferred this to the alternative. "End of May, when I arrived, this trail was waist deep in snow. I had two big barrels catching water off the roof, but every morning I'd find a dead mouse floating. I ended up drinking melted snow—oh, and pine needles. Ever try coffee flavored with pine?"

We broke into a clearing sprinkled with tiny alpine flowers, blue and red and purple and yellow and white. Above us, to the right, the rest of Jubilation soared rocky and massive. Scrub gave way to shale and scree. Then came boulders, sheer cliff and, thousands of feet above, the jagged, snow-capped peak.

To our left, down the mountain, an avalanche or rock slide had cut a swath through the forest. The scrub was waist-high and we enjoyed an unobstructed view of the valley, the Mistaya River twisting away. The clearing was noisy with chirping and buzzing and I slapped at mosquitoes and remembered hiking down off Desolation, what? fourteen years before? A seventy-pound pack on my back, my shoes worn through in the soles. Agonizing.

"Awake and alert," Frankie said as we re-entered the trees, the underbrush thicker here. "Keep an eye out for wood ticks."

I'd been listening to what sounded like a stream: "Say what?"

"No ticks in the Cascades?" Derisive, this, as if he'd finally caught me out, and I grinned at his post-California scepticism. "They're tiny insects, almost invisible, that hang on the leaves of plants," he said. "You brush the plants and the ticks cling to your clothes. They climb your leg, then your torso. They burrow into your hair, crawl into your ear—decidedly unpleasant."

"Shades of the Joycean earwig."

Frankie grabbed my arm, put a finger to his lips and pointed through the trees. A fawn stood splay-legged, drinking from a stream. Behind him, almost invisible, loomed a great-antlered elk. The animal gazed at us, alert and protective. We waited in silence. When the fawn finished drinking, the elk nudged its flank, then wheeled and shot into the trees: three leaps, a flash of white and he was gone. The fawn scrambled after him.

The sight moved us both. We fell silent, and in that silence Frankie became aware for the first time of our telepathic rapport. "We can hear each other."

"You finally noticed."

Spooked, Frankie withdrew.

Here, again, an avalanche had cut a swath through the trees. The stream tumbled past, its source a melting glacier far above. Frankie shrugged off his water carrier. He knelt beside the stream and scooped water into his mouth, then splashed his face. When he'd finished, I did the same. The water was freezing cold, invigorating.

Frankie made a mill race, uncapping the metal carrier and wedging it into the stream so water trickled bugless and sparkling into its mouth. Then he sat on a rock and I joined him. We chewed straws and sought shapes in the scudding clouds and I almost lost myself in a Haight-Ashbury acid flash.

Frankie kept me on the mountain: "So what's a miracle?"

For this I'd roughed out a plan, but I said: "Come again?"

"You knocked my scepticism, remember? So what's a miracle? Stumbling on those elk?"

"That was magical, not miraculous. A miracle implies divine intervention."

"Give me a for-instance."

"Well, the miracles I know best are my own."

Flatly, no question implied, Frankie said, "Your own miracles."

"The three I worked in my lifetime. But you've read *The Dharma Bums*."

"Loved the novel." He took a beat. "Didn't think it miraculous."

I laughed. "It isn't. But it does report two of my miracles. Remember how I cured my mother?"

"Can't say I do."

"We were living in North Carolina, my mother and me, with my sister and her family. It was 1956. The spring before Desolation. I was heavy into Buddhism and fancied myself a religious wanderer—a *bhikku* in modern clothes. I was roaming the world to turn the wheel of True Meaning and so gain merit for myself as an Awakener, a future hero in Paradise. I was praying and meditating and felt I was getting stronger, spiritually."

"You're kidding, right?"

"Memere came down with a bad cold. Her nose was running, her throat hurt. She was sneezing continually and getting worse. On the night of March 12, 1956—it was my thirty-fourth birthday—I lay on the back porch listening to her cough until finally I could stand it no longer. I sat up in my sleeping bag and meditated, went into a deep trance while concentrating on my mother's cold. Before long I had a vision, saw three images: Heet liniment, a bottle of brandy and white flowers."

"You had a vision of Heet liniment? Tell me you're kidding."

"By now it was midnight. I got out of bed, went into Memere's room and took away this vase of white flowers, bachelor's buttons. My sister had brought them into the house and scattered them everywhere.

116

I went and collected all these white flowers and put them out on the porch. Next morning, when my mother woke, I treated her with Heet and brandy. By night, she was cured."

"And that was your miracle."

"The first of three." I'd moved to a massive boulder that was flat on top, almost perfectly level, and I brushed it clean with my hand. "For a long time I thought it would be my last. I warned myself against becoming obsessed with working miracles. I mean, what a responsibility!"

Frankie snorted, shook his head: "I've heard ridiculous, but this beats all."

I positioned my hands on the rock and swung into a headstand, and Frankie laughed despite himself: "Now what?"

I began methodically lowering and raising my feet. "Not to worry," I said. "There's nothing sublime about this." I did twenty-five leg raises, added five for good luck, then quit and sat up straight. "Come to think of it, I used to do that even when I was drinking heavily. That's pretty miraculous, *n'est-ce pas?*"

The water carrier had overflowed and Frankie removed it from the stream. As he screwed on the top he said, "All right, I'll play straight man. In *Dharma Bums* there's a second miracle?"

"It was a prophecy."

"A prophecy's not a miracle. Not the way you've defined it."

"Don't be a pedant, Frankie. It counts, I tell you."

"Okay, but this better be good."

"The rucksack revolution. I predicted it in *Dharma Bums*. Prophesied that millions of young people would take to the roads with packs on their backs, having refused to worship the great god Consumption."

"Wasn't that somebody else's prophecy?"

"Gary Snyder gets an assist. But I was the one who put it in print."

"Tell me you're kidding."

I grinned and picked up the water carrier. Now it weighed at least sixty pounds and Frankie helped me into the harness. Then put his hand on my shoulder. "You're talking Jabberwocky —"

"Make that Kerouwacky."

"— but I can't stand an unfinished story. The third miracle?"

"That came later. I was living with Memere in Northport, Long Island. I had a painter friend, a Polish guy I called Stashou, and in New York City, commuting distance away, a girl friend named Dody who was also a painter."

"Wait! Don't tell me! You started painting."

"You got it. I was having visions and most of my work had a religious theme. I especially liked painting pietas—the Virgin Mary mourning over the dead body of Jesus?"

The water carrier weighed six tons and my shirt was getting wet from condensation. I decided to keep it short. "Finally, I had a vision of this cardinal, Giovanni Montini. I saw him wearing papal robes and painted him that way. Four years later—are you ready for this?—Montini became Pope Paul the Sixth."

"That painting was it?"

"Technically, it's nothing special—almost like a cartoon. But I gave the Pope these big blue eyes. They follow you around."

"You call that a miracle? Even if that painting did exist, it would prove nothing."

"Miracles never prove, Frankie. They signify and suggest."

I swung onto the trail, but hadn't gone twenty strides before I felt freezing water running down the backs of my legs. Condensation? "What the —"

"I forgot to tell you," Frankie said, deadpan. "You fill that old carrier with water, it leaks like one of your stories."

16.

Again it was 1966, Thanksgiving Day, and Frankie McCracken had arrived in California. Nineteen years old, a yea-saying rucksack warrior in jeans and a turtle-neck sweater, he'd hitch-hiked and ridden freights across the continent and stumbled into what looked like a social revolution.

That's what, three nights before, a sociology professor had called it as they rolled south in his Volkswagen van. "The Haight-Ashbury?" He raised his eyebrows. "You've never heard of the Haight?"

He rhapsodized for twenty, twenty-five miles, describing the Haight as the most interesting social experiment America had ever spawned. "But you've heard of Timothy Leary and LSD? Turn on, tune in, drop out?"

Frankie had read Leary's famous Playboy interview, found it fascinating and said so. And when the professor dropped him off in downtown San Francisco, he not only directed Frankie to the Haight but reached into his shirt pocket and took out a tiny ball of tinfoil. "This is all I've got with me. Just half a tab.

But it's primo acid—pure LSD." He handed Frankie the ball. "Wait for the right moment."

Now it was Thanksgiving Day, free turkey dinner in the Haight, and Frankie stood in the middle of a dirt-floor garage, the original Free Frame of Reference, grinning and nodding, unable to believe his stumbling good luck, a turkey leg in one hand, a cup of wine in the other, a half-tab of acid safe in his wallet.

The feast was courtesy of a group called The Diggers, self-styled Merry Men who regarded the Haight as a kind of Sherwood Forest. Beautiful people were everywhere. A guy in a W.C. Fields mask and an old top hat hovered over a turntable playing *Visions of Johanna*, the same verse, over and over again, Bob Dylan jeering repeatedly that little boy lost, he takes himself so seriously. Nobody minded. A girl wearing a see-through American flag and nothing else climbed onto a table and made like the Statue of Liberty. Nobody minded that, either—certainly not Frankie.

He stood nodding, guzzling red wine, stuffing his face with turkey. People were jostling him, climbing back and forth over a Mad-Hatter type stretched out on the floor, his arms crossed on his chest. Reaching for another cup of wine Frankie took an elbow in the ribs. Turned to face an older guy, mid-thirties, chubby, with a light-bulb nose, pale blue eyes and thin brown hair that hung lifeless over his ears.

The man said sorry. Frankie said no problem and suddenly he was talking, telling this guy that he'd hitchhiked and ridden freights from Montreal, that he was chasing experience, gathering material for a novel.

"Experience you want?" The man held out his hand. "My name's Oscar."

They both laughed. Turned out Oscar, too, was a writer, more specifically a poet, and that got Frankie babbling particulars: "I call my latest story *A Piece of Wandering Orgasm*. It's like my hero's . . . ."

"Sorry, a what?"

"*A Piece of Wandering Orgasm*. My hero's so alive he's experiencing orgasm all the time. You know, just walking around. It's an advance on Kerouac."

Oscar nodded as he listened to this nonsense, rocked back and forth on the balls of his feet, his hands in the pockets of his baggy green trousers, his paunch out over his belt. He reminded Frankie of a toy he'd had as a child, a roly-poly man he'd push over onto his back, but who always rolled to his feet again. Wanted to know if Frankie had published anything. "Oh, a couple of stories. I've got others making the rounds. What about you?"

"Short poems here and there," Oscar said. "The usual literary mags. Just finished a long one, though, a sixteen-pager. It'll be in an anthology that a friend of mine's putting together."

That got Frankie's attention. "An anthology?"

They chatted until Oscar said come on back to the house and read my poetry: "I share the place with some beautiful people."

"Hey, why not?"

A light rain was falling but Oscar's house was just around the corner, a two-storey Victorian that looked out onto the panhandle section of Golden Gate Park. "The Fell Street House, we call it," Oscar said, opening the double front doors and ushering Frankie inside.

Oscar shared the ground floor with a married couple, their disturbed son and a painter named Ruth, none of whom was home. Angry paintings adorned the walls, mostly of whores draped in American flags and surrounded by cars and airplanes and TV sets. "Ruth works part-time as a topless dancer in North

Beach," Oscar said, as if that explained the pictures. "She's a lesbian."

Oscar sat him down in an overstuffed armchair in the living room, handed him a hard-cover binder containing fifty or sixty poems, all neatly typed, double-spaced, and left him alone to read. The poem for the anthology, the sixteen-pager, was all about Oscar's early life but with African mythology mixed in: God laughed once, *cha*, twice, *cha cha*, seven times in all, created the world that way. All about the magic of New Orleans, how his mother conceived him in the back seat of a car and he never knew his father. Full of esoteric references and allusions and ending with a vision of Africa, a night-time initiation rite and naked thirteen-year-old boys prancing around a bonfire.

Fantastic. But Frankie admired even more a series of poems about terrible angels who couldn't tell whether they moved among the living or the dead. Their confusion had to do, somehow, with Eros and Agape, with Realizing Duality and The Seventeen Scale.

"Ah-gapay," Oscar said when Frankie asked him to explain. "Not 'agape' but ah-gapay. Eros and Agape, lust and compassion—they're two sides of the same Duality. The challenge is to realize this Duality by reconciling the opposites in experience."

"Run that by me again?"

Turned out Realizing Duality was the secret of The Seventeen Scale, a way of measuring writers. Only the greatest writers and poets, Oscar said, the ones who had Realized Duality, could hope to become Seventeens. They were The True Artists. Most writers were Sixes or Sevens, Eights or Nines. And it wasn't just a matter of craft.

A Nine could be as skilled as a Seventeen, as fine a wordsmith, but because he hadn't died and been born again, and so reconciled the Opposites, he could write nothing that would last—nothing that would echo forever in the minds of men. Ten was the turning point. A superb craftsman could become a Nine, but he couldn't get into those double digits, couldn't become an angel, unless he Realized Duality. And to do that he had to die and be born again.

"I don't understand."

"Duality isn't something you understand, Frankie. It's something you realize. You've got to die and be born again."

Impossible to imagine bafflegab more suited to a would-be writer, and a few days later, bent on Realizing Duality, Frankie sat in that same armchair waiting for his half-tab of acid to work the appropriate magic. He'd given up on a rational approach, having cross-examined Oscar in the sundry cafes and coffee houses of the Haight—The Blue Unicorn, the Donut Shoppe, the I and Thou. Oscar said Rainer Maria Rilke was The Greatest Poet Who Ever Lived, that his *Duino Elegies* had Transformed Poetry. He himself was probably The Greatest Poet Alive Today, if only because he treated the Duality of Love. "I am a bridge," he said. "A bridge you must cross."

Frankie understood that Oscar was gay. But he told himself: so what? That was part of the man's fascination. As a teenager, Oscar had peddled his ass in upscale Miami. Then he lost his looks and considered becoming a priest. Finally, he'd opted for poetry. And followed his muse wherever she led: New Orleans, San Francisco, New York City—round and round and round. Somewhere he married and tried to go straight. Somewhere else he divorced. For years he worked as a counsellor for disturbed children.

"Half a tab," he said, disappointed, when Frankie showed him the acid he'd received as a gift. "Not enough for both of us."

"Guess I'll have to do it alone."

"Your first trip?" Oscar shrugged. "No guide? It's your life, baby."

Frankie thought a moment, then said, "Maybe you'll be my guide."

"No way. Sharing a trip is one thing. Guiding's another."

"Oscar, you'd be perfect."

He shook his head: "Acid's like a pair of glasses. You can see more clearly. And you, Frankie—you'd see the evil in me but not the good."

"I'd see both."

"How could you, Frankie? You haven't Realized Duality."

"But that's what I want to do. Don't you see, Oscar? You're the perfect guide."

Now, at The Fell Street House, Frankie lounged in the armchair while Oscar sat reading on the inside stairs that led to the second floor. Nothing was happening. Frankie grew impatient, irritable, and was ready to pronounce the experiment a failure when the cross piece in the window opposite rushed directly at him, then rushed back into place again. It was like seeing it through the zoom lens of a movie camera. "The acid!" he cried. "It's working!"

Settling deeper into the overstuffed armchair, Frankie brushed one hand along its arm. His hand tingled pleasurably. He repeated the action. Felt even better the second time, all pins and needles. Both hands down his thighs. This was fantastic. The acid had sensitized his entire body. Frankie ran his hands up and down his legs, then noticed the mattress on the floor against the far wall. On the mattress lay an old pink bedspread covered with thousands of tiny ridges. Rougher texture.

"Where are you going?"

Frankie crossed the room and slid, face down, onto the mattress. "Oooooooooo." The feeling was unbelievable. His hands, his legs, his chest, his stomach—his entire body was pins and needles. "Ooooooooo." He began writhing against the bedspread, squirming. Oscar was standing over him, looking down, but he couldn't stop. "Oooooooooooo." Back and forth on the bedspread. "Ooooooooooo." Nothing but the bedspread. "Ooooooooooo. Oooooooooo."

"Frankie." He heard a voice. "Frankie." A hollow voice was calling his name. "Frankie, isn't there something you have to do?"

Something he had to do? Yes, there was—but he couldn't remember what it was. Didn't care. He wanted to continue making love with the bedspread. "Ooooooooo."

"Frankie." The voice persisted. "Isn't there something you have to do for Oscar?"

"Oscar?" The name sounded familiar but he couldn't place it. "Oscar?"

"Yes, Oscar. Don't be so selfish."

He looked up from the mattress and saw a man standing over him. The man's name was Oscar—but he knew nothing else about him.

"Frankie, you've been rolling around on that mattress for three hours."

He tried to stop writhing, couldn't. "Ooooooooooo, it feels good. It feels just so good."

"Look, Frankie." Oscar held a clock in front of his face. "Three hours."

"Three hours." The words meant nothing. Somewhere, Time existed. But that was in a world he'd left behind. Again he let go. "Ooooooooooooooo."

126

"Where's your Agape, Frankie? Your compassion? Think of Oscar."

"Oscar?"

"Yes, think of poor Oscar, sitting and watching this. Don't be so selfish, Frankie. Think! Isn't there something you have to do? Here, look at this."

Oscar sat down on the mattress and showed him a piece of paper. A poem was written on it. Frankie tried to read the poem but the typed words kept changing shape, bending and twisting. It was like trying to read in a fun-house mirror. "Footsteps on the stairs." He heard footsteps. "Not for me." The footsteps went past the door. "A bed, a chair . . . this tiny room . . . an unknown city." The poem blurred.

"What's the matter, Frankie?"

"Nothing. It's just —" His voice cracked. "It's just so sad, so lonely."

"Hey, now." Oscar patted his head. "Oscar's here."

Frankie buried his face against Oscar's chest.

A hand was unbuttoning his shirt. It was just a hand. It didn't belong to anybody. One button. Two buttons. Three. The hand was under his shirt, running lightly over his chest. This was wrong.

"Frankie." The voice again. "Frankie, will you wait here while Oscar goes to the bathroom?"

The hand belonged to Oscar. It was Oscar's hand.

"Will you wait, Frankie?"

"Uh hunh." If he didn't say yes, it didn't count.

"You won't move now? Promise?"

"Uh hunh." He watched Oscar go down the hall and disappear into the kitchen. Then he dragged himself from the mattress and stumbled across the room into the armchair. He hung sideways over the arm, noticed specks of white paint on the grey floorboards. He'd seen those specks before but now they arranged themselves into a pattern. Suddenly, the pattern changed, became more intricate. Then it changed again. Amazing. The specks didn't move but the pattern changed anyway.

And what was that—a foot? A foot and a leg? They were just sitting there by themselves. Frankie couldn't figure it out. No, wait! That was his own foot! And that was his leg! That foot and that leg belonged to his body! He sat up straight and looked down at his body. His body wasn't him. It was something he used. A vehicle. The real him was thinking thoughts. That body wasn't him at all. It was just a vehicle that—

"Frankie! You promised not to move."

A strange man glared at him from across the room. Oscar! The man was Oscar. But he was smaller than before, smaller and far away. In the distance, he sat down on the mattress. "Come here, Frankie." He patted the mattress. "Don't you want to realize Duality?"

"Duality?"

"You promised, remember? Are you going to break your promise?"

"I didn't promise."

"Yes, you did, Frankie. But it looks like I was right about you. You've got no compassion." Oscar stood up. "That's your problem, Frankie. You're selfish."

"I've got compassion, Oscar."

"No you haven't. Eros, baby! You understand nothing but lust. You'll never be anything but a Nine."

"A Nine!" This was terrible. Frankie couldn't remember what a Nine was, but he knew he didn't want to be one. "No, Oscar. Seventeen! I'll be a Seventeen."

"No way, baby." He shook his head sadly. This had been a test. Oscar was a judge of some kind, an agent for a higher order. Now the matter was out of his hands: "Nine."

"Seventeen." The room was hot. Stifling. Which way was outdoors?

"Sorry, Frankie. Probably you won't make Nine. You'll be an Eight."

"Seventeen!" He spotted a hallway, knew he had to get outside, pulled himself out of the chair. "SEVENTEEN!"

Again Oscar shook his head: "Seven."

"SEVENTEEN, OSCAR!" Yelling, Frankie made for the hallway: "SEVENTEEN! SEVENTEEN!"

17.

If human consciousness is a neural metropolis, then a psychedelic trip is an earthquake. It demolishes buildings, knocks out communications, creates chaos and confusion and plunges the city into wounded silence. And if that metropolis is a San Francisco of the Psyche? If it straddles a major fault-line? Well, then you've got serious trouble.

On Mount Jubilation, the shattering rush of Frankie's first acid trip brought me not only his exploded Haight-Ashbury but my own disastrous Newton Center, Massachussetts, where with Allen Ginsberg, in January of 1961, I visited Timothy Leary, the great guru-to-be, who was then a psychology professor at Harvard University and ostensibly hunting a cure for alcoholism.

Leary assured me that psychedelic drugs could work miracles, even change the world, because they made religious experience universally accessible. I popped his mushrooms and relived a nervous breakdown I'd had in the navy, where I'd ended up in the psychiatric ward—horrible days when I swore I could see inside other people's heads.

That first trip shook me to my foundations. But it didn't raze me. And later that year, when Leary produced more mushrooms in Ginsberg's New York City apartment, I chewed a dozen or so. Leary and I rambled through the snowy streets of the Lower East Side and tossed a loaf of bread like a football. Then I started hallucinating: buildings toppling, people turning into cackling demons. The usual horror show. Only this time everything happened on several planes simultaneously. Every act and utterance carried five or six different meanings.

Next day I awoke to myself—but I didn't feel the same. It was the morning after an earthquake. In some sectors destruction was minimal. In others, the quake had knocked out nerve centres and disrupted communications. I felt disoriented. If objects could change their essence without changing shape, a simple chair becoming a golden throne, then how did I know what I thought I knew? Modes of perception were conditioned responses. Reality was anybody's guess.

Despite my highly differentiated consciousness, then, and my thirty-nine years of experience, psychedelic drugs reduced me to adolescence. And here's the worst of it: the effect stayed with me. Months after that second trip, during a thirty-day drinking binge that brought me, red-faced and ranting, to an old favorite bar in Lowell, I met a ne'er-do-well steeplejack named Paul Bourgeois, an ex-thief who'd spent twelve years in jail. After listening to me rave drunkenly that my ancestors included not only French Canadians but North American Indians, Bourgeois concocted an insane story that spoke directly to the drug-traumatized twelve-year-old in me.

Bourgeois was Moon Cloud Chief of the Four Nations of the Iroquois. He'd just returned from Prince of Wales Island near the North Pole, where

131

three thousand of our people, half-French, half-Iroquois, were starving to death. Trouble was, nuclear submarines were cruising beneath the polar ice cap, polluting the water and contaminating the fish. The Moon Cloud Chief was on his way to Washington to complain. What's more, we were cousins, he and I, because two of the four tribes in the North were named Kirouac and L'Evesque—Memere's maiden name.

Yes, I believed this—even after I sobered up. I wrote letters to friends saying that soon I'd be heading North to join my Iroquois brothers. And I clung to this fantasy for six months. Eventually, I brought Bourgeois home to Florida where, under pressure from Memere, he confessed and made me listen.

Nobody could understand it—how a cheap con artist seeking beer money could snooker a world-famous author. But that was because nobody yet understood the destructive power of psychedelic drugs. Nobody realized that, even months after my second trip, my psychic defences were down.

Next thing I knew, Leary was hounding me to publish an upbeat letter I'd written after my first trip, when I was still innocent. I told him to forget it—that psychedelic drugs stupefy hand and brain for weeks and months. That tyrants and mad doctors would one day use such drugs to brainwash people, destroy their minds.

By 1967, six years after that second trip, Leary was jet-setting around the world chanting turn on, tune in, drop out. Ginsberg was travelling America urging every man, woman and child over fourteen to drop acid and welcome the ensuing nervous breakdown. And I was telling friends that I'd never fully recovered, and denouncing psychedelic drugs as a Communist plot to destroy the country. Metaphorical truth-telling, this—the only way I could hope to get through.

But these were the Oh-So-Hip Sixties, remember? So I was ridiculed and derided, labelled a boor and a has-been: Cracker Jack Kerouac, once King of the Beats, had become a know-nothing redneck, don't you know? A broken-down drunk.

But only half of that was true.

18.

All this came back on Mount Jubiliation as I swung along the trail from the stream, the leaky water carrier on my back. I was thirty-nine years old, remember, when I blew the psychedelic fuses—fully mature and not without achievements. A megalopolis in a world of cities—bedevilled by alcoholic slums, it's true, yet functioning, even celebrated. And still, from psychedelia, it took me months to emerge.

As for Frankie McCracken, despite his adolescent bravado and his wise-guy street-smarts, when he hit acid at age nineteen, he wasn't a city, much less a metropolis, but rather a hamlet with pretensions. Or maybe a town on a San Andreas fault. That first acid trip razed him, reduced him to rubble—though some inner core remained standing, some irreducible pillar. And, with all else in ruins, that core took control. The emergency system? The Self?

Put it this way: a rucksack warrior plunged into the Psychedelic Experience. A little boy lost stumbled out. Yes, Frankie was still able to function—to smoke grass and bum cheeseburgers and find places to crash.

But after that first trip he "understood" that some mysterious force had brought him to San Francisco for a special purpose. Taking acid had removed his blinders. Now he could discern hidden meanings. These meanings had always existed, but he hadn't been able to see them.

Suddenly, the world glowed with omens and portents. Events happened on several planes at once. During the acid trip, Oscar had made a pass at him. But that was just the surface. On a deeper level, he'd been acting for some mysterious force. He'd been testing Frankie—but for what? That was the question.

True, Frankie had fled into the evening shouting: "Seventeen! Seventeen!"

Yet somehow he'd passed Oscar's test.

Every day he visited the Fell Street House. Always Oscar welcomed him, though Frankie felt a new distance between them. What did that mean? He needed another sign, another signal. So he was thinking one afternoon as he arrived to find the house buzzing. He'd just missed meeting Jessica and Mitchell, the upstairs tenants. The city had shut off their electricity and they'd turned up at the front door to ask if they could run an extension cord.

Oscar had said yes, of course, and had helped Mitchell dismantle part of the makeshift barrier that blocked off the inside steps. Afterwards, Jessica had sat on those steps and read palms. Tarot cards, tea leaves—apparently, she did it all. Under a pseudonym, she wrote an astrology column for *The San Francisco Oracle*. Oscar said she was clairvoyant and that Mitchell was beautiful: "An archangel! A beautiful archangel!"

Frankie couldn't believe he'd missed them. Then Oscar said Jessica had invited him upstairs to read his poetry. And he didn't want to go alone.

That evening, after a dinner of brown rice and cabbage, Frankie followed Oscar out the front door and around the side of house. They climbed the rickety stairs to the second floor. Jessica opened the door. She was older than Frankie had expected, at least forty, and wore a floor-length blue dress and a black lace shawl. She led them into the dining room, dark except for three flickering candles. The air smelled of grass.

At the table sat a good-looking guy rolling joints. Neat and precise, wavy black hair, four or five years older than Frankie: Mitchell the archangel. He shook hands solemnly. Everybody sat down around the table and Jessica closed a hardcover volume that had been lying open beside her. Oscar said, "You've been reading by candlelight?"

"Just checking a reference," Jessica said. And as Mitchell rolled joints, she explained that the book was a hard-to-find Bible translated directly from Sanskrit, and incorporating much that orthodox Christianity considered apocryphal.

Mitchell sent a joint around the table.

Oscar had brought his red binder and the others passed joints as he read his poems by candlelight, using his hollow reading voice and finishing with the long work about God laughing seven times and creating the world that way. Everybody clapped and then Frankie must have missed something because Jessica was talking about reincarnation. "In the early eighteenth century," she said, "in my last life, I was an Indian princess."

Frankie said, "How do you know?"

"I remember."

"You remember a past life?"

"Oh, yes. Not everything but bits and pieces. I remember travelling through mountains in winter.

Yes." Jessica touched her fingers to the sides of her head. "Yes, that was the worst of the terrible winters." She was staring straight ahead, seeing nothing. "I almost died in the shadow of the tallest mountain in the world."

Mitchell handed Frankie the joint. He inhaled and passed it along without looking away from Jessica. Black eyes, black hair flecked with grey. Forty-five? Fifty? She was ageless, other-worldly.

After a moment, still gazing into the candles, Jessica resumed talking in a younger voice, a strange rhythm. "It was late afternoon when we reached the ridge that faced the tallest mountain. Grey Beaver said we'd camp there overnight and picked up his bow. He didn't have to tell me where he was going. We'd seen elk droppings on the trail and hadn't eaten meat for weeks. I tethered the ponies, built a fire and wrapped myself in buffalo hides. The baby was kicking inside me. I closed my eyes. When I opened them, it was night—and Grey Beaver hadn't returned. The wind was rising. I checked the ponies, then stoked the fire and curled up beside it."

Oscar offered Jessica the joint but she ignored him. She was entranced. Frankie sat opposite her, watching the candles dance in her eyes. He felt a mental bond between them. His head was buzzing with it. Jessica actually remembered being alive in the seventeen hundreds. This was mind-boggling—or maybe she was putting them on? How could he know?

Again Jessica started talking, the room silent except for her strange, young-woman voice. "When I woke it was morning. A cold wind was blowing snow into drifts and the ponies were gone. As I ate the last of the pemmican, I heard Grey Beaver calling me—not his voice, but his spirit. Telling me to hurry. I plunged down the trail, snow swirling around my knees, calling, 'Grey Beaver! Grey Beaver!' I felt him moving farther away. I tried to run but the snow got deeper and I kept falling and getting up, falling and getting up. Finally I couldn't get up any more. I lay there, exhausted, with the baby kicking inside me."

Again Jessica paused, only this time, as he stared, Frankie saw her face change. The lines around her eyes disappeared and so did her wrinkles. Her hair fell suddenly to her shoulders, thick and black and shining. For three seconds, four, the woman across the table from him was a beautiful Indian princess.

Then Jessica returned.

"Your face!" he said. "I just saw your face change!"

"Change? In what way?"

"You really were an Indian princess! You were . . . beautiful."

Jessica asked him to describe in detail what he'd seen. When he'd finished she smiled and said, "You see very clearly, Frankie. But why so surprised? You saw the face I wore during my last incarnation."

"That's just it. I've never believed in reincarnation. Though it fits, I suppose, with what I discovered on acid. With the idea that the body's a vehicle."

"Yes, the body dies but the self lives on, moving from one vehicle to another."

"But that changes everything."

"It's astonishing," Oscar said, standing up. "But you've been very hospitable and it's time for us to be off." He raised his eyebrows: "Shall we go?"

Frankie couldn't believe Oscar would leave now, in mid-discussion. Then realized, his head buzzing, that this was all part of The Test. If he wished, Frankie could leave now and forget the mysterious force. If he remained, Jessica would show him his next step. But everything took place on a number of levels.

Frankie had to play the surface game, too. "If it's okay with you, Osar, I'll stay a while."

Jessica patted Oscar's arm and led him to the door. Frankie shared another joint with Mitchell, still marvelling. When Jessica returned she resumed her story, described how she'd ended up giving birth in the snow. Then Frankie said, "What about Duality? How does that tie in?"

"Duality?"

"You know, Realizing Duality, reconciling the opposites. How does that fit with reincarnation?"

Jessica laughed and nodded towards Mitchell: "Maybe you should ask him. He's the wise one here."

"I'm not sure there is a connection," Mitchell said: "Duality is an illusion. All things are One."

"I don't understand."

Jessica laughed and said to Mitchell: "Wouldn't Charmian just love him?"

"With Charmian, who can tell?"

To Frankie, Jessica said: "If you're ever down in Carmel, you must look her up. Charmian Foster." She smiled a special smile. This was it. If Frankie wished to go forward, he had to visit Charmian Foster. "How do I get to Carmel?"

Mitchell said: "It's down the coast a hundred miles, maybe a bit more. On the Monterey Peninsula?"

"I leave tomorrow morning."

"I didn't mean for you to make a special trip," Jessica said. "Just that if you happened to be down that way you could —"

"No, no." At each step, obviously, he had a choice. "I'm going down anyway. I've got to go."

"As you wish," Jessica said at last. "But if you do see Charmian, don't tell her who sent you. Tell her . . . let's see . . . tell her you don't know whether I'm male or female."

Mitchell looked at the ceiling. He felt she was revealing too much. But Jessica touched Frankie's arm. "Tell Charmian you're not sure whether the person who sent you is a man or a woman."

19.

In the summer of 1960, six years before Frankie McCracken hitchhiked down the coast to Carmel, I made the same trip myself. I rode a bus south out of San Francisco down the Great Highway past those song-famous "little boxes made of ticky tacky," and soon found myself roaring down Highway One, which twists and turns and zigs and zags and climbs and falls along the California coast, offering vistas of craggy bluffs and windblown trees and the Pacific Ocean crashing white-capped over scattered black rocks. It's one of North America's great drives.

Carmel is just south of Monterey, which is where, as darkness fell, I got off the bus. I hopped into a taxi and rode fourteen miles to Bixby Creek Bridge, which is so photogenic, at least in daylight, that it turns up in tourist brochures. But now it was night and foggy and when I told the cabbie to swing right and follow the hard-packed Old Coast Road steeply downhill into the trees, he flatly refused—insisted that I pay him eight dollars and told me to hike the rest of the way.

I was making for Lawrence Ferlinghetti's cabin in the woods, which was destined to become the main setting for my last great novel, *Big Sur*. But I'd been drinking heavily, the night was moonless and loud with crashing ocean and I couldn't see ten yards through the fog, not even with my old brakeman's lantern. Somehow I lost the rutted dirt track. Finally I got scared and so bedded down where I stood, in a meadow.

Six years later and a dozen miles north, Frankie McCracken ran into no such trouble. Having ridden most of the way with a crazy old coot who insisted that the end of the world was at hand, Frankie hiked his last half mile in mid-afternoon, lugging his rucksack down a deserted two-lane highway.

The town of Carmel has long since become a boutique haven for the rich and wrongly famous, but when Frankie arrived in December of 1966, he stumbled into an ocean-front, gingerbread town with a spectacular, white-sand beach that stretched both ways forever.

He found a phone booth, flipped open the directory and right away, amazingly, found the number he wanted. A woman answered the phone. He said: "Charmian Foster? This may sound strange, but I've been sent to Carmel to see you."

"Not so strange. Who sent you?"

"The one who sent me said, 'Tell her you're not sure whether I'm a man or a woman.'"

Charmian said, "I see." Then: "A few of us are meeting tonight. Perhaps you'd like to join us?"

Frankie spent the afternoon on the beach, telling himself this was insane. Signs, omens, mysterious forces—what was he doing here? Then he'd remember his acid trip—how he'd seen for himself that reality was more complex than he'd dreamed. And what about Jessica's face? The idea of reincarnation had a literature behind it.

At seven o'clock, when he rang the bell of the cosy bungalow to which he'd been directed, a dazzling woman opened the door: big blue eyes, white-blonde hair to her shoulders, a shimmering floor-length gown, dark blue with silver stars. "Charmian Foster?"

Having shaken his hand, wide-eyed and smiling warmly, Charmian led Frankie into a sunken living room where three men and a young woman sat cross-legged on the floor. Made introductions. Frankie registered Kenneth as a lanky man with an Indian feather behind one ear. Wendy was about his own age, chubby and freckled. Patrick and Bradley were clean-cut guys in their mid-twenties. As he joined the circle with Charmian, Frankie spotted a red cross hanging over the fire place: "Are you Rosicrucians?"

"Very observant, Frankie. The answer is yes and no. But tell me: How is Jessica?"

So Charmian knew. He said Jessica was fine and described how, the previous night, he'd seen her face change: "She was once an Indian princess. Beautiful."

Charmian, nodding, looked around the circle, then back at Frankie: "What else?"

"It sounds insane," he said, "but I feel as if some mysterious force is guiding me."

"You're a seeker," Charmian said. Then briskly clapped her hands. "Let's begin."

She led Frankie to a couch on a raised platform and told him to lie down.

"Can't I stay in the circle?"

"You can rejoin us later. Right now we're going to release your astral body."

"My what?"

"Your spiritual body. Your higher self." She laughed, patted him on the arm. "Don't look so concerned. It needs to get out and breathe."

Frankie thought of Old Kerouac—remembered, vaguely, that in one of my novels I'd mentioned my astral body. *Desolation Angels?* He wished he'd read more closely. Something about relaxing and entering a trance?

Following Charmian's instructions, Frankie stretched out on the couch, his arms at his sides, and closed his eyes. Charmian rejoined the circle on the floor. Methodically, Kenneth had been dimming lamps and lighting candles. The darkened room fell silent and those in the circle—Frankie peeked out the corner of one eye—bowed their heads as if in prayer. Again Frankie thought of me, tried to imagine how I'd react in this situation, and willed himself to let go, to enjoy the flickering light.

"EEEEEEEE!"

The piercing scream jolted him upright: "What the— ?"

"Frankie, you've got to relax." Charmian stood up, chuckling, and came over to him. "That's just the signal to begin."

She settled him back down, returned to the circle and began again: "EEEEEEEE! EEEDLE EEEDLE EEEDLE EEEDLE EEEDLE EEEDLE EEEEEEEEE!"

Charmian screeched and warbled until she ran out of breath, then began sing-songing in a high-pitched voice, not making any sense: "Shayla-sooooooo, incubaaaaaaay, maninaaaaa, portoseeeeaaaa."

One of the men added a simple bass background: "Unga, toro, singa, medi, unga, toro, singa, medi"—sounded like Kenneth. Then came another female voice, Wendy, winding up and down against the cadence: "Haytanaya yoowayoowaooo, ganabayeeayee, aaeeaaeeaah."

144

Finally, Frankie could distinguish five voices, each of them chanting something different, Charmian's voice tight-roping high above the others. A man's voice stopped—the unga-toro bass. Out of the corner of his eye, Frankie saw Kenneth rise and stride into the kitchen. He could hear him bing-banging around, opening and closing doors. Running water? Smashing ice-cubes?

Kenneth returned to the living room carrying a pail full of water and smashed ice. This he sat on the floor in the middle of the circle. Then he rolled up a pantleg, pulled off a sock and, wincing, plunged his bare foot into the pail. Frankie almost laughed out loud. Kenneth clenched both fists. He stretched one arm upwards and the other towards Frankie, then closed his eyes and began rolling his head in time to the music.

The chanting grew louder, more intense. It reached a crescendo and then slowly tapered off as, one by one, voices withdrew. Finally Charmian chanted alone: "Shaylasooooooo, incubaaaaaaay, maninaaaaa, portoseeeeaaaa." She carried on for a few seconds, then warbled and screeched a finale: "EEEDLE EEEDLE EEEDLE EEEDLE EEEDLE EEEDLE EEEEEEEEE!"

Sudden silence. Kenneth went rigid.

"No, Frankie, don't get up." Charmian approached the couch. "We've released your astral body."

"How do you know?"

"I can see it, floating here above you. It's having a lovely time."

"My astral body? What's it look like?"

"Like your physical body, only lots of different colors. Look: can't you see it too, faintly?"

"No. No, I can't." Frankie squinted but saw nothing. "Maybe it's too dark."

"Not at all. I can see it quite clearly. But how do you feel?"

"Pretty good."

"Don't you feel—lighter?"

He considered this. "Maybe a little lighter."

"What are you thinking?"

Charmian was standing close to the couch, her leg almost touching his arm. She really was quite stunning. Should he lie? If she could see his astral body, probably she could read his mind. "I'm thinking that I wouldn't mind becoming your lover."

One of the men snorted. Charmian glanced over her shoulder and the noise stopped. "That's not unnatural. What about your astral body? Are you worried about it floating away?"

"Should I be?"

"No, no." Charmian laughed. "It's attached by a sort of umbilical cord."

"Will you be able to get it back in?"

"Oh, yes. But we'll give it a few moments. Obviously it needs some fresh air. Now, shhhhh."

Charmian returned to her place on the floor.

After a brief silence, again she screamed. Again she led a five-voice chant and finished with a shriek. Kenneth went limp. Groggily, he shook his head. He stepped free of the pail, dried his foot on a towel and carried his paraphernalia back into the kitchen.

Charmian said Frankie's astral body was back inside his physical one. She invited him to rejoin the circle on the floor, said: "Now's the time for questions."

"What was Kenneth doing?"

Charmian explained that he'd been acting as lightning rod. That releasing an astral body for the first time required energy. "With practice you can learn to release it yourself, and even to project it from place to place."

"But what's the connection between astral bodies and changing faces? And how does reincarnation fit?"

"It's the astral body that moves from one incarnation to the next."

"So when I saw Jessica as an Indian princess, I was seeing one of the faces of her astral body?"

Wide-eyed, Charmian nodded.

"What about you? Can you see faces?"

"Yes, of course."

"Can you see any of mine?"

"Frankie, I can see all of them. Some of your past lives were very noble indeed."

"So who was I?"

"It's best to explore past lives yourself. Kenneth was once one of Napoleon's soldiers. Wendy was lady to a knight of King Arthur's. Patrick, here, knows a great deal about several of his past lives. All of us lived in Egypt—back in the days of the pharoahs."

"Did I live then, too?"

"Yes, you did. That's often the way it works. Cyclical reincarnation. The same people turning up in different times, different places. Jesus and his disciples. Arthur and his knights."

"You mention Jesus. Was I around then?"

"You were."

Frankie didn't want to ask the question that popped into his mind, but could see no way around it: "Was I . . . was I Jesus?"

"No," Charmian said, unruffled. "No, Jesus was . . . a bit different. But you were close to him."

"Was I . . . one of his disciples?"

"Yes, you were."

"Which one?"

"I don't usually tell people about their past lives, Frankie. I prefer to let them find out for themselves." She looked around the circle. "But in this case, I'll make an exception." She smiled at him. "You were James."

"James the Brother of John and another one?"

Charmian beamed at her. "Very good, Wendy."

"Two James? Which one was I?"

"Which one do you think you were?"

"Which one was nearer to Jesus?"

Charmian looked at Wendy and nodded.

"James the Brother of John," she said. "You know: Peter and James and John."

"Was I The Near James?"

Charmian smiled. "That you'll have to find out for yourself."

20.

By the time we got back to the cabin I was soaked to the skin. Frankie had offered to take the leaky water carrier at the clearing, having laughed until the tears ran down his cheeks, pointing and saying, "Mister . . . Mister Omniscience!" But by then I was laughing myself and saw no sense in both of us getting wet.

The crack in the seam of the carrier was near the top, and in the cabin we emptied the remaining water into containers that didn't leak: a kettle, a dishpan, two pots and a bucket hidden beneath the makeshift sink.

Frankie went out to the tower and, as I changed my clothes, I gave myself over to rushes—heard the long, lonely wail of a train from Montreal and contemplated the significance and consequences of having a tragic father. Lost in this reverie, I was hanging my wet jeans and T-shirt on a front-yard clothes-line when Frankie appeared beside me: "Barometer's rising." He pointed north to where the sky was grey with scudding clouds. "We're in for a storm."

We spent the next couple of hours battening hatches. Frankie carried coal from the tool shed while

I swept the cabin. Together we split wood and stacked it on the front porch where it wouldn't get wet. Twice Frankie climbed into the tower to look around, but fire hazard was low and he didn't stay long.

I volunteered to cook supper and whomped up a meal modelled on one I'd shared at Ferlinghetti's cabin in Bixby Canyon just ten years before: potatoes wrapped in foil and baked in the wood-stove, along with hunks of roasted spam and cheese and a can of applesauce, all of it washed down, a departure here, with non-alcoholic cider.

Thunder rumbled as we ate and Frankie suggested that tonight I might want to sleep in the cabin. I told him I'd prefer to stay in the tower: "Less claustrophobic."

"Suit yourself." He looked relieved.

After supper, as we did the dishes—Frankie washed and I dried—I noticed a clutch of books on a shelf above the sink: *Drugs and the Mind, The Doors of Perception, The Varieties of Psychedelic Experience.* When I'd finished drying, I pulled out this last and sat down at the table.

While Frankie put away dishes, I flipped through *Varieties*, an academic tour-de-force by R.E.L. Masters and Jean Houston. Then opted for W. C. Fields: "Ah, yes, the psychedelic experience."

"No doubt you're an authority."

Back to myself. "I survived magic mushrooms, Frankie. But you're right. This psychedelic business has extraordinary dimension." I kept flipping. "Masters and Houston set up a four-tiered model of the unconscious. On the symbolic level, an acid-tripper encounters, let's see here . . . ."

Finally I found the right passage and coasted into it: "The acid-tripper encounters images that are 'predominantly historical, legendary, mythical, ritualistic and archetypal.'"

"That book blew me away."

"The subject may experience, blah, blah, blah . . . Ah, here it is. 'He may act out myths and legends and pass through initiations and ritual observances often seemingly structured precisely in terms of his own most urgent needs.'"

"Yeah, that's the stuff."

I kept reading aloud: " 'Where the symbolic dramas unfold, the individual finds facets of his own existence revealed in the person of Prometheus or Parsifal, Lucifer or Oedipus . . . ' and so forth." I snapped the book shut and shoved it back onto the shelf. "The Self fights back."

"You've lost me."

"Symbolic dramas, archetypal images. Under attack, bent on survival, the Self fights back." Ignoring his confusion, I stood up and stretched: "Let's go play horseshoes. Before the storm hits."

He bounced off the bed. "Didn't know you played."

"Don't expect much. I haven't pitched horseshoes since 1961, when I was gathering myself in Florida to write *Big Sur*."

"Yeah, yeah."

We put on jackets—the evening was cool—and brought the jug of cider.

The horseshoe pit was just south of the tower.

For three months Frankie had been playing nightly, steadily improving, and the first two games he killed me. Then, with a winning score set at twenty-one, he spotted me ten points. We played two games that way and still he won. He tossed at least one ringer each "end," and sometimes two. Finally, he suggested we retire to his favorite tree-stump and finish the cider.

"One more game," I said. "Loser makes breakfast tomorrow—and forget the handicap."

"You serious?"

"I'm feeling lucky."

After two turns Frankie was ahead eleven to
seven. Then he threw two consecutive ringers, which
gave him enough to win. I had one more toss. I turned
my back to the peg, flipped the horseshoe casually
over my head and heard it settle perfectly atop his two
ringers. We were playing last ringer scores all—another concession for my sake—so fifteen points were
mine. I'd won.

"What luck!" Frankie cried. "Okay, I'll make
breakfast. But let's play one more game."

This time, after three ends, Frankie tossed a
wobbly ringer, apparently a game-winner, and
grinned: "That's that."

Magically, though without panache, I topped it.

With his final shoe, Frankie threw yet another
ringer. Chuckling, he wiped his hands in the air:
"Who's the better man?"

I closed my eyes tight and spun around three
times. Then, my arm extended, hook-shot style, and
still with my eyes closed, I flipped the horseshoe
skyward. I opened my eyes and watched the wind
carry it sideways, this heavy metal horseshoe, and drop
it with a gentle thunk around the peg, a perfect ringer.
The game was mine.

"What a fluke!" Frankie clasped his head with
both hands and staggered around in melodramatic
circles. "Talk about a fluke shot!"

I had to laugh. "Magic is alive."

"One more game!"

"Sorry." I rubbed my shoulder. "Pulled my arm
with that last toss."

I picked up the cider jug and our two glasses and led the way to Frankie's favorite stump. Looking north from there, you could see half the valley. Frankie sat down on the gnarled stump beside me, still shaking his head. "Can't get over that fluke shot. Incredible." "I used to play pool," I said. "Every so often, I'd make what a friend of mine called a 'Jesus-Christ shot.'" Having refilled our glasses, I proposed a toast: "To Jesus-Christ shots!"

We drank and then I gestured with my glass at the clouds, now heavy and dark: "You were right about the storm."

Frankie sipped cider. "What did you mean earlier, when you said miracles signify and suggest, but prove nothing?"

We were still on track. "Miracles provide circumstantial evidence."

"Of what?"

"This and that. Looming sainthood, for example."

Frankie rolled his eyes but I had him: "You yourself once dreamed of sainthood."

"Long ago and far away."

"San Francisco? What, three years back? Maybe I should remind you, Frankie, that my novels crackle with proselytizing. I'm a not-so-secret general of the Jesuit and other armies."

"You mean Kerouac's stuff? Get serious."

"My second published story featured an angel."

"Maybe his early work. Before he matured."

"The *Dharma Bums* came later."

"An adventure story, mainly. The religion's irrelevant."

"*Au contraire, mon ami. Visions of Gerard, Dr. Sax, Big Sur*, even *Satori in Paris*—sainthood is always the subtext."

"What are you selling? Kerouac was an impulsive madman, a non-stop sinner."

"My impetuosity was a kind of faith—a reliance on the Dharma, on the idea that the universe is self-regulating."

"Kerouac was a drunk."

"Frankie, you're forgetting duality—the dynamic interaction of opposites."

"I don't believe this."

"In my case, addiction to alcohol and the quest for sainthood."

But all this was hitting Frankie too early and he shook his head, disgusted. I refilled our glasses with cider. We drank in silence, staring out at the mountains, the lowering sky. On my face I felt the first droplets of rain.

Frankie said, "So how'd you get onto this sainthood kick?"

"Runs in the family. When my brother, Gerard, was dying of rheumatic fever, age nine, local nuns gathered around his bed to record his last words. I was four and expected him to reappear after he died, huge and powerful and renewed, greater and more Gerard-like than ever." I took a sip of cider. "Sure enough, shortly after he died, I was lying in bed one night when suddenly there he stood, leaning over my crib, wide-eyed and wild-haired. My big brother, Gerard."

"So this weird fixation of yours springs from a dream you had at four?"

"Oh, I had many dreams. My mother kept a crucifix in her bedroom and sometimes in the dark I'd see Jesus glowing like a light. Once God spoke to me through that crucifix. He promised to save me, but said I had to suffer first and die in pain, frightened and despairing, tormented by doubt and ambiguity."

"You expect me to take this childhood stuff seriously?"

"Cut to Mexico City, 1950. I was twenty-eight. I'd just seen my first bullfight and found it revolting—brutal and bloody and senseless. To forget I smoked grass and focused on my writing. That's when I finally found my way into *On The Road*. Had a vision of myself as this Great Walking Saint."

"Drug-induced hallucinations." Frankie waved his hand dismissively. "Best put them behind you."

"North Carolina, 1955. No drugs. I was smelling flowers in the back yard. I stood up, took a deep breath—and woke on my back in the grass. I'd been unconscious, a neighbor said later, for about sixty seconds. That's when I had my vision of the Golden Eternity. Realized that Time is an illusion. That eternity is not just a long time, an eon, but has nothing to do with Time. That dead or alive, we all exist forever in the Golden Eternity."

"Mystical mumbo-jumbo!" Frankie said, snorting. "Kerouac drank and took drugs. He screwed anything that moved. He was a committed hell-raiser, an unrepentant sinner—and you're trying to pass him off as a saint?"

"A saint can serve God as a sinner."

"Ha! Try that one on a priest."

"I'm not here to defend conventional religion, Frankie, but certain men of the cloth might surprise you." Again I refilled our glasses. "One night in Northport, must have been the mid-sixties, a friend arranged for a nymphomaniac to visit me at my house. I didn't want to ruin her pleasure by coming too quickly, so before she arrived I deked into the bathroom and took care of business. Later, my friend told a priest. The priest said, 'That's charity! That's real Christian charity!' And demanded to meet me."

"Christian charity!" Frankie almost fell off the stump. "Deking into the bathroom to masturbate?" This time he couldn't stop laughing.

21.

In Carmel, California, having located Charmian Foster, Frankie crashed for two nights at a communal house shared by three of her disciples. The future looked bright—he was clearly on track—until the second evening, when Brother Patrick overheard Sister Wendy inviting Frankie to her room to give her a back rub. Until now, Patrick had been Wendy's lone back-rubber.

Brother Patrick was also, as it happened, the main payer of rent for the communal house. And next morning, though Frankie had declined Wendy's invitation, Patrick told him to clear out. He'd had a dream. Frankie was spiritually disruptive.

Frankie telephoned Charmian Foster. Brother Kenneth answered and said she'd temporarily left town, that she was attending a retreat. Frankie couldn't believe he'd finished learning from Charmian—the knowledge that he'd once been a disciple of Jesus gave him no sense of closure—and felt he had to remain in Carmel.

Room rents, however, were out of sight. A sympathetic waitress told him that rents were much lower in the nearby town of Pacific Grove. Frankie spent one night on the beach, shivering in his thin sleeping bag and hiding from patrolling cops, before he understood that her suggestion was a sign.

He hitchhiked across the peninsula to Pacific Grove and rented a room for a week. From there he contacted Charmian Foster, but Patrick had got to her and she wished him many noble lives: "Remember, Frankie: You were one of Jesus's chief disciples—one of the two James."

Great. But where did that leave him? Hanging out in the Pacific Grove Library, a long, low building, white with a red-tile roof and distinctive Spanish arches. He couldn't borrow books because he wasn't a member, and couldn't become a member because he wasn't a resident, but Frankie spent hours rummaging in the stacks and reading at tables.

The library had a copy of *Desolation Angels,* and in it Frankie found my single allusion to astral bodies. But my passing reference shed no special light and Frankie plunged into Rosicrucianism, read three or four contradictory tomes about venerating the rose and the cross and developing occult powers. Then he discovered Phylo and Nostradamus and wrestled with astral projection, planes of existence and ancient prophecies of doom.

Trouble was, Frankie could find no way to relate any of this to his own experience, to integrate it with what he'd learned since dropping acid. Since moving to Pacific Grove, he'd seen precious few signs. Had the mysterious force deserted him? He was out walking one morning, wondering about with this, when some clown in a passing car yelled: "Hey, hippy! Get a haircut!"

Frankie detested the term "hippy." Besides, his hair barely covered his ears. Only, what if that yell was an omen? Maybe the signs were there but, because of the mix-up with Charmian Foster, he hadn't been seeing them? On the other hand, what about money? He was down to four dollars.

Still, a possible sign was a possible sign. Maybe, for some reason beyond the physical realm, on another plane of existence, Frankie did need to get a haircut. He glanced down the street—sneaked a peek, really. No barber poles. Very well. He owed the mysterious force this much: If he passed a barber shop before he reached the end of the block, he'd accept the yell as a bonafide sign. Otherwise, no.

Ten strides more and there, painted on a window, Frankie discovered a red-and-white barber pole. Couldn't believe it. He peered into the shop. A trim, sandy-haired barber was dusting off an only customer. A poster proclaimed his prices. No way Frankie could afford a haircut, not even if he was meant to have one.

Still, a sign was a sign. He took two deep breaths and entered the barber shop as the other customer, an older man with a goatee, paid for his haircut and left. Frankie waited until he was sitting in the chair, a bib under his chin and the barber clipping away: "You aren't interested in reincarnation, by any chance? In planes of existence or astral bodies?"

The barber stopped clipping, stepped back and stared, open-mouthed: "Who are you?"

"That's what I'm trying to find out."

While the barber cut his hair, Frankie explained that he was being guided by some mysterious force: "An omen drove me into this shop."

The barber listened intently, then stepped around from behind the chair and extended his hand: "My name is Munsie. I'm a spiritualist."

159

Munsie went and sifted through a pile of maga-
zines and handed Frankie half a dozen: "Take a look
at these."

Instead of *Playboy*, *Time* or *Newsweek*, Munsie
stocked *The Winding Path*, the covers of which advertised interviews with beings who lived "on the other
side of the veil" and advice on how to stay on the right,
true path. Frankie flipped through several of these,
fighting to keep an open mind.

When the barber was done he swept aside his
cloth with a flourish: "The haircut's on me."

"Thanks, Munsie. This means more to me than
you realize."

"Listen, my wife and I are having a few friends
over tonight. An informal gathering. Why don't you
join us?"

Munsie and his wife lived above the barber shop
in a neat, two-bedroom flat. When Frankie arrived,
precisely on time, he found half a dozen people there,
most of them twice his age and prosperous-look-
ing—not a single pair of blue jeans among them. They
sat in the living room drinking tea and eating cookies
and discussing an acquaintance's passion for curing
women by laying on hands. A middle-aged woman in
a sequined dress motioned Frankie into the kitchen
and whispered, "Are you The One?"

"Which one?"

"The One we're awaiting?"

"I don't know."

Back in the living room, a red-faced man named
Gerald said: "Can you see auras, Frankie?"

"Auras? No, I can't."

"Don't be ashamed to admit it," Gerald said, his
voice booming. "We've all seen auras. Myrtle, you've
seen them, haven't you? Sure you have. Come on,
Frankie. Look at Myrtle. Can't you see her aura? Red

and blue and just a touch of yellow? I'm sure you can
see it. Don't be ashamed to say so. You can see Myrtle's
aura, can't you?"

Munsie said: "Gerald gets like this when he
drinks, Frankie. Pay no attention."

Later, as the party wound down, Munsie whispered to Frankie that he should remain behind: "I've
got something to show you."

When the two of them were alone, his wife
having said goodnight and disappeared into the bedroom, Munsie rooted around in a wooden chest hidden in a back-hall closet.

"Got it!" he said at last, producing a blue suede
jewel box. Munsie sat down on the couch, opened this
box and took out a two-inch prism: "With this we can
consult the spirits."

The sparkling, red-and-blue prism was attached
to a piece of white thread. Munsie took the end of the
thread between the thumb and forefinger of his right
hand and jiggled the prism up and down. "A pendulum, see?"

His wife emerged into the living room and
picked up a magazine. "Oh, Munsie," she said. "You're
not showing him that old thing?"

"I thought you'd gone to bed."

"It's just nervous impulses," the woman said.
"Been proven."

She spun on her heel and left.

"Pay no attention," Munsie said. "She has little
faith." He spun the prism with his finger. "When
people die, they don't assume new bodies right away.
For a while they live on in the astral state—pure,
disembodied spirits."

Frankie nodded, non-committal: "That fits."

"As spirits, they know things we don't. And
sometimes they'll answer questions for us." Munsie

jiggled the prism up and down. "They'll spin this pendulum clockwise for yes, counter-clockwise for no." He lowered his voice to a whisper. "Watch."

Munsie dangled the prism over the palm of his left hand. Staring hard, he called: "Spirits! Spirits, can you hear me?"

Nothing happened.

"Spirits! Spirits, please! Will you answer questions for Munsie the Barber? Spin the pendulum clockwise for yes, counter-clockwise for no."

Again nothing.

"Spirits, please! We wait with respect."

The prism began to spin clockwise.

Frankie looked at Munsie's right hand, the one holding the prism. It was perfectly still. Yet the prism spun faster. Munsie asked the spirits half a dozen questions. Had people enjoyed themselves tonight? Would Gerald ever emerge from his scepticism? Each time the spirits responded.

Frankie worried that Munsie was somehow moving the thread: "May I try it?"

The barber handed him the prism. Frankie suspended it over his left palm, careful to keep his hands steady. "Spirits," he called. "Spirits, will you answer questions for Frankie McCracken?"

Munsie said, "For Frankie the Seeker."

Nothing happened. Frankie handed back the prism. Signs or no signs, this business left him cold. But Munsie insisted that he try again. This time, at the barber's insistence, he said, "Frankie the Seeker." And to his surprise the prism began to spin. Yes, a mysterious force had guided Frankie to California. Yes, that force had wanted him to meet Munsie the Barber.

Munsie clapped his hands: "Ask a tough one."

"Spirits," Frankie called. "Spirits, listen. In one of my past lives, I was a disciple of Jesus—but I don't

162

know which one. Can you tell me? Was I the James of
Peter and James and John? The James who was nearer
to Jesus?"

Nothing happened.

Munsie cried, "Again!"

"Spirits, yes or no," he called. "Was I James, the
brother of John? Was I once The Near James?"

The prism spun slowly at first, then gathered
momentum and began to revolve.

"Frankie, you were James!" Munsie clapped his
hands. "The Near James!"

22.

c/o General Delivery,
San Francisco, California,
Dec. 17, 1966.

Dear Family:

Strange things have been happening to me and I
don't yet know what they mean. All I can tell you
is that I'm looking for myself. I hope what I find
will make you happier with me than you have
been.

I love you all very much.

I'm sorry I can't be home for Christmas. Thank
you for your kind wishes. You can be sure that
I'm thinking of you all. But I have to stay here in
California until I find out what it is I've been sent
here to learn.

If my last unemployment cheque has come, I
would appreciate your sending it along. Also, do
you know the precise time of my birth? Mom, this

is important. If you don't know to the minute, could you give me an approximation?

I wish there was more I could tell you. I am healthy. I'd like to send you all Christmas presents, but I just haven't got the money. All I can send is this letter and my love.

Joyeux Noel,
Frankie

P.S. Please don't worry about me. I've started working part-time at the post office.

23.

Nobody learns to be a writer. Not the way you learn to be an accountant or a plumber. You have to be born with a tragic father. So I declared in 1967 during my interview with *The Paris Review*. A wild generalization, I know, but I'd recently written *Vanity of Duluoz* so I'd been thinking about my own father, Leo Kerouac, and realizing yet again how large he'd loomed in my life.

On Mount Jubilation, at Frankie's unconscious prompting, I remembered how my father would arrive home late for dinner, having gone drinking with his cronies. Memere would call him a no-good drunken bum, a *vaurien* who cared nothing for his wife and children, and tell him she should have listened to her family, she should never have married him.

Leo would respond with something more charming still, maybe *ferme ta guèle, maudite vache*, shut your face, you god-damn cow, *avant que je te fous une baffe*. Before I shut it for you. And so the evening would begin.

On Jubilation, as I shed my wet clothes and hung them outside on the line, I remembered that when my parents fought like this I'd stand out in the back yard. From there, in the gathering dusk, I'd watch neighbor families in their kitchens eating dinner and imagine they were ghosts eating ghost food, and maybe I was a ghost too. I'd look up at the stars and wonder where the universe ended and think how small, really, my problems were.

If my parents' battle showed no sign of abating, I'd go for a long walk and end up sitting on the bank of the Merrimack River, listening to the rush of the water. Sometimes, from upriver, the long, lonely wail of the train from Montreal would reach me and I'd swear never to become like my father—never to become a drinker.

On Jubilation I discovered that, two decades after I sat on that river bank as a teenager, and not three hundred miles away, in Sainte-Thérèse-sur-le-lac, ten-year-old Frankie McCracken would hear the wail of a different train from Montreal—and the long, lonely sound would once again evoke a tragic father.

Frankie would lie awake in his bed waiting to hear the whistle from off in Coeur d'Aimée, one long *wooooooooooo*, one short, and then another long: *wooooooooooo, wooo, wooooooooooooooo*.

This would be any season but summer, because then the train came all the way to Sainte-Thérèse and Frankie's mother would take him and Janey and Eddie to meet their father. They'd walk up *Avenue des Archanges* and along the highway, *Chemin Saint-Esprit*, then turn up a dirt road lined with trees and bushes. At the train station—just an open shelter, really—the children would put their ears to the tracks and listen for the rumble that signalled an approaching train.

Far away down the tracks, a light would appear against the dark trees. As the train drew near in a long, slow curve, *wooooooooo, woo, wooooooooo*, they'd count the cars—usually six or eight, sometimes ten or twelve. Mothers would yell at children to get off the tracks and into the station. From inside, leaning out, they'd watch the engine thunder past, the engineer waving his big gloved hand, and then the passenger cars clank and shudder to a halt, the whole train steaming and hissing.

Frankie loved to see his father step off the train with the other commuters, his hat on his head, his suit jacket over his arm, his tie askew and his white shirt open at the neck. Down the dirt road they'd march *tous ensemble*, a family like all the others.

Only sometimes Frankie's father didn't get off the train. And they'd stand, the four of them, looking to see if they'd missed him in the rush—maybe up near the engine?—while the train pulled out and everybody else swung laughing down the dirt road.

That meant his father had stayed in town to drink. And his mother, biting back tears, would lead the family slowly home.

When Frankie had turned ten, she'd bought him an old bicycle to use on his *Gazette* route. Now she started sending him on it to meet the train—first the five o'clock, and then, if necessary, the five-thirty. It was his job to see that his father came straight home instead of stopping off at the hotel. "Mummy'll be mad," he'd tell his father. "She's been alone all day with the kids and needs a break."

"Yes, yes, I'm just going to unwind with a quick one. Tell your mother I'll be home soon."

That was in summer.

The rest of the year the train from Montreal came only as far as Coeur d'Aimée, and if his father wasn't home before seven-thirty, usually everybody would be in bed when he did arrive. Frankie would lie awake listening for the long lonely howl of the train whistle, which carried on the wind across the corner of the lake: *Wooooooooo, wooo, wooooooooooo*. At the sound, he'd roll over and look at the luminous white hands of his alarm clock.

Twenty minutes, his father took to get home by taxi. Five, ten, fifteen. Twenty minutes and in he'd come, go straight to the front room and dig out his gramophone. Wouldn't stop to remove his hat and coat. He'd crank up the gramophone, sit down at the kitchen table and start playing records, scratchy old 78s, the same ones over and over. *Dream when you're feeling blue. Dream, that's the thing to do. Just let the smoke rings rise in the air. You'll find your share of memories there.*

He'd sit at the kitchen table in his hat and coat, staring at the floor, listening to Frank Sinatra sing the same songs over and over. *Dream when the day is through. Dream, your dreams might come true. Things never are as bad as they seem. So dream, dream, dream.*

But go beyond twenty minutes. Frankie would hear the train whistle and wait. Twenty-five minutes, thirty, thirty-five. Forty minutes and he'd start praying for an exception—that tonight his father wouldn't come home at all. That tomorrow morning in Coeur d'Aimée he'd get off the train all the other commuters got on.

Everybody would see his father and know he'd been out all night drinking, but no shouting match would rip the wee hours open. Either his father would collapse into bed and his mother would call the office and say he was sick, or else she'd help him out of his crinkled suit and into clean clothes and ship him back to Montreal on the next train. Late for work, smelling of booze—but no shouting match.

That was the exception, because waiting twenty minutes beyond the train whistle usually meant

169

Frankie's father would catch the last train from Montreal and arrive home at quarter to two. Or else that he'd got out of the taxi at the hotel, *La Fin du Monde*, and would stagger home drunk when he ran out of money. Either way, bad news.

Frankie would wake to the creaking of the kitchen door. His father would stumble into the house, kick off his boots and throw his coat on the couch. Then, "Maggie, I'm hungry. What have we got to eat?"

"Keep your voice down," his mother would call from bed. "You'll wake the whole house. Your supper's in the oven, where it always is when you get home at this time of night."

His father would open the oven, take out his supper, let the door spring shut. He'd pull a kitchen chair away from the table, make a scraping noise on the linoleum floor. After a minute he'd throw down his fork, shout, "Maggie, this food's cold."

"What did you expect? Supper was on the table at six o'clock. If you'd get home here after work, like any decent man, you'd find your supper waiting."

"Guy slaves all day with a bunch of philistines, he's got a right to a hot meal when he arrives home. Get out here and make me something to eat."

"Make it yourself. What do you think I am? A bloody servant?"

From there the battle would escalate.

In his bed, Frankie would pull his pillow tight over his head to drown out the noise. Usually, after about half an hour, the shouting would subside. And he'd go back to sleep.

Then came the night his father lurched muttering into the house. He slammed the door shut and Frankie woke knowing that tonight would be bad. He checked his clock. Quarter to twelve, no trains due. His father had been drinking at *La Fin du Monde*.

Now he was pacing around the kitchen, making a strange smacking sound—pounding his fist into his hand? "Nine years I gave them." He bumped into a kitchen chair, knocked it over onto the floor. "Nine years of my life! And this is the thanks I get! Ingrates! Sons of bitches!"

"Maurice, stop slamming around. And shut up that swearing. The kids can hear every word you—oh, my God! Look at this mess!" His mother had risen and gone into the kitchen. "You're like a bloody two-year-old. Don't know enough to take off your boots when you come through the door."

His father banged his fist down on the kitchen table and the utensils rattled. "Don't give me any crap, Maggie. I'm not in the mood."

"Take your boots off, then."

His father resumed pacing. "I'll take my boots off when I'm ready." He banged a cupboard door shut—once, twice.

Frankie had never heard him this bad.

"They got me, Maggie. They finally got me."

"Who got you?"

Blam! Blam! His father was pounding the wall behind the oil stove.

"Maurice! For God's sake! You'll break your hand."

Blam! Blam! Blash! Something had given way.

"Are you satisfied? Let me see your hand."

"They got me, Maggie. They finally got me."

"Who got you? What are you talking about?"

"Those bastards at work." His father was crying. Could this be happening?

"Nine years it took them. But they got me."

"What do you mean, they got you?"

"They fired me, Maggie."

"Fired you? Oh, my God! What happened?"

"I borrowed some money out of the accounts receivable. So I could buy lunch."

"So you could buy beer, you mean."

"I was going to hit the bank and return it this afternoon, as usual. But the auditors came back."

"Weren't they in yesterday?"

"Somebody tipped them off."

"It's because of your drinking."

"Nine years of my life, Maggie!"

"They were looking for an excuse."

Frankie fell asleep to his father's sobbing.

In the morning, behind the oil stove, he found a hole in the wall. His father had punched his fist through the gyprock. Amazing.

24.

My favorite biographer, Gerald Nicosia, suggests that my obnoxious megalomania wasn't born until the mid-fifties, but he's too kind. In truth I always had a tendency to self-aggrandizement. As a boy I imagined myself the world's greatest writer, and at nineteen, when I had the first of my great waking dreams, I saw myself as the hero not of a story but a full-blown legend—notably, as the author of a book "so golden and purchased with magic that everybody smacks their brows." A couple of years later, when I cracked up at navy bootcamp, the Yossarian syndrome, a psychiatrist diagnosed me as "a schizoid personality with angel tendencies"—nineteen-forties jargon for megalomania.

The fifties did bring inflation. When I discovered reincarnation, I produced a list of past lives that included Honoré de Balzac and William Shakespeare, as well as two of the greatest-ever Buddhist saints. I admitted also to having been an Indian potboy and an English thief, but this was a story-teller's ploy, a sop to credibility.

The sixties? More of the same. In San Francisco, recently arrived, I declared that I'd been present at the crucifixion of Christ. Then, better still, that no, I wasn't, I couldn't have been because I would have tried to prevent it and that would have been recorded. Down the California coast, in Bixby Canyon, I decided that in a recent acquaintance I'd found Jesus himself, come again to lead his disciples on a march from California to New York and beyond.

Why do I rehearse this history? Because in it, on Mount Jubilation, I discovered resonances. Frankie McCracken's "angel tendencies" blossomed late in 1966, when he returned to the Haight knowing he'd been The Near James, but penniless and with no place to stay.

He ended up crashing at The Fell Street House. Two nights later, Ruth The Painter freaked out, began yelling that her home had become a madhouse in which she couldn't paint. She'd signed the lease and wanted everybody to get the hell out—everybody except a beautiful couple and their disturbed four-year-old son, but certainly including Frankie and Oscar and Bonnie Torn, a razor-sharp red-head who'd announced that a guy named Joe Bob was on his way to the Haight from New Orleans. That's what had set Ruth off, the idea of yet another addition to Oscar's ever-changing retinue—always somebody knocking on the door to see the poet-guru.

A fellow named Bernie was visiting when Ruth freaked—an ex-New Yorker in his late twenties. Bernie sported a green cowboy hat, held down an inside job at the post office and edited a literary magazine. This was the guy who was publishing Oscar's poem about God laughing seven times—though with Frankie this no longer signified.

Bernie lived in a two-room apartment, called it his Bunker, on the second-floor of yet another run-down Victorian mansion in the Haight. Said he had room for three people, no problem, and Oscar and Bonnie and Frankie gathered their gear and went with him.

Next day Oscar pacified Ruth The Painter and moved back into The Fell Street House. Frankie stayed on at the Bunker and watched Bernie and Bonnie became lovers. His own sex drive was dead, too many things on his mind, and he went for a lot of walks. Spent his days rambling around the Haight, smoking dope and watching for signs, and his nights on a mattress on the living-room floor.

One afternoon, while sitting under a tree in the Panhandle, getting high, Frankie spotted Oscar hurrying along Fell Street towards Bernie's Bunker. He took one last toke, then popped the roach and shouted and caught up. Oscar said, "Joe Bob arrived last night."

Frankie had never seen him so excited.

Mounting the stairs, he heard somebody wailing on a harmonica. Oscar said, "Joe Bob!" and started taking steps three at a time. The two of them burst into the Bunker and almost hit Bernie, who was dancing around the kitchen waving a ladle. He laughed and jerked his green-hatted head, hey, get a load of this, at the guy blowing harp in the corner.

Joe Bob was finishing a bluesy rendition of *When The Saints Come Marching In*, wailing away with his eyes closed. Even so he was strikingly handsome, mid-to-late twenties and Greek-looking, with well-chiseled features and wavy black hair. On the table in front of him stood a half-empty gallon-jug of red wine. He opened his eyes, surprisingly blue, but Oscar cried, "Don't stop!"

Joe Bob whooped at the sight of his old pal and started blowing for real, chuffing and wailing like a freight train. He rocked back and forth, stomping one foot on the floor so the whole kitchen shook but who cared? Bernie was dancing around clacking spoons. Joe Bob blew a fierce, howling riff and whooped a finale, but Oscar yelled, "Don't stop!"

So Joe Bob went at it again.

Oscar was laughing and crying and yelling, "Don't stop! Don't stop!" and finally Frankie couldn't stand it any longer, keeping it all inside. He spotted the wine and yes! grabbed the bottle, whipped off the top, and with Joe Bob wailing, Bernie banging spoons and Oscar crying, "Don't stop!" he lifted the jug and splashed wine into Joe Bob's black hair, half a glass, splashed it out, and Joe Bob looked up and nodded and kept wailing.

"Appreciated the gesture, man," he said afterwards, when everybody had collapsed and he was drying his hair with a towel. "Appreciated the gesture."

Turned out Joe Bob had been blowing harp for ten years, off and on. "Picked up my riffs from old blues men in Nworlins—cats like Jimmy Reed, Howlin' Wolf, Sonny Boy Williamson. Used to hang out after hours in the French Quarter."

Frankie said, "In New Or-leans?"

"No, Nworlins," Joe Bob said, laughing. "Nworlins."

To complement his drawl, turn it almost into song, Joe Bob had a deep bass voice. Blue eyes, pale skin, curly black hair: this was one beautiful cat. But see Joe Bob two days later, climbing the hill to the Drugstore Cafe between Oscar and Frankie, green duffle coat open to the elements, a long blue scarf hanging down his back. In one hand, dangling from a finger, Joe Bob carried his gallon jug of dry red wine. In the other, an old-favorite hardcover: Walt Whitman's *Leaves of Grass*, a large-format edition boldly illustrated in charcoal.

Oscar was celebrating Rainer Marie Rilke, droning on about angels and puppets, when Joe Bob cried: "Enough antiquated elegies! You want poetry?" He passed Frankie his jug, flipped open his Whitman and began reading aloud, marking the rhythm with his free hand: *"Afoot and light-hearted I take to the open road, / Healthy, free, the world before me, / The long brown path before me leading wherever I choose."* He declaimed the first stanza, really from memory, then snapped the book shut: "Now that's poetry!"

"Did you say antiquated?" Oscar sniffed. "Whitman was dying when Rilke was born."

"Nonsense! Whitman lives!" Joe Bob whipped out his blues harp, handed Frankie his *Leaves Of Grass* and, there on the street, swung into *When The Saints*.

Behind him, in Nworlins, Joe Bob had left a "too possessive" wife and a job as an artist in an advertising agency. Besides his Whitman, Joe Bob carried a single small suitcase: socks and boxer shorts, all neatly folded, two pairs of corduroys, three long-sleeved shirts, a thick blue sweater, two boxes of colored pencils, three harmonicas in different keys, a hard-cover copy of the *I Ching* and the manuscript of an unpublished novel he intended to rewrite.

Women were crazy for Joe Bob. When he wasn't drinking wine, spouting Whitman or blowing harp, he "balled chicks" on the mattress in the living room. Frankie remembered that in one of my books I'd spoken of "balling." *The Subterraneans?* Should he look it up? Occasionally, Joe Bob got orgies going, but usually Frankie watched from the armchair, declining to participate. Too many things on his mind.

By the time his mother informed him of the precise moment of his birth, he'd abandoned astrology and resumed vagrant reading. He discovered Meher Baba, would-be avatar of the age: "I was Rama, I was Krishna, I was this one, I was that one—now I am Meher Baba." Dismissed him as a charlatan. Gurdjieff, Ouspensky, the *Bhagavad-Gita*: none of them explained the mysterious force.

Frankie wondered about the *I Ching*, the *Chinese Book of Changes*. In the Haight that book was the Bible. Hadn't Kerouac mentioned it in *Dharma Bums?* Frankie badgered Joe Bob to show him how The Oracle worked and finally cornered him in The Hobbit Hole, which was just down the hall from Bernie's Bunker. Really it was a storage room, but Joe Bob had cleaned it out, christened it and installed two mattresses. Frankie sat on one of them, smoking dope, and Joe Bob on the other, drinking wine.

Joe Bob first warned Frankie against consulting the *I Ching* daily, as some people did. He himself intended to seek its advice only once—on the day he arrived at The Fork In The Road. Until then, he was content to lug it around in his suitcase.

Frankie nodded his understanding.

"The idea behind the *Book of Changes*," Joe Bob said, "is that everything's in harmony. Two opposing principals are at work in the universe—male and female, active and passive, creative and destructive. The *I Ching* calls them *Yin* and *Yang*."

"Eros and Agape?"

"Oscar's old favorites? Sure, why not? These principals are forces, really, and they push each other back and forth. That's where change comes from—from the interaction between these forces."

"Hence the name: *Book of Changes*."

"Right. Underneath change, though—and this is the secret—there's order." Joe Bob took another slug of wine. "There's order, only it has nothing to do with cause and effect. Everything's related, see? Everything's in harmony. At any given time, and in any given place, there's only one way things can happen. If I throw a penny into the air and it comes up tails, it's because that's the only way it can possibly come up at that time and place."

"Because everything's in harmony?"

"Exactly. And that's why the *I Ching* can answer questions. It uses the opposites, interprets them, to tap into the all-encompassing harmony."

Joe Bob began a complicated explanation of how to consult The Oracle by tossing pennies into the air and counting how they fall, heads or tails. But Frankie wasn't listening. What had Charmian Foster said? The same people cropping up in different times, different places.

He felt a tingling at the back of his neck. Once he'd been The Near James and here he was, returned to earth. Maybe the other disciples had also returned. Maybe they were gathering to perform some important task. When Joe Bob paused to sip wine, Frankie said: "Do you have a favorite disciple?"

"Come again?"

"A favorite among the disciples of Jesus."

Joe Bob laughed: "Frankie, I don't know about you."

"No, no. Listen, Joe Bob. Peter and James and John. You say everything's in harmony. What about John? You like John?"

"John? Sure. 'In the beginning was the Word, and the Word was with God, and the Word was God.' How's it go? 'In him was life, and the life was the light of men. And the light shineth in the darkness, and the darkness comprehended it not.' Great stuff!"

"That's it, then. You were John!"

"Frankie, what are you talking about?"

"Reincarnation. In a past life, I was James—The Near James. I found out in Pacific Grove. Maybe you were my brother John."

"You mean John, the disciple? I was thinking of the gospel writer." Frankie's face must have spoken because Joe Bob slapped his arm. "John sounds good to me, Frankie, even so." He rolled to his feet. "Come on, let's hit the Drugstore. I'll buy you a burger."

25.

Peruse any book about the Psychedelic Sixties and you'll find a paen to the so-called Human Be-In—and rightly. This was IT, the largest-ever gathering of The Tribe, and the first counter-culture event to come with a date attached: January, 14, 1967. Woodstock was still two years in the future when 20,000 people turned up simply to BE in Golden Gate Park—though half of them, it's true, believed a New World was being born and expected to witness a magical transformation, or at least a miracle of some kind.

Take Frankie McCracken. Lost in a maze of his own making, he pronounced the Human Be-In a bust. "I knew it," he thought as the event wound down. "I should have left San Francisco when Oscar did. I should never have waited around."

But all over the Haight he'd seen signs advertising the Be-In and its Beat-Generation stars, and so he'd waited, just in case. Now he stood in the trees at the edge of the Polo Grounds sharing a joint with a friend named Misty as countless beautiful people drifted past.

He'd arrived early that afternoon, having hiked through the park from the Haight, and found the field teeming with revellers in robes and costumes. Many rang bells or tambourines, while others carried mirrors or baskets of fruit or banners depicting the holy marijuana leaf.

The Diggers were doling out turkey sandwiches at makeshift tables, and white-robed acid-heads wandered through the crowd carrying brown paper bags full of LSD. They gave away thousands of tabs donated by the legendary Owsley Stanley: tiny pills called white lighting, the strongest acid yet.

On stage sat the stars of the show: Allen Ginsberg, Lawrence Ferlinghetti, Timothy Leary, Gary Snyder, Lenore Kandel, Michael McClure—everybody but Jack Kerouac. To Frankie that seemed wrong. Where was the King of the Beats? That's why he didn't drop acid, but merely pocketed a few tabs.

Even so, Frankie fought his way front and centre and listened while Lenore Kandel read from her recently banned *Love Book*, interested because she'd made a cameo appearance in my novel *Big Sur*. Lenore proclaimed that Love was God of the New Age, and then Timothy Leary was at the microphone, decked out in flowers and beads, daffodil in hand, denouncing fake-prop TV-set America. Drop out of high school, he said. Drop out of college, drop out of grad school, drop out as a junior executive, drop out as a senior executive, drop out and follow me. Finally he sat down on the stage and played patty-cake with a small girl.

The crowd loved it. Frankie was more interested in Gary Snyder, who figures hugely in *Dharma Bums*. The first step, Gary said, is to detach yourself from the plastic, robot Establishment. He rang a change on Leary: "Drop out, turn on, tune in."

This Frankie had done. But what was the second step? Suddenly here was Ginsberg, big black beard and glasses, hollering into the mike, urging people to seek the guru in their hearts and join the psychedelic renaissance. LSD was not the final answer, he said, but a revolutionary catalyst, and everybody who could hear his voice should try it. Every man, woman and child over fourteen should drop acid to induce, once and for all, a collective nervous breakdown in these United States of America.

With this Frankie had no problem. But where was Kerouac? Why wasn't I there? He was still wondering when, as Ginsberg led a Buddhist chant, Misty appeared beside him: "Knew I'd find you at the front."

They moved away from the stage and found a place to sit cross-legged, smoking grass, as rock bands roared on and off the stage. Quicksilver Messenger Service, Jefferson Airplane, Big Brother and the Holding Company, The Grateful Dead—later they became huge. Now Frankie lost himself in the music. During the Dead's set somebody set off orange flares. A parachutist floated to earth as the sun set and everybody said, "Ahhhhh!"

Was this the promised miracle? The vaunted climax? This parachutist? Secretly, Frankie had been hoping still for Kerouac—dreaming that I might make an appearance. Why not? Ginsberg was here. Also Snyder, Ferlinghetti, McClure. And he had no idea of my condition. But as the sun dipped below the horizon and Snyder blew on a conch shell, signalling the end, Frankie had to face it: Jack Kerouac wasn't going to make it.

The Be-In was a bust.

Ginsberg led a chant to the Coming Buddha of Love and urged people to stay and help clean up. Hundreds began picking up garbage. Hundreds more drifted away towards home. Frankie stood in the trees with Misty, sharing a joint and wondering how to explain his next move.

Misty he'd met three weeks before at the Diggers' Christmas Party. She'd sat down beside him, obviously tripping, and gently touched his face: "You're beautiful, man." She had frizzy, carrot-red hair and no place to stay. Frankie brought her home to Bernie's Bunker and there she'd remained, more friend than lover because he'd lost interest in sex. Mostly they rambled around the Haight blowing dope.

Misty was three years older than he was. She'd studied psychology at Berkeley. The summer before, while hitchhiking late to a class, she'd hopped into a van with three men. They'd driven her out of town and dragged her into some woods. "Please don't hurt me," she'd said. "Don't hurt me and I won't tell."

They'd left her in the bushes, bruised and bleeding. Misty hadn't told. Instead she'd dropped acid. The night she told him this story, Frankie hugged her until morning. But now he had problems of his own. Looked like the disciples were gathering in New Orleans. Joe Bob had left on Boxing Day: "See you in Nworlins, Frankie." Oscar had followed a few days later. Frankie didn't know which disciple Oscar had been, though he wondered about Judas. Anyway, Oscar had ridden a bus out of town. And that Frankie couldn't afford.

Now, as the Human Be-In wound down, he told Misty: "If Kerouac had shown up, who knows? But he didn't and the signs point to Nworlins."

"What signs? I don't understand."

"Neither do I, not completely." This business of gathering disciples was too insane to share, even with Misty. Frankie could hardly believe it himself. Having

survived a second tumultuous acid trip, however, just
a few days before, he clung to it secretly—a thread in
the darkness. "I just know I have to go."

"Okay, I'll come with you. I've got a few dollars.
We'll buy food, get pots and pans from the Goodwill
Store." She looked up at him eagerly, all wet-blue eyes
and carrot-red hair. "We'll camp out. You carry, I'll cook."

"I don't know, Misty." Frankie took a last toke,
exhaled and popped the roach. "The signs don't say
anything about bringing anybody."

Misty kicked at the grass with a moccasin. "I've
got a friend in Los Angeles. We could crash on the
way."

"As long as I'm in the right place at the right
time," Frankie said, "crash pads will take care of themselves."

Misty had tears in her eyes.

"Okay, okay," he said. "Maybe we're meant to
visit your friend."

Two days later, early, they rode a city bus to the
ocean and started hitchhiking. Between them, they
carried one rucksack, two sleeping bags and a burlap
sack containing three tins of spam, a bag of brown rice,
a box of quaker oats, half a dozen oranges, an alu-
minium pot, two bowls, two glasses and some basic
utensils. This was more than Frankie had bargained
for, but he was going with the flow.

By early afternoon they were standing on the
highway above Carmel. Frankie was wondering if they
were meant to visit Charmian Foster when a big
blonde woman, shoulders like a football player,
picked them up in a station wagon. He told her they
were going to Nworlins and she said she'd drive them
thirty or forty miles. Turned out she was going to Los
Angeles, but she had several stops to make so she
couldn't take them all the way. Half an hour down

the highway, she started asking where they wanted
out.

This was Big Sur country—nothing but trees,
cliffs and sun-dappled ocean. Frankie studied his map.
Maybe the woman would change her mind? But no.
Instead it was, "Here? What about here?" Finally they
passed a stone building on the coast side of the
highway. It looked like an old-fashioned inn but was
really a restaurant. Surely the occasional car would
emerge out of there? Frankie said, "Here."

Misty made a face: "You sure?"

The blonde woman pulled over and let them
out. She squealed her tires as she drove off, left them
surrounded by evergreens and silence. The restaurant—which was, as it happens, the cliff-top "Nepenthe" that I myself had visited just six years
before—was a quarter mile back. They waited. Two
cars passed going the wrong way. Otherwise, nothing but silence.

Frankie needed to relieve himself, walked
down the highway, stepped into some bushes. Standing there, he spotted a dirt road—an old fire road, by
the look of it—winding down through some woods
towards the ocean. A padlocked gate blocked the
entrance and a sign said: "Private: Keep Out."

Misty liked the idea of camping near the ocean
but balked when she saw the sign. Frankie tossed his
rucksack over the gate and climbed after it: "The fact
we're here is an over-riding sign."

Misty shrugged and followed. The fire road
wound down the hill, thick with pine needles, overgrown with grass. Evergreens shut out the sky. They
stopped to rest and heard water running—a stream?
The road became two rutted tracks. Misty twisted her
ankle. "Let's forget it," she said, wincing. "Go back up
and hitch until dark."

"No way." Frankie strode ahead. "I'm not quitting. This road can't go down forever."

Abruptly, he hit level ground. The track became a footpath. Frankie trotted into a clearing, found himself in a valley between two steep hills, almost cliffs. The woods hid the highway. Here the stream ran loud. A few steps more and there it was, tumbling across the path near a circle of rocks—a fire pit. In the pit lay half a dozen blackened tin cans. Beyond, almost lost in the evergreens, somebody had built a pine-bough shelter. "Misty! We've found Shangri-la!"

"Incredible," she said, catching up. "How'd you know this place was here?"

Frankie shrugged: "Just followed the signs."

They dropped their gear, followed the path along the stream to a grassy knoll and stood in the wind looking out at the ocean. The waves were two feet high. They picked their way down onto the rocky beach, threw off their clothes and waded into the water, freezing cold. Misty climbed onto a rock and stood naked, the wind whipping her hair into a carrot-red mane. Surprised by her beauty, her womanliness, Frankie plunged into the January ocean.

Afterwards, back at the shelter, he zipped their bags together, then built a fire. Misty cooked a meal of rice and spam. They ate it and washed their dishes in the stream, then watched the fire burn to ashes. The embers looked like the lights of a city seen from above. They went to bed and made love.

Next morning, over porridge, they agreed the ocean was too cold and rough for swimming. Frankie wanted to loaf around camp and read about Taoism, which tied in with the *I Ching*. Misty wanted to get back on the road. Frankie said nobody would be guided into Shangri-la one day just to leave the next. But she worried about their trespassing. Grudgingly, Frankie relented.

By the time they'd broken camp, the sun was above the trees, the day too hot to be perfect. They started hiking up the path, stopped at the clearing to take a last look around. Might be faster, Frankie realized, to climb one of the hills to the highway. Misty wasn't so sure but yes, yes, he insisted, it'll be faster. And when he started scrambling up the easier-looking face, she followed.

At first the slope was no problem: hard ground, long grass, forty-degree angle. Then the grass became sand, shrubs and bushes, and the hill almost a cliff. Misty said he was climbing too fast so he took her awkwardly bundled sleeping bag, slung it over his shoulder and pressed on.

Gradually, Frankie drew ahead. Soon he forgot everything except the cliff, the sun beating down and the sweat rolling off him. Fifteen minutes up, he hit a loose, sandy spot. He scrambled upwards, breathing hard, and stopped to wipe his face only when the worst was behind him.

Misty called: "Frankie! It's too tough."

"We're almost there," he hollered. "Can't quit now."

Again he began beating his way up the cliff. His rucksack was heavy and Misty's bag awkward but he wouldn't quit. Root by root, he clawed his way upwards. Finally, he hauled himself over a ledge onto level ground and, puffing, stood up. Before him—why was he surprised?—sat the restaurant they'd passed on the highway: "Nepenthe."

Trouble was, a dense thicket stood between Frankie and the restaurant's deserted patio—a dense, chest-high thicket of thorn bushes roughly thirty yards deep. He tried going one way, then the other. Finally, he scrambled down the cliff and, working hard, came up in another spot. The thicket was waiting.

Frankie tried using his rucksack as a shield, ramming his way forward. Cut his arms, his hands. He flailed at the thicket with his rucksack: whack! whack! whack! then stood breathing hard, fists clenched. He could see the restaurant, the patio chairs neatly stacked. The highway was beyond. But he couldn't get through. They'd have to go back to the bottom and take the road.

Frankie shouted for Misty. She didn't respond and he yelled again. This time she hollered back, but from oddly far away. Then he spotted her—kneeling by the stream, madly waving a washcloth. She'd gone back down without telling him. There he stood, hot and sweaty from trying to beat his way through a thicket for both of them—or so he told himself—and Misty was cooling off down by the stream.

Frankie grabbed his rucksack and the sleeping-bag bundle and started scrambling down the hillside. This was much faster than climbing up but not fast enough for him. He flung his rucksack out into the air and watched it roll and bounce down the cliff into a clump of bushes. Down he went after it in great, skating strides, sand pouring into his shoes. He reached his pack and flung it again, watched it bounce and bang down the hill, throwing off clouds of dust.

Finally, sweating and furious, he reached the stream. Misty was drying herself on a towel. "Poison oak up there," she said. "Here's some soap. Better wash."

Frankie grunted, waved away the soap and emptied his shoes of sand. He drank from the stream, splashed water over his face and hands, then picked up his rucksack and Misty's sleeping bag. "It's getting late," he said, and led the way, silent, up the fire road.

They dumped their gear at the side of the empty highway. No cars coming either way. Misty wandered

189

down the road and stood tossing stones into the trees.
She had a surprisingly good arm. Frankie sat down on
his rucksack. In his anger he'd ignored Misty all the
way up the fire road, but now he watched her throw
stones: frizzy, carrot-red hair, a checkered workshirt
three sizes too big, tired old jeans wearing through in
the seat. Suddenly he had tears in his eyes. He joined
Misty and threw a couple of stones himself. "You wait
and see," he said. "Some guy'll come around that
corner and drive us all the way to Nworlins."

"Frankie, I'm thinking of returning to the Haight."
She tossed a last stone. "We've got no money, no food.
I haven't seen my friend since college. What if —"

"Go with the flow, Misty. How do you think we
found Shangri-la? Nothing can go wrong if we follow
the signs."

"Let's hitch both ways, then. Whichever way we
get a ride, that's the way we're supposed to go."

"We're supposed to go to Nworlins."

"Maybe not right away. In the Haight I could
make a couple of deals. Get some bread together.
Then we could leave again."

"The signs are pointing south now."

"Says who? Let's hitch both ways and see."

Frankie looked up and down the highway. If
they were in the right place at the right time, and
heading in the right direction, they'd never get a ride
back to the Haight. But fifteen minutes later, when an
old white panel truck shuddered to a stop in front of
them, it was heading north—back towards San Francisco. The driver said, "Hop in."

He was fifty, maybe more, wore baggy grey
trousers and a crinkled white shirt. Hadn't shaved in
three days. "Where you goin?"

"We were going to Nworlins," Frankie said.
"First stop Los Angeles."

190

"Los Angeles?" The driver looked from Frankie to Misty and back again. "You want to go to L.A.?"

"That's where we were going," Frankie said. "Couldn't get a ride."

"Hell, I'll take you to Los Angeles, that's where you want to go. San Francisco, Los Angeles. It's all the same to me."

Frankie raised his eyebrows at Misty but she turned and looked out the window. The choice was his. "If it's all the same to you," he said, "let's go to Los Angeles."

The driver didn't stop. He slowed down and made a U-turn and again they were heading south. Frankie said, "Fantastic!"

Misty stared out the window.

After a few moments, the driver leaned forward, looked over at Misty. "Sure a lucky fella, have a little lady like her. Hey!" He called around Frankie over the roar of the engine. "What's your name, anyways?"

"Misty."

"Misty? Mine's Hap."

"Mine's Frankie."

"Pleased to meet you. Hey, Misty. You wanna sit in the middle here."

"I'm okay, thanks."

"Suit yourself." Hap sat back in his seat. "Lemme know if you change your mind."

Hap launched into a monologue about the importance of friendship and Frankie admired the scenery: to the right, precarious trails zig-zagging along cliff-faces, and to the left, the sun-dappled Pacific Ocean, its waves splashing white over the brown and black rocks that lined the coast.

Hap was talking about an older guy who'd picked up a couple of hippies. "They all became buddies. Started living together, having good times."

191

KEN McGOOGAN

Frankie glanced over at Misty but she was leaning against the window, her eyes closed. He couldn't
get comfortable, kept crossing and uncrossing his
legs. The truck would start rattling at sixty miles per
hour—Hap demonstrated—and so, at fifty-five, they
droned through the afternoon into evening. Head-
lights came on. Frankie started to nod and Hap nudged
him, said he'd be more comfortable by the window.
"Misty won't mind sitting in the middle."

"Misty's asleep." Frankie gritted his teeth and
willed his eyes to stay open. After another hour Hap
pulled into a restaurant, said, "Let's get some grub."

In his pocket Frankie had pennies and
dimes—all that remained of their money. "If it's okay
with you, we'll wait here."

"What's the matter, no dough?" Hap looked
around him. "If'n I had a little lady like you, Misty, I'd
know how to take care of her." He got out on his side
of the truck, then stuck his head back in. "Come on,
the both of you. It's on me."

Hap bought hamburgers, french fries and coffees all round, then talked only to Misty. Wanted to
know where she came from, what her parents
did—teachers, both. Frankie went to the washroom.
When he returned Misty was telling a story about
growing up in Fresno and she and Hap were laughing
like old friends. Frankie relaxed a bit, took his time
with his coffee.

All night long they drove, Hap at the wheel.
Misty dozed fitfully. She was willing to sit in the middle
but Frankie was bent on being The Protector. Tried to
stay awake, to "yeah" and "uh-huh" Hap into thinking
he was following his non-stop monologue, which had
two themes: that hippies and old-timers had more in
common than he realized, and that he was a lucky
fellow to be with a young woman like Misty, and if Hap

had someone like her, he'd know how to take care of her.

Would this ride never end? Apparently not, because just after midnight the radiator boiled over. Hap carried a can of water in the back but they had to sit on the side of the highway until the engine cooled. They resumed driving, but twice left the highway for coffee. The third time they halted, at a truck stop, Hap bought everybody steak and eggs. Not a bad guy, Frankie decided—if only he'd quit hustling Misty.

The sun was coming up when they reached the outskirts of Los Angeles. But hallelujah! Misty dug out her friend's address. Frankie checked the map and located the street. Hap said he knew the area, that he'd deliver them to the door. Half an hour later, with traffic building, they pulled up in front of a dilapidated rooming house in a run-down section of town.

All three of them piled out of the truck. Hap and Frankie stretched their legs while Misty walked to the door and rang a bell. She rang three times. Finally the door opened and she disappeared inside. A few minutes later, she returned, looking glum: "My friend moved out two months ago. Didn't leave a forwarding address."

"Did you check the phone book?"

"Yes—and she's not in it. I also called and inquired about new listings." Misty kicked at the sidewalk. "I don't know, Frankie. No money. No place to crash. Maybe we should go to Fresno. Stay with my folks a while."

"Fresno? That's back the other way."

Hap said: "You want to go to Fresno, Misty? No problem."

"Come on, Frankie. We'll get some money together, then go to New Orleans."

"But we're halfway to Nworlins now!"

"Have you looked at a map lately? You go ahead if you want, Frankie. I'm going to Fresno."

"Sure, go ahead," Hap said. "I'll take Misty to Fresno, no problem."

Frankie took Misty by the arm and led her down the sidewalk.

Hap stood leaning against the truck.

"Listen, Misty," he said. "You can't go to Fresno with that guy! He's dangerous."

"Hap? He's just a lonely man who needs company."

"Yeah, sure. And those three guys who picked you up in Berkeley were lonely, too."

Misty flushed. "I can't skulk around forever because of one bad experience. If you're so worried, why don't you come with me? We can leave again when we have money."

"Listen, Misty, the disciples are gathering in Nworlins. I should be there."

"What disciples? What are you talking about?"

"Oh, never mind." It sounded insane, even to him. "Give me a moment, will you?"

Across the street an empty building site was strewn with rubble, overgrown with grass. Frankie walked out into the vacant lot, dug a rusty tin can out of the dirt with his toe and stomped on it. What was Misty trying to do? He shoved his hands into his pockets and jingled the last of their money. Misty and Hap were leaning against the side of the truck, eating popcorn out of a brown paper bag. He couldn't leave Misty alone with this guy. But Fresno? No way the disciples were gathering in Fresno.

Now he understood why Joe Bob carried the *I Ching* everywhere. This was a Fork In The Road. But wait a minute. Maybe he didn't need the *I Ching* to see which way the signs were pointing. *Yin* and *Yang* remained operative. Frankie fumbled the coins out of his pocket and, in his cupped hands, shook them like dice. There was only one way these coins could fall at this time and place. All he had to do was interpret their meaning. If more coins came up heads, he was supposed to go to Fresno with Misty. If more came up tails, he was meant to leave her with Hap and go on to Nworlins.

Frankie tossed the coins into the air, watched them fall to the ground, bent over and counted: one, two, three heads. And tails? One, two, three. He counted again. Three heads, three tails. Couldn't be right. He kneeled, searched the dirt. Nothing. The signs weren't pointing either way. How could that be? Still on his hands and knees, Frankie looked up at the sky. Choice! He had a choice to make.

Finally he stood, pocketed the coins and looked over at the truck. Misty waved. Hap was standing at her elbow, talking, talking. Maybe the disciples were gathering in Nworlins. But no way he could leave Misty alone with this guy. He walked back across the lot and climbed into the truck: "Fresno, you say? Let's do it."

26.

Rain spattered the tower windows and thunder rumbled through the Rockies. I lay in darkness, my jacket an uncomfortable pillow, and renounced the trio bound for Fresno in favor of larger ironies. In November of 1966, when Frankie rolled into the Haight chasing his mythical, larger-than-life Kerouac, a yea-saying Canuck who roared back and forth across the continent with wild-eyed buddies, or else sat cross-legged and alone, seeking enlightenment on isolated mountain-tops like Jubilation, the real me was fighting to survive in New England: fat and old and red-faced and lonesome, I was marrying the virgin Stella, real name Stavroula Sampatacacus, so she would take care of my newly paralyzed mother.

And early in 1967? When Ginsberg, Ferlinghetti and Snyder were chanting *om sri maitreya* into the setting sun, and Frankie half-heartedly with them, actively regretting that I hadn't parachuted into the Be-In? Why, I was late-night drinking in Lowell, Massachussetts, sitting in my living room with a Canuck buddy, ridiculing hippies for trying to storm the gates of heaven—later I tempered this judgment—and denouncing Timothy Leary as a fraud and a charlatan, a verdict I never did soften, damning him not only for his Pied-Pipering but for my own magic-mushroom descent into a psychedelic maelstrom, an experience I'd barely survived.

From out of nowhere came a flash of Frankie's father stumbling out of *La Fin du Monde*, making for home in an evil condition. That swept me, sobered, back to Jubilation, where between lightning and thunder I counted nine seconds. What was the factor? Six seconds per mile? Again the sky lit up. I counted seven and thunder cracked. I focused on Frankie in the cabin and chuckled as he rose grumpily to dress and dash through the storm.

In the darkness, by touch, I found a candle. I crawled out of my bag and lit it on third try, just as Frankie arrived and began pounding on the underside of the trap door. "Kerouac! Open up!"

"Where you been?" I helped him into the tower. "I've been watching the light-show for hours."

"The hell you have." With the inside of his arm he wiped his forehead, then jerked his thumb at the candle. "I would've have seen the light."

Frankie sat down at the table-top and flipped open a notebook. I stood beside him and for the next half-hour we watched the storm worsen. Wind howled through the valley and rain smashed the windows in waves. The tower creaked and groaned and Frankie glanced at me in the flickering candle light. Whenever lightning struck he'd scribble a note about where. But mostly, like me, he stared at our reflections in the windows, waiting for flashes to light up the valley and marvelling at the ferocity of the storm.

Again I found myself remembering San Francisco. By the fall of 1952, my affair with Carolyn

Cassady had spawned jealousy and reprisal and I was living like a hermit in the Cameo Hotel, corner of Third and Howard. In my room I had nothing but Bibles to read—one left by the Gideons, the other a midget New Testament I'd stolen from a Fourth Avenue bookstore after the owner tried to cheat me in a trade. When I grew too tired to write, I'd lie on my bed and read about Jesus.

Standing now in the tower on Jubilation, I remembered being buffeted by ideas and revelations. The Bible itself, I realized, by making concrete a literary tradition extending over centuries, and having a beginning, a middle and an end, a discernible development, the Bible itself proved the existence of God.

To Frankie I said: "I just understood why I found solace in the Bible long after my favorite Zen *koans* had lost their power."

"Here we go again."

"The Bible reflected that unbroken continuity through Time, that unprecedented parade of poets and prophets, seers and saints."

"Hey, why not?" Frankie said as he scribbled a note. "You've already told me you're a masturbating Roman-Catholic saint."

Out popped W. C. Fields: "Close, my boy, but no cigar." Back I came: "I'm still on the road, Frankie—not yet a saint and not exclusively Roman Catholic or even Christian. I sing the crucifix but also the Star of David. I sing the *Tao Te Ching* and the *Tibetan Book of the Dead*, the *Vedas*, the *Koran* and the *Avesta*. I sing alchemy and individuation, Bach and Picasso, Carl Jung and James Joyce. I sing the beatific consciousness and the ananda state in which one enters into immediate relations with the Absolute. Truth is One, Frankie, though saints and sages call it by many names."

"You're out of your skull."

"In the One World Church of Yesterday's To-morrow, which in the Golden Eternity is always with us, myriad are the kinds of saints." Even to myself I sounded like a mad revivalist, but this was my story and I was reveling in it. "The Christians among them emerge from the ranks of nuns and priests, seers and monks and prophets. And the Mahayana Buddhist saints, the so-called *Bodhisattvas*, are near rela-tives—though not Christian."

"Wait! I remember! The Arhat enters into nir-vana, but the *Bodhisattva*, whose essence is perfect wisdom, returns to relieve others of suffering and illusion, right?"

"Frankie, you amaze me."

"What disturbs me is the reek of self-righteous-ness." Lightning stabbed a nearby mountain and Frankie scribbled a note. "This karma business. You know: 'I'm spiritually advanced enough to seek en-lightenment because I've lived wisely during countless past lives. You're a crippled beggar because you've sinned shamefully.'"

"Smug and self-righteous, no question."

"A second ago you were singing *Bodhisattvas*."

"There's no room in the Golden Eternity, Frankie, for earthly dogmatism."

"Your Golden Eternity's full of holes."

"Buddhism's designed for a specific audience, Frankie. Consistent within itself, it's at once a spiritual philosophy and a work of art through Time. It's an elaborate construction, a glorious intellectual edifice. Like Christianity, only Eastern."

"I get it: consistency before truth."

"Put it this way, Frankie. To achieve sainthood outside of Time, and so join the great parade, you must demonstrate that others perceive you as holy."

"No fear of that happening with Kerouac."

"Saints are simply heroes, Frankie, who have given themselves to God. Some saints establish an ethical standard: Gandhi, say, or Francis of Assissi. But not all saints embody a superior morality. Some are great teachers—think of Augustine, of Thomas Aquinas. Others are mystics like Edgar Cayce, Neal Cassady's old favorite. Others still are prophets: Nostradamus, Mohammed."

"And wait, let me guess! Jack Kerouac—The Great Walking Saint!"

I sniffed: "I'm registered in that category, yes."

"Why am I listening to this stuff?"

"Better than staring into the void?"

Lightning cracked an eggshell pattern across the sky and thunder boomed. "Now I remember." Frankie scratched a note in his log. "I need all the distractions I can get."

"Don't worry, the tower's grounded. I checked. Even if we're hit directly, the lightning will just go 'psssst' and shoot down the wires into the ground."

"Where were we? Still on the road?"

"These days, many religions and churches simply proclaim their saints—the Eastern Orthodox Church, for example. Other institutions are even less formal. But eventually, a variation on the old Roman Catholic process wins out: 'B and C,' we call it."

"Okay, I give up."

"Beatification and Canonization. It's a tricky business. Part One requires two witnesses: a postulate of the cause, who makes the case for sainthood, and a devil's advocate, who reveals the sinner's underbelly."

"These two characters stand before a tribunal and thrash it out?"

"Metaphorically, yes. But this happens in Heaven, Frankie. It's a matter of record."

"You've spent time on this."

"In my case the postulate of the cause is a biographer—or will be. Some time during the next fifteen years, a man named Gerald Nicosia will publish a biography citing the visions, the miracles, the religious poems. Showing how Beat means beatific. He'll sing *Dr. Sax* as the first post-modern novel and make the case for yours truly as a hillbilly scholar and hokey, come-as-you-are saint."

"And the devil's advocate?"

"An English professor from old Stinktown on the Merrimack—a man named Charles Jarvis. In Time he'll testify first. Even as we speak he's scribbling away at his nasty palimpsest, poking around in the dark corners of my sometimes squalid life."

"We're back to masturbation."

"And worse, I'm afraid. Jarvis will portray me as an obnoxious megalomaniac. He'll ridicule my accomplishments as a football player, claim I owe them to my father. He'll attack my image as a sailor. My visions he'll attribute to my brother, Gerard."

"No doubt it gets darker."

"Bigotry. Male chauvinism. Sexual perversity. Jarvis will mention my love for black panties, garter belts and stockings. He'll describe certain embarrassing homosexual episodes and weep crocodile tears over my alcoholism, lamenting that a bright-eyed Endymion should have come to living out his final days as a loud-mouth booze-hound in fatigue pants, a dirty workshirt and a hunter's cap."

"But you look great! How—" Frankie slapped his forehead. "What am I saying?"

"Fortunately, Nicosia wins the argument."

"And you're beatified. Presto!"

"Well, three miracles enter into it. But I've described those."

"Ah, the miracles. You worked them during your life-time, right?" Frankie thought he had me and didn't wait for an answer: "Bad news, pal. I've remembered something. To count towards Beatification, miracles must be accomplished after death."

"In the Roman Catholic tradition, yes, that's true. But in the One World Church of Yesterday's Tomorrow, temporal order and the death of the body mean a great deal less. And this is where you enter the tapestry."

"I'm not entering anything."

"Frankie, what if I said I needed your help? As ex-King of the Beats, I'm venerated. And I've been beatified. But I've yet to be canonized. I'm still on the road to Great Walking Sainthood. And your hunch isn't far off. I've yet to accomplish my first posthumous miracle."

Before Frankie could respond, lightning crackled and the world exploded around us. The tower shook, the candle guttered out, we tumbled to the floor.

"Frankie, you okay?"

"*Câlisse!*"

"No blasphemy, please. You want to get hit again?"

"*Câlisse de tabernac d'hostie de sainte-ciboire de saint-sacrament!*"

Still on my hands and knees, but getting into the spirit of Frankie's rebellion, I shouted into the engulfing blackness: "You! Hey, you! I dare you to do that again!" Nothing happened. "*Calvaire!*" I said. "*Mon ecoeurant!*" Still nothing. I cut loose with my scariest Shadow laugh: "*Mweee heee heee haa haa haa!*"

"Jesus! Enough of that."

"The Shadow knows!"

202

"The hell he does. The Shadow said the tower was grounded. That even a direct hit would zip harmlessly into the ground."

"Guess it depends."

"Wait! I've got it!" Frankie snapped his fingers. "This was your posthumous miracle! You've saved our lives!"

Cut to W. C. Fields: "No miracle, my boy. Just a cut-rate synchronicity." Back to myself. "Sometimes, Frankie, I despair of you."

"Do me a favor, Kerouac. Until this storm blows over, no more talk of sainthood."

27.

From Fresno, Frankie returned alone to San Francisco and found Bernie's Bunker thick with strangers. Even the Hobbit Hole was occupied. His third night back, Bernie flipped out like Ruth The Painter before him, stood on his bed in his jockey shorts and green cowboy hat yelling that he'd grown tired of working at the post office so freeloaders could sit around blowing dope and everybody but Bonnie Torn could get the hell out.

A few moments later, while people packed, Bernie announced a second exception—ah, the ethos of the Haight—but Frankie felt compelled to show solidarity with the ousted, most of whom he hardly knew, and kept stuffing gear into his rucksack. He spent that night on a bench in The Panhandle, and subsequent nights at either the Free Frame of Reference, a Digger-run crash pad, or the Hare Krishna temple next door. Both were elbow-to-elbow sleeping bags and noisy into the wee hours, but better than sleeping in the rain.

While living at Bernie's, Frankie had eaten regularly, simply by being around at meal-times. Now he discovered the importance of the Diggers. Every day at four o'clock, two or three of them would drive up to The Panhandle in an old Dodge truck. They brought garbage cans, presumably pristine, full of hot cabbage soup. You presented your bowl and they doled it out free, along with chunks of day-old crusty bread.

One afternoon, as he waited hungry at the usual spot, Frankie found himself remembering Los Angeles and wondering yet again whether he'd made the right choice. Since returning to the Haight he'd spotted not a single sign. When he wasn't thinking food, he rambled the streets wondering why this might be.

A few miles out of Los Angeles, with Hap yakking non-stop, he'd let Misty sit in the middle. She and Hap talked while he stared out the window, his mind whirring. Joe Bob had said everything was in harmony—and so predetermined. How, then, could he have made a choice in that vacant lot? If he'd really made a choice, then Joe Bob was wrong—and so he'd been wrong about Joe Bob. That meant the disciples were NOT gathering in Nworlins, which made sense because The Near James was heading for Fresno.

This satisfied Frankie until he found himself scratching his neck for the third time and realized he was itchy all over: his neck, his arms, his hands, his face. Misty took one look and said, "Poison oak. You'll need cortisone shots. Don't worry, I know a doctor."

Hap pulled into a gas station and Frankie went to the washroom. Hot water eased the itching and he stood patting his face with wet paper towel. What would have happened, he wondered, if he'd left Misty with Hap and made for Nworlins? Instead of being safely on his way to a doctor in Fresno, he'd be going crazy with itch on the highway south of Los Angeles. Frantic with poison oak, alone with a few lousy coins in his pocket. He grinned at the queer, puffy face in the mirror. He'd made the right choice.

In Fresno, Hap said goodbye with tears in his eyes. Misty made peace with her parents, school teachers who were worried sick about her. They let him sleep in their guest room. Somewhere, Misty found money for cortisone shots. After a couple of days, the poison oak disappeared. Misty drove him to the highway in her mother's car. She was thinking about returning to Berkeley: "Maybe there's something in it, after all."

At the highway, when she kissed him goodbye, Misty cried and Frankie realized he'd never see her again. But he didn't let it touch him. He didn't let it touch him until years later, when he cried more than once over what he'd lost.

Back in the Haight, Frankie reasoned that if, in that vacant lot, he'd made a right choice, then he'd avoided a wrong one. The old Yin-Yang. Nworlins would have been the wrong choice. But maybe, in that time and place, being who he was, he could not have made a wrong choice. Maybe that was how events were predetermined. You had a choice but, being who you were, there was only one choice you could make. So Joe Bob had been right. But that meant he'd been John, the brother of James, after all. And the disciples might be gathering in Nworlins without him.

Round and round he went until the day he waited hungry and the Diggers failed to bring their travelling soup kitchen to The Panhandle. Frankie emptied his shirt pockets, looking for change—and turned up a tab of acid. The last of the white lightning from the Human Be-In. Discovering this tab now was a sign, no question. To see clearly, he needed another trip.

Evening was falling when Frankie popped.

He walked off the initial rush, which made him feel nauseous, in Golden Gate Park. Next thing he knew, the sky was dark. A light rain was falling. He stood in a circle of blowing palm trees. If the disciples were gathering in Nworlins, what was The Near James doing in the Haight? Maybe Charmian Foster had lied. Was that a possibility? Maybe he'd never been The Near James. But what about Munsie The Barber?

Looking up into the gathering storm, Frankie addressed the Mysterious Force: "Please! I don't know who you are, or what, but I can't take any more of this confusion!" Crying, he fell to his knees. "Please! I'll go anywhere, I'll do anything, only please, I can't take any more of this, I just can't take it any more!"

Oscar stood leaning against a palm tree, shaking his head. "Don't you remember, Frankie? You have to die and be born again."

Then he was gone.

Frankie stumbled to his feet and trotted off towards the ocean. Realized as he ran that he'd become part of a living tapestry. He couldn't see the whole pattern, but now at least he knew what next. In the distance, and then not so far away, thunder rumbled. Frankie felt he could run forever, no problem. He ran until he spotted the Dutch windmill that marked the end of the park, then slowed to a fast walk.

The wind had picked up. The light rain had become a downpour. On the Great Highway, drivers were using high beams and windshield wipers. Frankie looked both ways and crossed. A sign said, "Drownings occur due to heavy surf and severe undertow. PLEASE REMAIN SAFELY ON SHORE."

No, it didn't apply to him.

On the beach Frankie removed his sweater and workshirt. His T-shirt he pulled halfway over his head, but the rain felt cold and he changed his mind. He

removed his boots and socks. Dressed only in jeans
and T-shirt, Frankie trotted to the water. The ocean
was roaring white, spectacular. He waded into the surf
and right back out. The pounding rain felt warm. But
he had to die and be born again. He stepped into the
freezing cold water and forced himself to stand ankle-
deep. Frankie waded out until rolling ocean reached
his knees. His feet grew numb.

He forced himself farther still, to where waves
crested and toppled, crashed white around his hips.
The cold was terrible. Frankie stood hugging himself
against the wind, his teeth chattering. At his ankles he
felt an undertow. He looked back at the shore but no,
he wouldn't quit. A car went by on the highway. Then
another. Okay, three more. One. Two and three. He
wasn't ready. But he turned and forced himself to
walk. Step, step, step. Now he was beyond where the
waves broke, with ocean swelling around his chest.

Lighting crackled across the sky, startled him
into slow-motion running. Despite himself he angled
shoreward until again he was knee-deep. He charged
back and forth parallel to the shore. Lightning continued to explode over the city but Frankie stopped and,
breathing hard, stood hugging himself. Again he felt
an undertow. Again he looked at the beach but CRACK!
He had to die. CRACK! He had to die and be born again.

And again Frankie was running, only this time
he ran out straight out. The water reached his thighs,
CRACK! swelled and rolled around his waist, CRACK!
CRACK! Frankie stumbled and pitched forward and
suddenly he was under, tumbling, spinning. He felt
the undertow and look, there was the surface, shimmering above, and no! No! He didn't want to die!

Frantic, he made for the surface. His chest burst-
ing, he broke into the air and managed a breath but
now he couldn't touch bottom, the water was over his

head. Frankie swam desperately for shore. Finally, he managed to get his feet under him but the waves knocked him down and again he was tumbling, the undertow fierce. Again he fought his way to the surface and stood up and this time, with the lighting cracking overhead, he staggered ashore, fell onto the sand and lay panting.

Where were his clothes? Frankie trotted back and forth in the pounding rain, unable to find them. Maybe the missing clothes were a sign. Maybe, despite himself, he'd died back there under water. Maybe he'd died and already he'd been born again, into another world—a world in which his clothes would look out of place. They'd disappeared because they'd mark him out as a stranger.

The rain sluiced down in sheets and Frankie started to shiver. No use hunting for his shirt, his boots and socks. They were gone. Up the nearest steps he stumbled and looked both ways. A hundred yards down the highway, through the rain, he spotted what looked like a restaurant. He ran towards it through puddles, his jeans going squish, squish, squish. Strangely, he felt great. He'd died back there underwater and already he'd been born again. He couldn't believe how good he felt.

The restaurant looked all too familiar: a counter, some stools, a dozen formica tables. The far wall was mirrors from the waist up. A waitress stood at a sink, her back turned, washing coffee mugs. Frankie stepped to the counter, then remembered he had no money and looked around. Two men, clean-cut sales types, sat at a table in the middle of the restaurant, the only customers.

Did people in this world speak English? Frankie walked over and enunciated clearly: "Could either of you spare enough for a cup of coffee?"

One man stared through him. The other looked at his bare feet, then at the footprints he'd left on the floor: "I give only to those who wear shoes."

The first man snickered.

The same old world. Inside, he'd known it. But did that mean he hadn't died underwater? That he hadn't been born again? Frankie walked to the rear of the restaurant, sat down on a stool and studied his reflection in the mirror. He tried to dry his face with the inside of his arm.

Beside him, in the mirror, the waitress appeared. An older woman, she reminded him of Jessica, once a beautiful Indian princess. "Can I get you something?"

"If you don't mind, I'd like to sit and get warm."

The waitress nodded. She started to speak, then decided against it and walked away.

Frankie stared at himself in the mirror. He was dripping wet: his hair, his face, his clothes. But he'd stopped shivering. He didn't know anything any more. But remembering Jessica had given him an idea. Staring hard at his face in the mirror, he silently addressed the Mysterious Force: "Please! I don't know who you are, or what, but I need another sign. If I really was The Near James, then please: let me see my face as it was then."

In the mirror, his face changed. His jaw grew fuller, his nose smaller. The laugh marks around his mouth disappeared. He gazed at himself in the mirror. The face looking back was his own face—but purified, somehow. Perfected. It couldn't be improved upon and remain his. There, in the mirror, staring back at him: The Near James. He'd been beautiful. He looked like . . . an angel.

The waitress appeared in the mirror carrying a cup of coffee. She said, "On the house."

Back came his old face—but he'd seen the truth. Now he knew for sure: The Near James. Whatever he'd got wrong, that at least he'd got right.

"Why do you look so happy?" the waitress asked. "You're soaking wet and shivering with cold. Why so happy?"

The two salesmen had stood up to leave. Without thinking, but loud enough for them to hear, Frankie said, "Because all who don't love will be destroyed."

"Pardon?"

"That's why I'm happy. Nineteen hundred and sixty-seven years we gave them." He gestured towards the departing salesmen. "All those who haven't learned how to love will be destroyed!"

28.

Cut to the Drugstore Cafe, corner Haight and Masonic, which had lately become the loud-beating heart of the Haight. Physical appearance? Distinctive corner entrance, huge windows along both streets, high ceilings, overhead fans and four sturdy pillars, strategically placed and graced with full-length mirrors. There was a wooden counter at the rear of the restaurant, and waiters shouted orders through a window in the wall behind it.

Seven nights a week, the Drugstore was standing-room-only frenzy starting at around seven. Other times, the place was quiet and Frankie had been nursing a coffee for an hour one afternoon when Bernie swept into the restaurant and rushed over to greet him: "Frankie, I've been feeling bad about what happened. But I'm vacating the Bunker, going back to New York. And get this: the guy who's subletting the place? I didn't tell him about the Hobbit Hole."

"He doesn't know it goes with the Bunker?"

Bernie shook his head, gleeful. "A cat could move in, maintain a low profile and stay forever, rent free. Look! I brought you a front door key!"

That afternoon, having thanked Bernie pro-
fusely, Frankie collected what was left of his gear and
moved into his new digs. The Hobbit Hole was a gable,
really, and he was too tall to stand upright even where
the ceiling peaked. But this was a minor inconven-
ience. The place was a perfect base from which to
pursue his quest.

Lately, Frankie had started smoking quantities
of grass with a newcomer to The Haight, an "older
guy" of twenty-six. Toby had recently been discharged
from the army and didn't want to talk about Vietnam.
He'd driven across the continent in a rattle-trap Chevy
that served now as his crashpad. He was clean-shaven,
short-black-haired, and some people said he was an
undercover cop: a Narc. Frankie figured he was too
straight-looking—and far too heavily into drugs.

"I guess this is fair, man," Toby said one evening
as they swung across the Panhandle towards the Hobbit Hole. "I supply the grass . . . and you supply the
place to smoke it."

Frankie laughed uneasily. He felt guilty about
not inviting Toby to share the Hobbit Hole with him.
But he needed his privacy, his solitude, to continue
his search. He said: "Who told you the world was fair?"

By now, with so many old-timers having split,
Frankie's only long-standing friend was Mitchell, the
beautiful cat who lived with Jessica in the upper half
of the Fell Street House. More than once Mitchell had
turned up in the Panhandle as Frankie waited, spoon
and bowl in hand, for the Diggers to arrive with
cabbage soup, and insisted on treating him to dinner.
He worked as a waiter in the Cafe Cantata, an uptown
restaurant, and kept urging Frankie to find a job.

"Too distracting, Mitchell. Something BIG is
happening here. I've got to figure out what."

Still, Frankie appreciated the dinners. And he was delighted to run into Mitchell at the Psychedelic Shop one evening, surrounded by incense and sitar music and flipping through the latest San Francisco Oracle. Doubly delighted, because back at the Hobbit Hole he'd stashed a lid of Toby's grass. This was his chance to say thanks.

Soon the two of them were sitting cross-legged on the mattresses in the Hobbit Hole, sharing a joint. Mitchell was at peace with himself, Frankie realized. Always sported well-washed blue jeans, a clean sports shirt, a tweedy grey sports jacket. Didn't go in for gaudy. Frankie remembered meeting Mitchell the night he'd seen Jessica's face change. Oscar had declared him an archangel. And when he'd asked Jessica about Duality, she'd laughed and nodded at Mitchell: "He's the wise one around here, not me. He's the one you should be asking."

At the time, Frankie had thought she was being modest. Now, in the Hobbit Hole, he wondered. His last acid trip, when he went to the ocean, had reawakened him. He'd been seeking the other disciples, hoping one of them would know what they were all doing here. But he'd been The Near James—one of The Big Three. Which of the other disciples would know more than he did? Now he was back on track.

Having lit a third joint, Frankie held his breath and stared hard at Mitchell, silently asking: "Please, I've got to know. If you are The One I'm looking for, then let me see your face as it was then—back when I was The Near James."

Suddenly, Mitchell wore a square beard. His black hair, which fell almost to his shoulders, turned brown and curly and short. He looked older—ancient. His was the wisest face Frankie had ever seen. The change lasted only a few seconds but that was enough.

214

"Mitchell! It's you!" Frankie averted his eyes, ashamed, suddenly, to look into the face of his friend. "What can I say?"

"Say about what? Frankie?"

"Can you . . . can you forgive me?"

"Forgive you for what?"

"For not having known you sooner."

"What are you talking about?"

"Mitchell, I've just recognized you." Frankie looked into his friend's face and again found the square beard, the quiet wisdom—and lost it. "I've just seen your true face, Mitchell. The one you wore when I was The Near James."

"What exactly did you see?"

"You're the one, Mitchell. In a previous life, you were Jesus—The Son of God."

"We're all sons of God, Frankie. Though sometimes, it's true, I've felt singled out. Almost as if I've been chosen. What exactly did you see?"

Next morning, when the grass wore off, Frankie had trouble believing what he'd seen: Mitchell? The Reincarnated Jesus? No way he could tell people. They'd think he'd gone nuts. If it was true, all he had to do was wait. Mitchell would achieve full consciousness and reveal their new purpose.

Meanwhile, it was dope-smoking as usual.

Two days after he recognized Mitchell, Toby produced three lids of dynamite Mexican grass: Acapulco Gold. He told Frankie about it, excited, one night at the Drugstore. Why not go to the Hobbit Hole and test it? Why not, indeed? As they swung down Masonic, Toby made his usual joke about how fair it was: he supplied the grass and Frankie supplied the place to smoke it: "Sometimes I wish it was the other way around."

"No luck finding a room?"

Toby shook his head. .

Moved by a new spirit of generosity, determined to be worthy of his recent discovery, Frankie said: "You can crash at the Hobbit Hole, you know. Any time you really need a place."

"You mean that?"

"Well, it's small. And I like being alone. But any time you really need a place, sure."

At the Hobbit Hole, Toby rolled up three or four bombers. From toke one, Frankie knew this was no ordinary grass and he exhaled saying: "Wow! Is this cut with something?"

Toby laughed: "Don't think so—though it's got a kick." He started rapping about some chemical he'd tried two days before. "Like acid, only better. I'm getting more. If you like, we can drop together."

"Good stuff?"

"Something else, man." Toby shook his head, handed Frankie the joint. "I saw all kinds of things. Saw myself as I really am."

"You saw your face change?"

Toby nodded, holding his breath. Maybe he was another disciple? "What exactly did you see?"

"I'd rather not talk about it, man. Here, your toke."

For a while they smoked in silence.

Usually, Toby was non-stop talkative. Tonight, for stretches, he stared at the ceiling in silence, distracted, and finally Frankie asked what he was thinking. Toby said, "About how our actions have consequences."

"What do you mean?"

"Oh, I don't know. Take baseball. If you keep dropping easy fly balls, you get benched. Or out in the working world, you steal from the boss, you wind up in jail. Only it's not always that clear. Wouldn't it be

216

great if we could always anticipate the consequences
of our actions?"

"Don't you anticipate the consequences of your
actions?"

"No, not always. Do you?"

"Sure."

Toby raised his eyebrows. "You always anticipate the consequences of your actions?"

"Sure, I do." For an instant Frankie felt uneasy,
though he didn't know why. He took another toke and
the feeling passed. "Sure, I always anticipate the consequences of my actions."

Toby waved away the joint.

Frankie sucked on it, held his breath and wondered: Was Toby trying to tell him something? What
did he mean—that he'd seen himself as he really was?
Was he a fellow disciple? Should he tell Toby that he'd
located the Reincarnated Jesus? Frankie stared hard at
his companion, calling silently to see his real face.
Suddenly Toby's face changed—and Frankie gasped.

He'd expected nothing special—nothing, certainly, to rival his discovery about Mitchell. But Toby's
short black hair crept to a "V" down the middle of his
forehead. His ears became pointed. Two little horns
sprouted at the corners of his forehead. Suddenly, for
eyes, Toby had two round, black holes. The Devil! His
friend Toby was the Devil himself!

All this in an instant. Frankie gasped—then
caught himself. Toby grinned and held out the joint.
Deliberately, not wanting to reveal what he'd discovered, Frankie grabbed his workshirt, scuttled across
the room and stumbled out the door.

"Hey, man! What's happening?"

Down the stairs he ran with Toby calling after
him: "Hey, man! Hey!" Down the stairs, out the front
door, into the street. Frankie ran all the way to the Fell

Street House and raced up the back stairs, where he banged on the door and suddenly there He was, Mitchell himself, and Frankie was out of breath but safe—safe with the Son of God. "You won't believe this," he said, "but I've been smoking dope with the Devil himself!"

Inside, Mitchell told Frankie to relax, made him sit down and tell the story. Then, unflustered, serene, he launched into one of his convoluted sermons. "Mind and matter, spirit and body—there's a division of sorts in death. But for the living, Reality is One." He drew a circle in the air with his hands. "The whole supercedes and contains all polarities. Christ and the Devil, like any pair of opposites, are parts of the same whole." Again the circle. "Two sides of the same coin."

"Mitchell! The Devil himself!"

"The first step towards achieving wholeness is to become conscious of division. Of Yin-Yang. Yet reality is One." A third time, the circle. "Imagine a twisting line down the middle."

"Yes, but Mitchell! I've been smoking dope with the Devil himself!"

Eventually, Frankie calmed down. Still, he was surprised when Mitchell glanced at his watch and said, "Wow, man—time for bed." He'd worked all day, he explained, and had to meet Jessica early next morning, returning by bus from visiting her sister. Frankie said he didn't want to leave—that the Devil himself might be waiting at the Hobbit Hole. Mitchell said no problem, Frankie could spend the night on the couch. He dug out a sleeping bag, insisted he didn't mind and toddled off to bed.

Frankie turned off the lamp, tried to get comfortable and realized the couch was too short. He got up, unrolled the sleeping bag onto the floor and crawled into it. Then he lay in the dark, his mind spinning. Probably the Devil was still toking up in the Hobbit Hole. Or else he'd gone to the Drugstore Cafe and would be stuffing his face.

At that his mouth watered and Frankie realized how hungry he was. Today, again, the Diggers had failed to show in The Panhandle. He crawled out of the sleeping bag and made for the kitchen, stopped halfway there. Was he really going to raid the Son of God's refrigerator? He shrugged off his qualms. Mitchell wouldn't mind. As quietly as he could, he checked out the fridge—and was appalled to find it almost bare: a loaf of bread, a jar of dill pickles, a bowl of rice. Dismayed, he thought again of the Drugstore Cafe, where for sure somebody would buy him something to eat.

Trouble was, Frankie realized as he pulled on his jeans, the Devil might be at the Drugstore. But then, so what? Duality made his presence inevitable. The Son of God was in The Haight, so the Devil had to be here too. Jesus implied Satan—that was the nature of things. He had nothing to fear. In fact, as he quietly let himself out the door, Frankie realized that he found it exciting, the prospect of fencing with the Devil himself.

Yet when he walked into the Drugstore a few moments later and saw Toby sitting alone in a corner, Frankie went cold. He stared hard, checking to see whether he'd made a mistake, but no! Again the black "V" of hair down the forehead. Again the tiny horns. Toby was the Devil himself—though nobody else could see it. The Devil himself was waving at him in the Drugstore Cafe.

Toby came over and punched him gently on the shoulder. "Hey, man. You okay? What's the idea, splitting like that?"

"Listen, Toby. I know you're the Devil."

"Come again?"

"I can see you, understand?" Black holes for eyes, peaked ears. "I can see that you're the Devil."

"The Devil?" Toby laughed and threw his hands in the air. "Okay, I'm the Devil."

"That's who you saw yourself as, isn't it? The other day?"

"Maybe it is—but so what?"

"So what? Toby, do you want to die?"

"Who said anything about dying?"

"The Devil doesn't know how to love, Toby. And all who don't love will be destroyed."

"Man, that grass really kicks in, doesn't it?"

"If you don't want to die, you'll have to change your ways. Can't you change your ways?"

"I don't know, man." He shook his head. "I think it's too late for that."

"Listen, Toby, I just realized something. Maybe you haven't been able to love because you've felt that nobody loves you. If you know that somebody loves you, then maybe you'll be able to change your ways."

"Gee, I don't know, man."

"Toby, this is no joke. Listen: I love you even if you are the Devil. I know you're the Devil and I love you just the same. So you're saved! Don't you see? You're saved!"

"Sure, man. I see!" Toby danced around, shaking his hands in the air. "I'm saved! I'm saved!"

A woman walked by carrying a tray full of food and Frankie remembered why he'd come. He looked around. The Drugstore was jumping—yet, strangely, he didn't know anybody else in the place. Not well enough to approach. Only the Devil. He said, "I need to be alone a moment, Toby. To think."

"Sure, man." Toby slapped his shoulder. "I understand."

Frankie stood near the counter and watched Toby resume his seat. Sometimes he looked like a normal man. Other times, like the Devil himself. No way Frankie could ask the Devil to buy him something to eat. He looked around the Drugstore, but nobody new had arrived. Well, why not ask Toby? He was saved, wasn't he? Frankie loved him even if he was the Devil. Why shouldn't the Devil buy him something to eat?

Frankie walked over to where Toby was sitting. Again he saw the short hair, the horns, the black holes for eyes. He shook them off: "Toby, I haven't eaten a thing all day. Would you mind buying me something to eat?"

"Hey, man, you should have said something sooner!" Toby jumped up and led him back to the counter. "What would you like?"

"Well, a hamburger would be great."

"Oh, I think we can do better than that."

Two jumbo cheeseburgers, Toby ordered, with a double order of fries and two chocolate shakes. As they stood waiting for their number to be called, Frankie's mouth watered. He felt uneasy, waiting with the Devil. Yet he didn't feel he could walk away, not when the Devil was buying.

Finally, a waiter called their number. Toby paid at the cash, picked up the tray and led the way back to the table. As he set the tray on the table, he turned, thoughtfully, and gestured with his hand: "You know, man, I bet you can just see the evil pouring from my face."

Again Frankie saw the "V," the black holes, the tiny horns: "Yes, I can see you're the Devil."

"That's fair, then." Toby nodded. "You save me . . . and I buy you a meal." He paused, rubbed his chin. "But you know, man . . . that's almost like . . . making a bargain . . . with the . . . ."

He didn't have to finish. Frankie flashed to their talk in the Hobbit Hole, remembered boasting that he always anticipated the consequences of his actions. The Devil had tricked him into making that claim. Because now, if he took the food, he would complete a bargain. And everybody knew the consequences of making a bargain with the Devil.

"Sit down, man," Toby said. "Let's eat."

"No, I don't want it!"

"Come on, Frankie. I was teasing."

"You're not saved at all! I'm not making any bargains with you."

"Okay, okay. I understand." The Devil picked up the tray. "But here: if you don't want it, give it to somebody else."

Frankie reached for the tray, then caught himself. He couldn't give away the food unless he first accepted it as his. And the instant he did that, he'd completed a bargain. "No! That food's not mine to give away! It's yours and you can do what you want with it because that food has nothing to do with me!"

Frankie wheeled and ran for the door, left the Devil holding the tray and calling: "Hey, man! I was just kidding!"

Down Masonic he raced, down Masonic and into the Panhandle. He checked to make sure nobody had followed, then stood in the trees and looked up at the night sky. What deviousness! Obviously, the Devil had plotted the whole exchange, step by step, from before they toked up in the Hobbit Hole, and—oh, Christ! Frankie had told the Devil he could stay with him any time he really needed a place.

He'd been referring to the Hobbit Hole but the Devil would twist his words, argue that Frankie's "place" was really his body because that was where his spirit lived. He'd return and try to take over his body, arguing that he really needed a place to stay and Frankie had invited him. He'd throw out the spirit of The Near James!

Frankie spun on his heel and started back the way he'd come. He had to confront the Devil and tell him no! No, he wasn't welcome to crash, not ever, not under any circumstances, no matter how badly he needed a place! He rushed up Masonic and re-entered the Drugstore—but now the Devil wasn't there. Frankie elbowed his way to the counter, but no. He checked the washroom, no again.

By now the Drugstore Cafe was choked with people, standing-room-only, the air thick and grey with cigarette smoke. Frankie had to find the Devil and tell him no, but he was hiding in the smoke and noise, tell him no he wasn't welcome to stay, not under any circumstances, but as he pushed through the coffee line a big guy in a jean jacket, looked like a Hell's Angel, said, "Watch where you're going, man," and suddenly the whole Drugstore went over, everything shifting at once and demons! Nothing but demons!

Frankie could see it all, the truth of where he was, and everything clicked into place. Nobody in the Drugstore had gotten excited about the presence of the Devil. They could see him as clearly as he could, but they expected him to be here. The Devil was their leader. The Drugstore was headquarters. Frankie was in Hell!

As he started for the door, it hit him: the Hobbit Hole! The Devil had gone back to the Hobbit Hole. Frankie had to confront him there, tell him that he wasn't welcome to crash, not under any circumstances, because if he didn't the Devil would take over his body and oh, Jesus, where was Mitchell? Where was the Son of God when he needed him?

As he pushed and shoved towards the door, desperate to get outside, demons all around him, Frankie heard a woman laugh and say, "Decisions, decisions." He stumbled through the door, tripped and sprawled onto the sidewalk thinking, hey, wait a minute, maybe those words were meant for me—a signpost. Decisions, decisions—and why did he have to confront the Devil?

If the Devil did return to take over his body, couldn't the Son of God defeat him? But maybe alone Frankie could defeat the Devil. Maybe that's what he was supposed to do here on earth this time around. Never mind the Reincarnated Jesus. Maybe the Near James was in training to become Number One Son.

As he stood up and brushed himself off, Frankie realized he had to choose, *Yin* or *Yang*, like with Misty and the coins. That meant a right choice and a wrong choice. He looked up at the night sky, the few visible stars. Frankie had to choose between the Son of God and the Devil himself. Put that way, the Son of God was clearly the right choice. Forget trying to go it alone. Frankie swung down Masonic and broke into a trot. If the Devil did try to take over his body, he'd ask the Son of God to protect him. The Reincarnated Jesus. Why not?

29.

On Mount Jubilation,
where I'd grown accustomed to flashbacks and jump-
cuts, I learned that Frankie had long since decided his
father was two different people. This came as I lay in
darkness, listening to the approaching thunderstorm.
Sunday afternoons, Frankie would watch his father,
stone-cold sober, shuffling around the back yard in
baggy grey pants that proclaimed the man—ten years
old, three sizes too big, held up by a piece of rope.
He'd be working on some project. Frankie could
always tell if his mother had assigned the job because
then it needed doing.

Yesterday the temperature had hit seventy degrees and the storm windows were still in place. The
toilet was backing up into the bathtub and the drain
needed to be dug out. The spring flood had abated
and three loads of sand had to be spread around the
yard so the man next door couldn't pump water out
of his basement onto their property.

Easily distinguished from these projects were
those his father devised for himself. Envisaging a hal-
cyon summer of back-yard soirees, for example, his

father extended a rickety, waist-high platform from the rear of the house. Then mounted an immense wooden bar on this structure. That evening, while the family ate supper, a loud crash interrupted the blaring TV. Frankie was first into the yard. There, on the ground, lay the bar, splintered, irreparable, the platform having collapsed under its own weight.

Or again, after months of denying it, his father admitted that the back-yard shed was an eyesore. In a frenzy he went at it, ripping and tearing and banging, until finally the structure lay in pieces around him. Then he realized, with surprise, that he had no place to store his tools, his plywood, his old bicycle parts and mattresses. And so, using the materials he'd just ripped apart, he knocked together a second shed, put it in the other corner of the yard—and got upset, started yelling and waving his arms, when Frankie told him it looked just like the first.

Sober, Frankie's father was all entertainment, all drama, histrionics and broad gestures. "Clean-up brigade!" he'd cry. "Fall in, people! You're in the Air Force!"

This was when Frankie's mother was working in Coeur d'Aimée as a cleaning lady and his father was in charge of the house. "Twenty minutes to inspection! Get everything out of sight! I don't care what you do with it, just get it out of sight!" And he'd lead the children in a mad dash around the house, sweeping floors and fluffing pillows and tossing toys into baskets.

Or at lunch, Janey would declare that she didn't feel like eating. His father would address the ceiling: "You don't feel like eating?" Out he'd dash from behind the kitchen counter, pretending anger. "What's the matter? Beans not good enough for you?"

"I'm not hungry."

"Not hungry? People are starving in China! And you tell me you're not hungry?"

The children would giggle.

"Laugh!" He'd take little runs at them, one arm raised as if to deliver a backhand. "Go on, laugh! The fat of the land! You kids are living off the fat of the land and don't even know it. Just you wait. The Depression's coming. You'll find out."

The Other Man usually surfaced at night, after his father visited the hotel. He'd return a different person. Sometimes he'd sit and listen to Sinatra. *Without a song, the road would never end.* Other times he'd roar and slam around the kitchen, cursing and swearing about how it's a jungle out there, dog eat dog but the game is rigged, the fix is in and the little guy stands no chance.

Occasionally, the Other Man came out on a Saturday afternoon. Of all the chores Frankie did for his mother, fetching his father from *La Fin du Monde* was the only one he hated. He'd pedal up *Avenue des Archanges*, park his bicycle against the hotel and step out of the sunshine into the smoke and beer-smell. His father would be sitting in a corner with four or five cronies, talking French. "*Ah! Mon garçon! Viens ici, Frankie.* Come. Sit down."

Frankie would say no, he couldn't stay. But his father would take his arm and sit him down and offer him up to a circle of laughing, red-faced strangers. As soon as he got a chance, Frankie would tell his father why he'd come. Maybe the sink was blocked. Or the electric pump had broken down and they had no water. "Mum says you've got to come home."

"I'm on my way," his father would say.

But instead of rising he'd order another round, one for the road. Frankie would try to escape: "See you back at the house."

"Nonsense," his father would say. "I'll just be a minute here. Want a beer? A coke, then. Sure you do. Waiter! *Garçon! Un coke s'il vous plait.*"

And for the next fifteen or twenty minutes, until his father was ready to leave, Frankie would endure an endless hell of drunken table-talk and din.

Then came the Saturday in 1962, Frankie a hyper-sensitive fifteen, that Uncle Henry arrived unannounced. He'd bought a Rambler and wanted to show it off. Under orders from his mother, Frankie rode his bicycle up the street, parked it beside the hotel and slipped inside. He found his father alone in a cornerl, looking worse than usual. But he didn't realize how much worse until, after half an hour of entreaties, he finally got him outside.

Desperate to leave, Frankie hopped onto his bicycle. His father wobbled away from in front of the hotel. He tripped, almost fell, and sprawled across the hood of a parked car.

"You okay?"

"Give me a hand here, son." His father righted himself, but didn't take his hand off the car. "I can't seem to walk properly."

"All you've got to do is try."

His father took a couple of wobbly steps, still holding onto the car. Then he stopped, stood shaking his head. "Damn it!"

Frankie got off his bike and leaned it against the phone booth. He went over to his father, put his arm around the man and moved him away from in front of the hotel. "I'm just going to get you started."

Father and son walked fifteen or twenty yards along *Chemin Saint-Esprit*, then turned down *Avenue des Archanges*.

It was Labor Day Weekend, the end of summer. The sun was shining, the sky blue. People were laughing and talking in their front yards, drinking cokes, swinging in hammocks.

Frankie removed his father's arm from his shoulder and stepped away. "Okay, I've got to get my bicycle. You go on ahead."

His father came unsteadily to a halt, stood weaving in the sunshine. "I can't, son. Can't make it alone."

"Sure you can. You've got to!"

His father held out his hand.

"*Câlisse!*" Frankie again threw his arm around his father and got him walking. Halfway down the street, he saw her: the French girl he'd worshipped all summer. Petite, energetic, always laughing, today she wore white shorts and a sleeveless white sweater. She was playing badminton with her older brother. Now she spotted him and looked quickly away, pretending not to see. Frankie let go of his father, hissed at him: "Stand up straight, Dad! Walk!"

His father stood swaying in the middle of *Avenue des Archanges*. "Can't make it alone, son."

"You've got to." Frankie started briskly down the street. "Come on."

His father didn't move. He rested his chin on his chest. Then, as he stood there in his Hawaiian shirt, swaying back and forth, he started crying.

"Dad! For God's sake!"

"Can't make it, Frankie." His father reached out his hand. "Can't make it alone."

The girl Frankie loved had stopped playing badminton. She and her brother were staring, wide-eyed. The whole street was watching.

"Dad, I'm leaving now." Frankie took a couple more steps. "Come on, Dad. Please!"

"Go get your mother, Frankie." His father was blubbering. "Get your Uncle Henry. They'll help me."

Frankie turned and started home, then stopped and looked back. His father was standing in the middle of the street, blubbering like a two-year-old. "Jesus Christ, Dad!"

Frankie whipped out his handerkerchief, ran back and thrust it at his father. He helped him wipe his nose, his mouth, then draped his father's arm around his shoulder and, head high, looking neither right nor left, moved slowly down the street.

30.

While Frankie McCracken was in San Francisco, barely surviving his baptism of fire, water and foreign substances, I was in Lowell, Massachussetts, writing *Vanity of Duluoz*, my painfully Christian last novel. The book takes place in the mind of Jackie "St. John" Duluoz on Good Friday and frequently erupts into passages of confused testimony. We're talking the kind of witness I offered Frankie on Jubilation, when I evoked that "unbroken continuity of poets and prophets through Time."

This whole line of Biblical thought was born in San Francisco in 1952, when I was living at the Cameo Hotel and reading nothing but Bibles. I was earning six hundred dollars a month as a railway brakeman, sending most of that home to Memere and living on seventeen bucks a week. My rent took four dollars and twenty cents of that, and I'd eat breakfast at the Public Restaurant around the corner on Howard, where you could get three eggs for twenty-six cents, toast and coffee included.

Why do I rehearse all this? Because fifteen years later, Frankie McCracken did his own stint at the Cameo. Take it from the letters that hit me on Jubilation . . . .

March 7, 1967.

Dear Mum:

Sorry I haven't written sooner but lately I've been run off my feet. I've taken a job as a bicycle messenger with Golden Gate Delivery Service and spend eight hours a day pedalling up and down hills. I carry a walkie-talkie—actually strap it around my chest—and make $1.40 an hour (plus $7.50 a week if I work all five days).

I realize that I could have got something better, Mum, but right now this is what I want to do. The job leaves me time to think. I wasn't really working at the post office earlier, as I said I was. I just wrote that so you wouldn't worry. But now you needn't worry so I can tell you the truth.

I'm staying downtown at a hotel called the Cameo. A friend lent me enough money to pay the first week's rent and I'll remain here until I can afford to move. I found a Gideon Bible in the dresser so I've got something to read. Certain recent experiences have given me a new perspective on religion and I've got some catching up to do.

Maybe you could send the Montreal Library the money they're demanding? Tell them I lost the books. You've long since paid back the $25 I lent you before I left home. Figure out what I owe you and I'll pay it back as soon as I can.

That's all for now. I am well and trust that you and the others are too. Write soon and let me know how everyone is doing.

Love,
Frankie

P.S. I almost wrote "Jack." That's what they call me all day on the walkie-talkie. They already had both a Frankie and a Frank. When the dispatcher asked me for another name, out it popped: "Jack."

*

March 25, 1967.

Dear family:

I hope you are all well, as I am. Janey, thanks for your letter. I'm glad to hear you've received a raise and no, I haven't made any girls pregnant lately, ha ha. As for Thibideau's wedding, I'm afraid I can't make it because I won't be in Sainte-Thérèse.

I'm still working as a messenger for Golden Gate Delivery. I've discovered that when my deliveries exceed a certain number, a commission arrangement comes into effect. My Gazette-route bicycling is paying off. These past two weeks I've cleared $67 and $68.

The big news is that I've moved into a rooming house on the outskirts of the Haight-Ashbury. There's a kitchen down the hall, so once I get the hang of it I'll be able to cook my own meals. I already make my own lunch, usually peanut butter sandwiches, and bring it to work in a lunch box so I can have chocolate milk to drink (out of a thermos).

My daily routine starts at 6:45, when I get up and do a few stretches. For breakfast I make eggs or pancakes or porridge and toast. Then I put on my uniform—blue pants, shirt and jacket with crest—and ride the city bus to work. I get on my bicycle and pedal like crazy from 9 to 12:30 or so, then take half an hour for lunch. I go again until 5:30, after which I ride home on the bus (15 minutes) and make supper. I do the dishes, take a bath and read until bed time.

Mostly I read the Bible. After a long, long search, and much, much to my amazement, I have discovered that the Bible is the only book that even begins to explain everything that has happened to me. I see now that I was brought here to find this out.

Lately I've been thinking a lot about all of you and I've realized that your problems are my problems. I'm enclosing a money order for $50, which you should use to pay off some of the bills. It's a first instalment. I've decided to stay here in San Francisco, working as a bicycle messenger, until all our bills are paid off.

Please don't try to make me change my mind. Much as I miss you all, every single one of you, this is the way it must be done.

Your loving son and brother,
Jack

*

April 8, 1967.

Dear Mum:

Enclosed is a money order for $100—instalment number two. You needn't worry, Mum, that I'm doing without anything I need. The question is:

what do I really need? And the answer, materially, is food and shelter.

As I've already told you, I eat well. Usually I have pancakes for breakfast—12 to 14, which I make using three eggs. For lunch I eat three sand-wiches (meat, cheese or peanut butter), plus half a dozen cookies and an apple or a banana, and drink a thermos of carnation milk mixed with chocolate.

For supper I fry up a pound of meat or fish and have it with potatoes or rice and a small can of vegetables. Sometimes I cook spaghetti. As for shelter, my room is small but the rent is only $10 a week. Besides a bed, I've got a dresser, a small table and a chair—all one person really needs.

Mum, about those clippings you sent, hoping I'd see some job I like and "come home right away." Believe me, I look forward to that. But I will do it only when all our debts are discharged. I've told you this before, but I see you didn't take me seriously. Now I've told you again. If you check the Bible, you'll see that my parents' debts are my debts as well.

I think often of all of you there in Sainte-Thérèse. Incredible that you've still got snow on the ground. (All I see here is rain.) Glad to hear you've finished Eddie's room with gyprock. That should warm it up a bit. Also glad that you're finally putting in a water-heater. How's Expo coming? Most of the exhibits ready? Please write soon as it's always good to hear from you.

Your loving son,
Jack

P.S. Sorry you find it strange that I sign my letters "Jack." But that's what they call me all day and I've grown used to it. In a funny way "Frankie" is dead.

*

April 25, 1967.

Dear Mum:

Not to worry about me being drafted by the American Army. I have a social security card (needed it to work) but no draft card. I'm not on file with the draft board, so how could they draft me? God's army is the only one I care to join.

I was sorry to hear that Janey is doing so much partying. Why not give her a Bible to read? As for Eddie's long hair: if he wishes to wear it long and the school authorities permit it, then why not? He will, in time, learn that "fitting in" and doing what everybody else does is no way to live.

The apostle Paul wrote, "Doth not even nature itself teach you that if a man have long hair, it is a shame unto him?" In time, Eddie will realize the truth of this—and then he will get his hair cut.

Enclosed is another money order for $100. I'm glad to hear you're putting the money to good use. But, Mum, you've again said "come home" when I've told you that I'm not coming home until we've paid off our debts. Please note: I did not say, nor have I ever said, "Until I have paid off our debts." I will come home when WE have paid them off—the whole family.

This does not mean that I expect or ask anything of anybody else. If I have to discharge the debts alone, I will do so. I would hope, however, that each of you will remember, when you are buying something you think you need (alcohol, for example), that you will not see me again until that something has been paid for in full.

You asked, Mum, whether I go to church. The answer is no, I don't, because I have found no church that teaches what Jesus taught. Those I have visited appear to be places where people go to show off new clothes. Please note: I do not say categorically that's what they are, for I neither judge nor condemn. I say that's what they appear to be. I see no connection between going to church and following Jesus.

And I hope you believe me when I say that what Jesus taught is true. For he said, "Seek and ye shall find; knock, and it shall be opened unto you." And, "Wheresoever two or more are gathered in my name, there also will I be." And again, "He that loveth me will be loved by my Father, and I will love him, and will manifest myself to him." Jesus manifested himself to me, Mum. So I know what he says is true.

Yes, I too found it amazing. Believe me, I looked everywhere for answers, and when at last I looked to Jesus, there He was. Please remember when you read these words that this is your son and brother talking. Not some phoney street corner prophet. I knocked and Jesus opened—and so I know that the Bible is true.

Love,
Jack

P.S. Sorry to hear the lake's flooding. Surely the water won't rise as far as the house? Keep me posted.

*

May 9, 1967.

Dear Mum:

That's terrible news about the flood. The whole back room? I wonder if Thibideau's parents still have that extra rowboat? If the flood gets worse, maybe you could borrow that?

At this end I'm doing well at Golden Gate Delivery, clearing roughly $85 a week. I'm starting work now at 8:30 and finishing at 6, which explains the difference. One of the guys will soon switch onto a motorcycle and when he does I'll be able to start at 8. Then, by pushing just a bit harder, I should be able to clear $95 or $100 a week, which would mean I could sock away $65 or $70. Numbers like those soon add up.

I've decided that, as long as you are doing all right in Sainte-Thérèse, instead of sending money in dribs and drabs I'll stash it in a bank and send it in larger chunks. That'll save us the cost of countless small money orders. Don't worry about anything, Mum. Just keep paying the bills as best you can. When finally I do return home, they won't exist. All you have to do is believe in me. I've told you I can do it and I will.

In answer to your question, yes, I do spend most of my time alone—or at least without the company of other human beings. I get up around 7, eat breakfast and get to Golden Gate Delivery for 8:30 (soon to be 8). I pedal the downtown hills until 6 p.m., delivering letters and small parcels, and usually get home around 7 o'clock.

After eating supper, I prepare the next day's lunch. By the time that's done, it's 7:45. I relax for 15 or 20 minutes, then do some upper-body exercises (push-ups and sit-ups). Around 8:30 I take a 20-minute bath, and then I read the Bible until 10 o'clock, when I turn out the light.

On weekends I take long walks, often through Golden Gate Park, where I read in the sun. I also spend a lot of time at the public library, in the religion section. I do my washing Saturday night and shop for groceries on Friday, right after work. Or else Sunday, if I'm too tired.

I did have one friend, a guy named Mitchell, but I thought he was somebody he wasn't and we've drifted apart. I don't mind because nobody is alone when God is with him.

Remember: God so loved the world that He gave his only begotten son, that whosoever believes in Him should never perish, but have everlasting life. Jesus told us to love one another as he loved us—and then laid down his life to show us what he meant. That's what every one of us should be doing, each in his own small way.

Your loving son,
Jack

P.S. Don't worry about my address. Keep my mail coming c/o General Delivery.

*

May 21, 1967.

Dear Mum:

Jack Kerouac's family was once tested by water, as I recall, so I'm relieved that you weren't flooded out. But if the water ruined the linoleum in the back room, you have to replace it. What else can you do? At least the foundation's intact.

I can't tell you how sorry I was to learn that Dad refuses to change his ways. Surely in time he'll realize that drinking isn't going to solve anything, but will only make life worse, both for himself and others. I do hope, however, that you aren't nagging him. That would only aggravate an already bad situation, as I'm sure you know by now. Tell Dad no, I'm not writing any more. Just these letters. That which comes not of faith is sin.

I'm glad you've decided that, except for the flooring, you won't buy anything more on credit. That will be a big help. For my part, I'll continue saving until I've got enough money to pay off the remaining debts. Maybe you could send me a list of what we owe? I've started going into work at 8. The weather has been warming up some—85 degrees the other day. A little too hot.

Mum, you've once again asked that I reconsider what I'm doing. But Jesus taught that any man who looks back after he has taken up the plow is not fit for the Kingdom of Heaven. Also, he rebuked the Pharisees for teaching that freedom means saying to your parents, "It is a gift by whatsoever thou mightest be profited by me." So, all I'm doing is my duty.

Your loving son,
Jack

P.S. Just received the Expo '67 Gazette you mailed ages ago. Thanks for sending it. Having looked it over, though, I honestly can't see what the fuss is all about. Vanity.

*

June 7, 1967.

Dear Mum:

I'm afraid there's not much news at this end, either. In fact I have no news at all. Sorry if I've been "lecturing" lately. I'll try to stop.

I enclose a money order for $50 as you said you were short. Naturally, I'll send money whenever you need it. I would prefer it, though, if you could hang on and meet the payments until I can get enough cash together to pay off everything at once—which I will certainly do.

I stress certainly because last letter you said "if" a couple of times, as in "if" I am still saving to pay off the bills. Mum, that's the only reason I'm still here in San Francisco: to save enough money to pay off the bills.

Now that I think about it, maybe you could send me details of what you pay each month? Please do this soon, and include the totals outstanding at each place, as I'm anxious to know where we stand.

Thanks for sending Thibideau's wedding photo. I'm sure she's a lovely girl. As the apostle Paul wrote, "Better to marry than to burn."

Good news that Eddie is taking over the Gazette route. It's a chore, but looking back, I realize I enjoyed those summer bicycle rides, those cold winter walks. Remember when those men stole our boat during the flood? And I went and took it back, left them stranded?

That's about it for now. Hope everything is going well there, with a minimum of bickering and arguing. I miss you all.

Your loving son,
Jack

*

June 24, 1967.

Dear Mum:

Thanks for the partial list of debts. I'd expected worse. Why, Ogilvy's department store can be discharged in four months. You say we'll never get quit of bills because something new is always cropping up. You forget that once the debt is zero, you'll be able to pay cash for everything you buy—and put money in the bank besides.

The only way we'll succeed, though, is if you stem the tide of new bills until I can reverse it. I hope you'll send a more complete list of debts as soon as possible, including details about Household Finance, Uncle Henry and Lobey's Men's Wear.

My address, since that's the third time you've asked, is 1436 Grove Street. Please keep my mail coming to General Delivery, however, as it might get lost if it came here to the house. In an emergency you could call Golden Gate Delivery Serv-

ice (626-6788). That's it for now. I miss you all
very much.

Love,
Jack

*

July 17, 1967.

Dear Mum:

There are several reasons why I couldn't do what
I'm now doing from Sainte-Thérèse or even
Montreal.

1. The temptation for me to let bills slide would
be much greater and we might never get out of
debt.

2. The temptation for you folks to spend money
on goods you don't really need (eg. alcohol)
would be much greater. You might say, "Well,
with Jack helping, we can afford this little extra"—when you wouldn't really need it.

3. Most important, if I were there the family
would lack incentive. If Jesus had NOT gone
away, he would have saved nobody. If I were
home, Dad would have no reason even to consider going on the wagon.

Believe me, I'm at least as anxious as you are to
get the bills paid off. I'd like to move on to doing
something else. But this is the only way. So, if you
can, please continue meeting the payments without my help—as you've done in the past. Then,
in no time at all, we'll be free: no more bills
hanging over our heads.

You asked about my future. I have no idea what I'll do, Mum, but "getting ahead" or "becoming a success" are out. I don't worry, however: "Consider the ravens: for they neither sow nor reap, which neither have storehouse nor barn, and God feedeth them: how much more are ye better than the fowls?"

I'm sure that, once we've discharged this debt, God will reveal a new task. Please send a complete financial statement with your next letter.

I was about to close, but remembered something else. How do you make those special muffins? And what about that meatball stew? Can you think of anything else that would be good for supper—quick and easy to prepare and not expensive? I'm getting tired of eating the same meals over and over. I've gleaned a few recipes from package-backs but I know you've got "secret methods." What about those donuts you used to make?

Love to all,
Jack

*

Aug. 12, 1967.

Dear Mum:

From your latest I deduce the following:

Hot water tank	$146
Electric	365
Sewing machine	285
Ogilvy's	60

You didn't count the flood repairs, but I estimate	500
Lobey's Men's Wear	200
Uncle Henry and Household Finance probably	1,750
GRAND TOTAL	3,306

Don't be discouraged, Mum. The debt isn't that bad. I do wish you'd send me precise figures, though, for the last two items. If I had exact totals and details on the payments (amounts and frequencies), I could make some accurate projections about how long this will take us. Might surprise you.

At this end, I've been working from 8 to 6 for some time now, setting daily delivery records and clearing $110 a week. We haven't had rain for a while and that helps. When it rains I have to wear a wet suit, jacket and pants both, like when I picked tobacco. That slows me down. Also, the streets are treacherous, especially the ones with cable-car tracks.

Yes, I read the Bible nightly. Also, I've been investigating the Protestant Reformation, mainly William Tyndale and Martin Luther. Following Jesus is not just a matter of doing our best, as you recently suggested. As Luther pointed out, our best is simply not good enough and deserves nothing but death and destruction. That's why God sent Jesus into the world. Because alone we can do nothing.

Now, once we believe that Jesus saves us not because we deserve it, or because we're doing our best, but simply because he loves us—why, how can we avoid loving our fellow man? How can we avoid changing our ways?

Write soon and let me know how you're doing.

Your loving son,
Jack

*

Aug. 24, 1967.

Dear Mum:

Enclosed is a money order for $1,000.

I'd intended to save until I could pay off the bills in one shot. After thinking about it, though, I decided instalments of $1,000 would be best. For one thing, we'll save money by reducing the interest payments on what we owe.

I don't want you to say, or even to think, that my paying off the bills is anything but a duty. As the Bible says, "He who does not provide for his own, and especially for those of his own household, has denied the faith, and is worse than an unbeliever."

You said in your last letter, Mum, that God doesn't want us to suffer. That's true. But I'm not suffering. Everything I do, I do of my own free will—for God has set me free. I act, not because I must, but because I'm grateful for the gifts God has given all of us.

Mum, I hope now you'll stop worrying. We'll pay off the bills. If I were alone, it's true, I might not be able to finish. But nobody is alone when God is with him. It is not me who will pay off the bills, but God, who is working through me. And God can never fail.

So please don't fret. This is only the first $1,000.

I hope everyone there is well.

Write soon, Mum.

Love,
Jack

31.

But we've left too many gaps. Let's take it from two days after Frankie realized he was in Hell, when he arrived home to find a note pinned to his door: "WHOEVER YOU ARE: This storage room, otherwise known as The Hobbit Hole, belongs to my apartment. Vacate it within twenty-four hours or I call the police."

Again Mitchell urged Frankie to find a job, any job. But now, having cast his friend as the Reincarnated Jesus, Frankie felt compelled to heed his advice. The Hip Job Co-op, a store-front volunteer agency, sent him downtown to Golden Gate Delivery Service, which was perennially short-staffed. The dispatcher hired him on the spot.

On the strength of this job, Frankie borrowed twenty-five dollars from Mitchell and, to save on bus fare, rented a stop-gap room at a downtown hotel—a fleabag called The Cameo.

The night before he moved, he spotted Toby out front of the Psychedelic Shop, spun on his heel and hurried the other way.

"Frankie! Wait up!"

"Get out of my life, Toby. I know who you are."

"Okay, okay. Just answer one question: What did you do with the grass I left at the Hobbit Hole?"

"The Gold? I flushed it down the toilet."

"The whole lid? You're putting me on."

"No, I'm not. I know you're the Devil, Toby. Anything to do with you is Evil."

Frankie left him on Haight Street, one hand over his eyes, muttering and shaking his head. Never saw him again. Later, he'd wonder if Toby's superiors pulled him out of the Haight or assigned him to another department.

Newly installed at the Cameo, disoriented and subject to a capricious achetype, a white-water initiation, Frankie spent his days pedaling a one-speed bicycle around the San Francisco streets. Nights he was too beat to do anything but read. Curious about his past life as the Near James—just how important had he been, anyway?—Frankie began perusing a Gideon Bible he found in his hotel room.

Six weeks of immersion was all it took: Mitchell wasn't the Reincarnated Jesus, after all. God had used Mitchell to lead Frankie to the bonafide Son of God. The Mysterious Force had been God The Father driving him to repentance and baptism, to death and rebirth. The Devil had turned up to steal the baptismal gift of the Holy Ghost—a gift evidenced by Frankie's vision of himself as an angel—and Jesus had manifested himself to save him from the marauding Devil.

For the first time since he'd dropped acid, everything made sense. And one Sunday afternoon, fresh from John's gospel account of the crucifixion, Frankie fell to his knees in the Cameo Hotel and said the Lord's Prayer for the first time since childhood.

Had he once been the Near James? This no longer mattered—though the Bible didn't quite rule it out—because there remained the spectacular style of his salvation, starting with the storm-tossed baptism. Obviously, he'd been chosen to perform some important task. God would show him what it was. All he had to do was wait.

But living at the Cameo meant always eating out. This was expensive. Three weeks, it took him, to repay Mitchell's loan. He needed a place where he could cook. He searched the Haight but beautiful people were arriving from all over the continent, many with flowers in their hair. Vacant rooms didn't exist. And no way Frankie could re-enter the communal life—not after what he'd learned at the Cameo.

He broadened his search area. Finally, one Saturday afternoon, while rambling the outskirts of the Haight, he spotted a Room-For-Rent sign. Rang the bell but nobody answered. Three times he returned and at last a big woman answered the door. She ran a blacks-only rooming house, didn't want trouble and showed him a window-less cell—by far the lesser of two rooms, he learned later, then vacant. Perfect, he insisted. No, he didn't mind sharing kitchen and bathroom.

Next day, though it took him weeks to realize it, Frankie became the only white person not in the rooming house but the neighborhood. And so he remained for the next several months—months that, I noted on Mount Jubilation, produced not a single race-related incident. True, Frankie didn't go looking for trouble. But six nights a week he ate in the communal kitchen and one of the roomers became almost a friend. This was a woman named Lurline, who hummed bluesy tunes while she cooked supper for her live-in boyfriend. A couple of times she bent over in front of him and her dress fell open and he had to leave the kitchen to avoid temptation.

But the only real problem at the house was a dock worker called Big Man. This giant stevedore lived at the end of the hall and invariably greeted Frankie with a too-hearty slap on the back. All the roomers feared Big Man. Lurline said he had a mean streak. Just before Frankie had arrived, another roomer had accused him of stealing food from the fridge and Big Man threw him down the stairs.

One night Big Man brought home a woman. Two o'clock in the morning, they started shouting about money. Big Man told her to get the hell out. She said not until he paid her. From his bed, Frankie heard a crash and then slapping. He was pulling on his jeans and screwing up his courage when, crying and cursing, the woman burst out of Big Man's room. She ran past his door and down the stairs, then stood outside on the sidewalk yelling that Ernest was a liar and a cheat. Finally Big Man exploded out of his room, charged down the stairs and chased her into the night.

Frankie considered moving—but briefly. He had other things to think about. Somehow, he had to emulate Jesus, who'd sacrificed himself to save the world. A life-time ago, when he'd left Montreal, his mother had wanted him to stay home and help out with the bills. The money worries, Frankie decided, were a symptom. The root problem was his father's drinking.

Gradually, drawing on what he'd discovered at the Cameo, Frankie devised a plan. He'd lay his life on the line, as Jesus had done, by remaining in San Francisco until the family was out of debt. If his father loved him, the man would quit drinking. It was simply a matter of will power. Frankie imagined himself returning home to a debt-free family headed by a teetotaller.

But look at him zipping around San Francisco on a heavy-duty, one-speed bicycle, a walkie-talkie strapped to his chest, resplendent in a blue uniform: light blue shirt, dark blue slacks and matching jacket, a crest on the back proclaiming "Golden Gate Delivery Service." Up Bush Street, down California, swing along Montgomery to Market, down Sixth onto Mission, up Seventh, out to Van Ness and then back all the way to Sansome, up Washington, whatever the weather, round and round and round.

A bicycle messenger had to respect the cable-car tracks, especially on rainy days. California Street was the worst, and several times Frankie caught a tire in a track and crashed to the pavement. Parked cars were a less predictable hazard. Once, while whizzing along Montgomery, he glanced over his shoulder as a driver opened his door and whap! Frankie went sprawling, found himself on his back in the middle of the street, helpless in the path of a monster truck. At the last possible instant the driver swerved, honking furiously, and avoided hitting him.

Three months into the job, the dispatcher began loud-hailing Frankie as the best messenger in the history of Golden Gate Delivery Service. His secret? Non-stop revision. Like his fellow bicycle messengers, Frankie knew every back alley and shortcut in the downtown core. But often a messenger would have a dozen deliveries in his basket and three pick-ups to make. As Frankie pedaled, he'd work out the most efficient order in which to proceed, and he'd keep revising that order as he received new calls, save himself a minute here, a minute there. Those minutes translated into more deliveries—and earnings.

Even so, it took him five months to sock away one thousand dollars. He mailed off the money order, then waited. His mother was strangely slow to respond. When she did write, her letter of thanks was more troubled than thrilled. She worried about him constantly, she said, and again urged him to return home. His father had no intention of giving up drinking and felt Frankie was trying to blackmail him. That was the word he'd used. Blackmail.

That night in bed, as he read and re-read his mother's letter, Frankie remembered a night he'd almost forgotten. He was fourteen, fifteen at most. His father was working in Montreal, selling shoes in a department store, and when Frankie woke to the creak of the kitchen door, he automatically checked the clock. Quarter to twelve. No trains due: the old man had stopped off at *La Fin du Monde*.

His father stumbled into the house and shut the door behind him. He kicked off his boots, threw his coat on the couch: "Maggie, I'm hungry. What have we got to eat?"

Frankie's mother told him to keep his voice down, he'd wake the kids. His supper was in the oven where it always was at this time of night. Having retrieved and tasted the meal, his father threw down his fork and yelled that this food was cold: "Guy slaves away at work all day, he's got a right to a hot meal. Get out here and make me something to eat."

"Make it yourself," his mother responded. "What do you think I am? A bloody servant?"

The usual exchange. Frankie pulled the pillow over his head but it did no good. And tonight the battle took a twist: "To hell with this," his father said. "I'm going back to the hotel. Give me ten bucks."

"You're not going back to the hotel. You've had enough drink for one night."

"That thirty dollars I gave you yesterday—where is it?"

"That money's for bills. The milkman, the baker,
the grocer—I can't look anybody in the face any more.
Have to send Frankie to the store so we can buy a can
of beans. If we don't pay something this week, we
won't be able to—Maurice! Get out of that!"

His father had stomped into their bedroom and
was opening drawers, banging them shut. "I've had
enough shit, Maggie. Where's that money?"

"I've already told you. There is no money for
drink. Get out of my dresser. And shut up that talk.
The kids can hear every word you say."

"Let them hear! I'm the king around here! I'm
the king of this fucking castle and I'll say what I please.
I'm warning you, Maggie. I want that money and I'm
going to fucking get it."

"Over my dead body, you will."

"All right." His father was back in the kitchen.
"All right, if that's the way you want it." Slamming
around among the utensils.

"Drink, drink, drink!" His mother had followed.
"Don't you see what you're doing? You're destroying
yourself with drink."

"See this, Maggie? Where's that fucking money?"

"Put that down, you bloody fool."

"Where's that money, Maggie? Tell me or I'll kill
you! I'll fucking kill you!"

This was the worst yet. Frankie leapt out of bed and
ran into the kitchen. His father stood in the middle of the
room, hunched over, swaying, still in his white shirt, his
tie askew. In his right hand he had a butcher knife.

"Go back to bed, Frankie!" His mother was in
her night gown, her black hair loose to her shoulders.
"Right this minute."

"I won't." He edged around his father, the linoleum cold against his bare feet. Went and stood beside
his mother. "Not until he leaves."

254

"Mommy!" Janey came running out of the girls' room. "Mommy, are you all right?"

"Now look what you've done." His mother took Janey in her arms. "You'll have the whole house up in a minute. You kids go back to bed. Come on, Janey."

Frankie said, "I'm not going back to bed."

The butcher knife gleamed. His father swayed, almost fell over, caught himself. He stank of beer. "Okay, smart guy." He laid the knife on the counter. "You've been asking for it." He put up his fists. "Now you're going to get it." He swung at the air in front of Frankie's face. "Come on, smart guy. What's a matter?"

"Maurice! For the love of God!"

His father looked huge—far bigger than ever before. His knuckles were white, his eyes bloodshot.

"What's a matter, smart guy?" He took another wild swing. "What's a matter? No moxie?" He put one fist behind his back and shook the other in Frankie's face. "Look! Look, smart guy! One hand! I'll take you with one hand!"

Frankie's mouth went dry. He couldn't breathe. He clenched his fists but didn't move.

"Or no! No!" His father fell to his knees, still with one hand behind his back. "Look, smart guy! I'll take you like this."

Janey started to cry.

"What's a matter, smart guy? No moxie?"

Frankie stepped forward: "Get up."

His mother grabbed him by the arm. "Maurice, have you gone mad? Picking a fight with your own son?"

"He's got no moxie." Frankie's father was still on his knees, one fist in the air. "No fucking moxie." He banged his fist on the floor. "Me! I'm the one who had moxie! I'm the one who had talent." He banged again. "Never had a chance. Fifteen years old! Out to work in a glove factory!"

Both fists at once, hunched over, banging, punctuating his words. "I'm the one had talent!" *Blam!* "But it was out to work!" *Blam!* "Out to work in the glove factory." He switched to open palms, kept slamming them on the floor. "Never got a break." Blam! "Never had a chance." *Blam! Blam!*

His father started to cry. Frankie stood over him glaring, clenching and unclenching his fists. The old man kept pounding the floor and blubbering, repeating the same empty phrases. Finally, still crying and sporadically banging, but with just one hand, he rolled over onto his side and, to Frankie's surprise, passed out into a deep sleep.

His mother put Janey to bed.

Frankie picked up the butcher knife and marvelled at how it gleamed in the kitchen light. His mother returned to the kitchen, took the knife and put it away in the drawer. She looked down at his father, sprawled on the floor, snoring. "It's drink that does it," she said. "Drink makes him this way."

She knelt, untied his father's shoes and pulled them off. "Help me lift him onto the couch."

"Let's just leave him there."

"Take his arms, Frankie."

He helped her swing his father onto the couch, then kissed her goodnight and went back to bed. For a while he could hear his mother moving around the kitchen, cleaning up the mess. Finally, she, too, went to bed.

Now, in San Francisco, as Frankie pored over his mother's latest letter, he felt that long-ago night in the pit of his stomach. How could he have imagined his father would stop drinking? Instead, he'd accused Frankie of blackmail. So be it. If his father wouldn't stop drinking, he'd pay off the bills single-handed. He'd do it alone.

But for seven, eight months, Frankie had been working like a slave, living like a hermit—and he'd sent home only one thousand dollars. Ahead of him stretched eighteen more months, maybe twenty-four, as arid and lonely as the past six. Trouble was, he'd sworn in the name of Jesus that he wouldn't return to Sainte-Thérèse until they'd paid off all the bills. Round and round he went, and finally he drifted off knowing there was no way out . . . .

He found himself on a cement terrace, looked up and saw guess who? Yours truly, descending a broad spiral staircase. He ran up the stairs and seized my hand: "I've missed you, Jack—more than you know."

I shadow-boxed at him, laughing, then threw my arms around him and thumped him on the back. Together we came down the stairs. We walked to the edge of the terrace, which was encircled by a balustrade and overlooked a great city.

Night was falling. Clusters of people stared up at the sky, obviously waiting—but waiting for what? Suddenly a sleek, ultra-modern train, shining silver with blue stripes, glided through the sky towards us, silently laying tracks as it came. Directly overhead, the train made a U-turn, then glided back the way it had come and disappeared into the distance.

Seconds, this took, while everyone watched, and then the train was gone but its tracks were left hanging in the sky. Everybody could see where it had passed. Frankie found this amazing, but nobody else cared so he shrugged and said, "Must be nothing," and turned away.

I tugged at the sleeve of Frankie's jacket—he was wearing his messenger's uniform—and pointed at the tracks: "Look, Frankie. It made tracks and left them behind."

He nodded: "You think it means something?"

"Fearful sights and great signs."

The phrase rang a bell but didn't make sense.

"What are you tripping on, Jack?"

"Nothing but Jesus."

"Jesus?" Suddenly he was all ears. "What do you mean, Jesus?"

"The Shadow knows, Frankie." I punched his shoulder, then wheeled, strode to the spiral staircase and began to climb. Troubled, Frankie watched me disappear into a mist, then moved to the edge of the terrace. He stood looking out over the balustrade at the skyline of the city, frowning: What had Kerouac been trying to tell him?

Thock! Before his eyes, a tall building disappeared. *Thock! Thock!* Two more were gone—sucked down into the earth like carrots in a Bugs Bunny cartoon. *Thock! Thock!* Then *whisk!* A new building. *Whisk! Whisk!* New buildings popped out of the ground to replace the old ones. *Whisk! Whisk!* These buildings were larger, more numerous, more beautiful. *Whisk! Whisk! Whisk!*

As the city grew, drawing nearer, Frankie turned to the people around him and pointed at the shooting buildings: "Fearful sights and great signs." As he spoke, he recognized the phrase. It came from the Bible. Fearful sights and great signs would precede the end of the world. A silent sky-train laying its own tracks. Buildings shooting up out of the earth. That's what I'd been trying to tell him. These were the fearful sights, the great signs. This was the end of the world.

Frankie began pleading with those around him, pointing at the tracks in the sky and the shooting buildings, saying, "Fearful sights and great signs!" But people turned their backs and walked away. Nobody understood what he was talking about. Suddenly he knew what people had to do. "Give glory to God," he said. "Give glory to God!"

But nobody paid any attention.

Now came a tingling sensation, his whole body buzzing, and Frankie realized that the Holy Ghost had come upon him, breathing him full of authority, so now he was no longer pleading but speaking loudly, assertively, telling people: "Give glory to God!" Then it was no longer Frankie speaking at all, but the Holy Ghost speaking through him, enunciating clearly, using his voice to command people: "Give glory to God! Give glory to God!"

People ignored him. Panicking, confused by the rocketing buildings, they charged back and forth across the terrace. And even as they spoke, Frankie and the Holy Ghost through him, the buildings grew bigger and more beautiful, *thock! thock! whisk! whisk!* and then WHISK! one glorious building erupted out of the earth and filled the entire skyline.

It glowed beige and beautiful and strangely old-fashioned, almost ancient, with a roof that sloped upwards from two sides then broke into a pinnacle. A giant clock dominated the face of this peak and as Frankie read the time—what? not two minutes to twelve?—the beautiful building cracked and crumbled to the ground, smoke billowing.

Then the other buildings, all the magnificent skyscrapers, started tumbling, smashing into each other, crack! crack! and as people cried, "Earthquake!" Frankie felt himself swung up off the terrace and redeposited, as if by an invisible rope that reached up to heaven. Now he was shouting, or the Holy Ghost was shouting through him in a loud voice, enunciating clearly: "Give glory to God!"

Black smoke billowed over the terrace and everything was chaos as the city crumbled, people

259

screaming and running but not knowing what to do. Frankie kept telling them, shouting: "Give glory to God! Give glory to God!"

But nobody paid any attention and again he was swung up off the terrace, only this time he wasn't returned and tears rolled down his cheeks as slowly he felt himself reeled up into the sky, as if by a giant winch, still extending his arms and shouting, "Give glory to God! Give glory to God!"

And even as Frankie swung upwards, the loud voice and his own voice were one, but suddenly his own voice stopped speaking and the loud voice said once more, this time to Frankie, enunciating clearly: "GIVE GLORY TO GOD!"

He awoke sitting upright in bed, trembling, with the loud voice, the voice of the Holy Ghost, ringing around him, commanding him clearly: "GIVE GLORY TO GOD!"

Frankie sat a moment, stunned, then flicked on his lamp and looked at the clock. Quarter to five. He climbed out of bed, sat down at the small table in his room and, at the top of a blank sheet of paper, printed: "A VISION OF THE END OF THE WORLD."

Then he began to write . . . .

32.

The morning after the lightning storm, I awoke in the tower to find a slow-motion river of grey-white clouds churning through the valley. It tumbled past Jubilation just below the tower, spraying the windows with foggy wisps. I'd been contemplating Frankie's vision of the end of the world and what it implied, so the river became a rough sea and I stood alone on a ship's bridge, a captain navigating the difficult passage between the clashing rocks of Scylla and Charybdis.

A vision sweeps you through those rocks, I realized. That's the magic of it. For a time you sail boldly in the sunshine of conviction. No more confusion, no more angst, no more existential keening. In their place, transcendent innocence. Surely nothing is more beautiful than manifest commitment to spiritual truth, however partial that truth, however childish its expression?

For months after my fainting vision of the Golden Eternity, I fancied myself a special, solitary angel, a messenger sent to show people by example that they were living the wrong way. A man is Beat, a writer-friend once suggested, when he wagers the sum of his resources on a single number. Make that Beatific, I thought, contemplating my all-time favorite Frankie—the one who plunged into the streets of San Francisco with a stack of pamphlets under his arm. But the morning sun was burning holes in the cloud cover. As the valley floor became visible, the illusion of rolling seas faded and I abandoned ship for breakfast. Frankie whomped up buckwheat pancakes. We washed them down with coffee, then checked the tower for burn marks. Found nothing. It was as if the lightning storm had never happened—except that, with fire hazard at its peak, Frankie had to climb into the tower and stay there.

This was to be my last full day on Jubilation and I'd decided to look around. After cleaning the breakfast dishes, I packed a lunch, shouted *à bientôt* and followed a trail around the back of the mountain. For an hour I climbed, emerging from the dwindling forest onto an almost vertical desert of shale and scree and giant boulders.

Eventually I arrived, as Frankie had promised, at a mossy plateau radiant with alpine flowers. Far below, in a dark green valley, an ice-blue lake fed into a river that meandered into the distance, brazenly turquoise. Snow-capped mountains rolled away to the horizon, and as I ate my peanut-butter sandwiches I remembered looking north from Desolation Peak, seeing clouds of hope drifting in the sky above Canada, and thought how right it was that in the spring of 1967, while Frankie was in San Francisco, transforming himself into Saint Jack of The Sixteen-Page Pamphlet, I made my final trip to his native city.

I'd recently unearthed some notes I'd written years before, plans for a novel about French Canadians in America. *The Vanity of St. Louis*, as I called it, would focus on my own ancestors. It would open in *la belle province*, then move south to the dark mill towns of New England. To do the requisite research, I'd applied for a Guggenheim Fellowship, said I wanted to visit Quebec. I didn't get the grant but never forgot the project and was brooding over it in Lowell when a film crew arrived from Montreal—half a dozen guys wearing beards and granny glasses and black leather coats.

They were shooting a TV documentary about New England Canucks and including footage from bars like The Three Copper Men and Nicky's, my brother-in-law's place. No way they could have missed me, a celebrity writer roaring around in red flannel shirt and green workman's pants, talking homespun French to anybody who'd listen or else falling to my knees to warble Sinatra: *I guess I'll have to dream the rest* . . . .

My performance earned me an invitation to appear on a TV talk-show called *Le Sel de la Semaine*. A couple of years before, in France, people had laughed at the way I spoke French. But in Montreal, I told myself, I'd be a prodigal son returning home. I didn't realize that *la belle province* was still emerging from *La Grande Noirceur*. That I'd be visiting a Quebec that was hankering after Europe, not celebrating North America—a Quebec in which *bien parler c'est se respecter*, and where a Parisian accent was still *oh! la la*.

My brother-in-law Nicky drove us to Montreal.

At the studio they sat me down with a supercilious talk-show host in front of an audience, turned on the lights and rolled 'em. *M'sieur Chose*, as I called the host, Mister Something-or other, wore shirt and tie and shiny suit, while I was decked out in too-short corduroy slacks, tired desert boots and a sports shirt open at the neck, a white T-shirt underneath.

The worst of it was that, every time I spoke, the studio erupted with laughter. At first I didn't under-

263

KEN McGOOGAN

stand it. Then I realized that these sophisticated Montrealers were laughing at my old-style French, learned from Memere—at my *pataraffes* and *chalivaris*, the language recognizable but definitely not *à la mode*. I was less a prodigal returned than a faintly embarrassing curiosity.

That night, with Nicky and a couple of would-be poets, I started drinking at *Taverne de Trappeur*. We moved to the Jazz Club and then The Black Bottom, one of Frankie's old-favorite bars, and ended up at a brothel where I listened to Billie Holiday on the juke box and paid three times to take a woman upstairs and never went. Eventually I passed out under a table.

I never did get around to writing *The Vanity of St. Louis*, and this I regretted even as I sat on Mount Jubilation, smelling the alpine flowers and looking out at the white-capped Canadian Rockies.

Later that afternoon, having retraced my steps, I approached the lookout through the trees and heard Frankie using his two-way radio, a note of urgency in his voice: "Jubilation Lookout calling Saskatchewan River Crossing . . . . "

He waited a moment, then tried again. "Jubilation Lookout calling the Crossing. Come in, please."

From the ground, I called: "What's up?"

Frankie stuck his head out the open window. "Smoke! Come take a look." ·

I scrambled up the ladder. Frankie helped me into the office, handed me binoculars and pointed: "Look down there. Near the highway. The rock cut."

Black smoke was billowing skywards. "I don't remember lightning striking there."

"I don't, either. Maybe it hit while we were scrambling in the dark. Who cares? We've got ourselves a fire."

264

"I don't know, Frankie." I peered again through the glasses. "The smoke's oddly close to the highway."

"Jubilation Lookout calling Saskatchewan River Crossing. Jubilation Lookout calling the Crossing. Come in please."

"Mobile Unit here. Go ahead, Jubilation."

"Smoke! I see black smoke near the rock cut."

No response.

"Mobile Unit, do you read me? We've got a fire to fight!"

"We read you, Jubilation. Where's the smoke?"

"About three miles south of the station. Just off the highway near the rock cut."

Another silence.

"This is Jubilation Lookout. We've got a fire blazing. Do you read me?"

"Jubilation, we're parked at the rock cut south of the station. Along with a big yellow garbage truck. Can you see us?"

I handed Frankie the binoculars: "There's something yellow down there, just right of the cut."

Frankie peered through the glasses, then returned to the radio. "Mobile Unit, I do see yellow in the trees. And lots of smoke."

"The fire's under control, Jubilation. The driver of the garbage truck put it here. His load caught fire and he dumped it."

"He dumped a fire on the side of the highway?"

"That's right, Jubilation. In a clearing here. The forest is safe."

Frankie hesitated, then said, "Okay, Mobile Unit. Saw the smoke and thought I'd better check."

"Thanks, Jubilation." There was laughter in the warden's voice. "Mobile Unit clear."

"Jubilation clear." Frankie slumped in his chair and covered his eyes. "I've done it again!"

"The smoke was real enough."

"But I leapt to the wrong conclusion."

I swung into Sinatra: *Dream, when you're feeling blue / Dream, that's the thing to do.*

Frankie got to his feet, faced the open window and howled: "*Aaaaggggghhhhh!*"

I glanced at my watch. "Almost dinner time."

"*Aaaaaaggggghhhhh!*"

"What do you say we have some cider?"

Frankie stepped back from the window. "Don't you remember? We finished it last night."

"No, I've got one more jug. Found it in my pack this morning."

Frankie just looked at me.

Leaving the window open so we could hear if the warden radioed, we climbed out of the tower. Frankie went and sat on his favorite gnarled stump while I fetched the cider and glasses. I returned triumphant and, as I poured drinks, Frankie said, "You know, I could have sworn you turned that pack inside out last night."

I handed him his glass: "A toast, then! To miraculous discoveries."

We drank.

Then Frankie said: "I've been thinking about this elaborate fantasy of yours—Kerouac and the miracles? I still don't understand your game."

"Let's suppose, Frankie, that a posthumous miracle needs verification."

"I knew you weren't finished."

"A miracle-worker needs an articulate witness with enough courage to testify." I joined Frankie on the stump. "My first challenge, outside of Time, was to find that only right Angel."

"Will I never learn to shut my mouth?"

"A welter of would-be writers, veterans of the rucksack revolution, were clamoring for the job, none of them consciously. I had to narrow the field. But how can I explain this? It's like running variables through a computer."

"What? You mean punch cards?"

"Oh, right—1970. Put it this way, Frankie: I came up with a short list of candidates."

"Wait. Let me guess. My name was on it."

"Not because you're a genius."

"Hey, I admire you, too."

"It's a matter of correspondences. But my information was sketchy. I was seeing through a glass darkly and couldn't read all the signs."

"Not more signs."

"I had to focus on each prospect in turn. Found one guy turning acid-freak, another disappearing into artificial intelligence."

Frankie tried Sinatra: *Dream, when you're feeling blue / Dream, that's the thing to do.*

I grinned but persevered. "Others were tougher to eliminate. One French Canadian in particular. Victor-Levy Beaulieu?"

"The name's vaguely familiar."

"He's written two or three books. Next year he'll write one about me."

"That's rich!" Frankie slapped his thigh. "Tell me, Kerouac, do you like next year's book?"

"Not much. It's too sloppy. Beaulieu will have me visiting France three years early. He'll say I wrote *Big Sur* when I was barely thirty and call Mardou Fox a prostitute. And he'll refuse to correct even what he discovers to be false. Instead he'll warn readers to distrust his chronology."

"That's a logical extension of the spontaneous method."

"It's a cop-out. Sheer laziness—though Beaulieu will defend it as creative freedom. He'll contend that I didn't achieve greatness because I clung to literal truth, recreating only what I'd experienced."

"An interesting idea."

"Wildly off-base. Go back to *Dr. Sax*. Sure, I wrote about Beaulieu Street—see what gave me pause? But also I created Snake Castle and Count Condu and the Master of Earthly Evil."

"So what does Beaulieu get right?"

"He understands, despite himself, how profoundly French-Canadian I am. And how this influenced my life, mandating my relationship with Memere and even my blood-brotherhood with Neal Cassady."

"I've never thought of Kerouac as profoundly French-Canadian. Slightly, maybe."

"That's why I'm glad Beaulieu's around. But he wants to see me as the end of something—the end of Quebec out there in the world—rather than as the continuation of something else. His exclusionary politics flash only in French. I knew for sure he wasn't you when I turned to religion, discovered that he rejects my Beat saintliness."

"So who doesn't?"

"Ah, but Frankie, you remain open to magic. No way Beaulieu would even have heard me out."

"I'm having trouble myself."

"I hated to forsake Beaulieu, mind—the French-connection so palpably right. But then I realized that a variation might turn up in a Montrealer whose mother tongue was English. I focused next on you. And the signs flashed an all-inclusive yes."

"What do you mean, signs?"

"Parallels, portents—knots in the twisted rope of a shared fate. The tangled ancestry, the alcoholic father. The bizarre presence of Sinatra. Finally, here you wcrc on Jubilation, floundering. I knew I'd found you."

"I'm not floundering."

"Twenty-three and tractionless. Writer's block. God is dead."

"God IS dead!"

"You've driven away the woman you love."

"I didn't drive Camille away. Who knows? Maybe we'll get back together."

"Better hurry, Frankie. And be ready to grovel."

"Okay, how do you do it? Having read my manuscript, you extrapolate?"

"I've never read your manuscript."

"So what are you? Some kind of mind reader?"

"Not exactly. When you enter the body you accept limitations. But I do get rushes, flashes. I see things."

"And you want me to believe you're Jack Kerouac, returned from the dead?"

"What if I do?"

"That you're a miracle worker on the road to great walking sainthood?"

I nodded vigorously.

Frankie knocked back the last of his cider. Shaking his head, he got to his feet and placed his empty glass on the stump beside me: "Mister, I don't know who you are or what. But I do know you're out of your mind."

"I need your help."

Frankie snorted, spun on his hell and strode away, calling over his shoulder: "I've left madness behind, pal. You've got the wrong guy."

269

33.

The morning after he had his vision of the end of the world, Frankie McCracken ate breakfast as usual. Then he folded up his uniform—his blue shirt and trousers, his jacket with the crest on the back—stuffed it into a grocery bag and carried it downtown to the office. The dispatcher couldn't believe he was quitting. "What do you mean you had a vision? We'll put you on a motorcycle. Think of it, Jack! Your own motorcycle!"

On his way home, Frankie rented a typewriter.

For the next ten days, he sat hunched over the tiny table in his room, pounding away, writing a manuscript he called WHAT GOD HAS DONE FOR ME. Sometimes, when he thought of taking this out into the streets, the mortification involved, Frankie would weep and pound his pillow. Then he'd remind himself that he had a responsibility. The end of the world was at hand. God had chosen him to deliver the news. Frankie imagined himself glorified, looking like the angel he'd seen in the mirror at the ocean, a latter-days prophet sitting, if not at the right hand of Jesus, then certainly at his left . . . .

WHAT GOD HAS DONE FOR ME

I didn't believe in God and wasn't looking for him. In fact, I had gone far the other way. But God was looking for me, and although I didn't deserve it, He took me and showed me The Truth.

For my part I kicked and fought against Him as hard as I could. I just didn't want to hear about Jesus. But God was merciful and finally He did so many things for me that I couldn't deny The Truth any longer.

These are the things that God has done for me—and I haven't deserved a single one.

Before God did these things, I didn't believe in Jesus. But now I know that Jesus is true. Whoever believes these things also believes in Jesus, and whoever believes in Jesus knows these things are true . . . .

While working as a bicycle messenger, Frankie had visited every print shop in San Francisco. Now he shopped around and opted for Blue Print Service & Supply, which offered to print one thousand copies of *What God Has Done For Me* for just under two hundred dollars. That would do for a start. If God wished to extend his readership, obviously he'd have no trouble.

Frankie dropped off his double-spaced, sixteen-page typescript and made sure he was home, two days later, when a truck delivered sixteen thousand single pages. He bought a stapler and spent three days collating. The morning he finished, Frankie mailed a copy of the pamphlet home to his mother. Then he picked up thirty copies, as many as he could comfortably carry, and headed downtown.

For the next three weeks, every day except empty-streets Sunday, Frankie made this trek twice daily—first at noon and again at four-thirty. Short-haired and clean-shaven, dressed in blue jeans, a clean white shirt and a tweedy grey sports jacket gone in the elbows, he'd station himself at some busy intersection and hand a copy of his pamphlet to anybody who'd take one. Afterwards, walking home, he'd find six or eight copies that had been tossed onto the sidewalk or into the gutter. These he'd retrieve and, if not badly damaged, distribute again next day.

Reactions varied. Second time she saw him, a flirtatious receptionist from an office where Frankie had frequently delivered envelopes shook her head sadly: "What a disappointment you've turned out to be." Later, an older woman, tears in her eyes, took his arm and told him, yes, she believed—but even Frankie could see that she was disturbed.

Then came an energetic, white-haired man with an intelligent face—looked like a retired professor. He debated Frankie at three different intersections:

"Why are you throwing yourself away like this?"

"What I've written is true."

"You mean you believe it's true."

"What I believe and truth itself happen to coincide. If you believed *What God Has Done For Me*, you'd know there's no time."

"You're a clever young man, but you're project-ing. You should be off studying at some university."

"This is the end of the world."

When finally he'd handed out all but one of his pamphlets, and with the world lingering stubbornly, Frankie gravitated to the public library. He'd bring his lunch and spend whole days there, poking around in the religion section. He tried using the *Book of Daniel* to situate himself in time, and specifically to calculate how many days, weeks or months remained until the end of the world—but quickly gave that up. He ex-plored the Protestant Reformation in some depth, and was especially taken with the martyr William Tyndale, who was burned at the stake for heresy. Then he moved on to theologians like Karl Barth and Teilhard de Chardin, but their Christianity, compared with that of Tyndale and Martin Luther, lay dead on the page. Theology seemed beside the point, but what was he supposed to do now? Make more copies of *What God Has Done For Me*? That would mean resuming his job—and God had just ordered him to quit. Go else-where and repeat his performance?

Frankie was wrestling with these questions one grey afternoon as he made his way home from the library. What he badly needed, he decided as he crossed a vacant lot and swung onto Grove Street, was another sign from God. He needed another sign to tell him what next. Lost in thought, Frankie was half a block from home before he noticed the white man sitting on the front steps of his rooming house. He hadn't seen another white man in the neighborhood since he'd arrived. This one wore a brown sports jacket, a white shirt and tie. Frankie kept walking, then stopped. The man stood up.

Frankie spun on his heel. He took two steps back the way he'd come—then wheeled again. It was like someone had kicked him in the stomach. Gasping for breath, doubled over, he grabbed a railing and steadied himself. This was impossible. His father was home in Sainte-Thérèse, drinking and running up bills. He couldn't be here in San Francisco! Yet here he was, trotting towards him: "Frankie! Frankie, are you all right?"

Breathless, unable to speak, Frankie lowered himself onto the nearest steps. He sat shaking his head as his father patted his shoulder: "You all right, son? Don't try to talk. Just take it easy."

Talk about shock. Nothing could have rattled Frankie more than to find his father in San Francisco. The moment he spotted the old man on the front steps of the rooming house, his unorthodox Christianity was doomed—though he didn't realize it.

Frankie pulled himself together and invited his father into the house. The visitor sat on the single chair in the room, a flesh-and-blood apparition, while Frankie stretched out on the bed. He was still too stunned to talk and his father described his train ride, coach-class, across the continent from Montreal. The people he'd met, the sights he'd seen. Then he produced photographs of Sainte-Thérèse—of the house, of his brother and sisters, his mother. After about ten minutes, apropos of nothing, Frankie blurted: "You were supposed to put that thousand dollars against the bills. Not spend it on a train ticket."

"Your mother and I talked it over, son. We thought visiting you was more important."

"When did you decide that?"

"A couple of weeks ago. After we received your typewritten story."

"My pamphlet? Why did YOU come instead of her?"

"I wanted to come, Frankie. And one of us had to stay with the kids."

"What about your job?"

"I had another week of holidays coming and figured I might as well use it." His father stood up. "Look, why don't I go back to my hotel room, get cleaned up. Maybe we can have supper together?"

This Frankie welcomed. Everything was happening so fast. Having said goodbye to his father, he stretched out on his bed and closed his eyes. He could see his parents sitting in the kitchen at Sainte-Thérèse, talking about him. Obviously, they didn't believe the end of the world was at hand. They thought he'd gone nuts. But then, hadn't the Bible warned him? No man is a prophet in his own land. Probably his father would try to talk him into returning home. This visit was a last temptation, a final test. Frankie steeled himself.

The next three days he spent rambling around San Francisco with his father. They rode cable cars, window-shopped in Chinatown, ate lobster at Fisherman's Wharf. For eight months Frankie had lived like an urban hermit and the city's vitality knocked him out. So much activity still going on! But again the Bible came to his rescue: "They did eat, they drank, they married wives and were given in marriage, until the day that Noah entered the ark, and the flood came and destroyed them all."

Alone at night, shaken despite his resolution, Frankie reviewed the experiences that had brought him to this moment: the storm-tossed baptism, the manifestation of Jesus, the temptation by the devil, the vision of the end. No getting around it. He'd seen what he'd seen, and what he'd seen proved that the end of the world was at hand.

His father listened patiently, but preferred to reminisce about his own boyhood. Strolling along The

Embarcadero in the sunshine, he recalled the impact of the Great Depression: "Paw had been working the race tracks here in the States, mostly Chicago. But then the Depression got worse and the American government barred Canadians from those jobs. Paw returned to Montreal and rented a big old place on Cathedral Street, you remember it? Turned it into a rooming house."

"Dad, none of that matters any more."

His father took out a pack of cigarettes and stood staring out at the freighters in the harbour. "We all had to help out—cleaning rooms, preparing meals. Sometimes the roomers couldn't pay the rent. When I was fifteen, I got my first full-time job—making gloves in a factory in Lachine. I wanted to stay in school but I was the oldest of five kids. Worked six days a week, ten hours a day. Seventeen bucks a week, they paid me. And I was glad to get it."

"Dad, didn't you read *What God Has Done For Me?*"

"I read it, son." Slowly, his father lit a cigarette. "I'm just not sure what it means."

"This is the end of the world!"

His father clapped him on the shoulder. "Come on, Frankie. I'll buy you a coffee."

And so it went.

Frankie wanted to talk apocalypse and his father wanted to talk anything but. The next afternoon, having walked through Golden Gate Park to Ocean Beach, the two stood in the sand and Frankie said: "This is it. This is where God baptized me."

"Don't move." His father was looking through the lens of his camera. "Great shot. Perfect." He removed the camera from his neck. "Here, Frankie. Now you take one of me."

His father removed his shoes and stepped into the water up to his ankles. "Commemorate my visit."

"Dad, there's no point commemorating anything. This is the end of the world, remember?"

"Careful you don't shoot directly into the sun."

Later, they went to the restaurant down the highway, where Frankie had seen his face as that of an angel. The mirrors were gone. Over coffee, his father said he'd once had a religious experience of his own. "Not a major one, like yours. But I remember it vividly. Never told anybody, not even your mother."

Then he described how, shortly after losing his job with Blue Cross, he was walking home one night from Coeur d'Aimée. He'd gone into Montreal to apply for a sales job and found it already taken. On his way home, he stopped off in Coeur d'Aimée for a couple of beers. Missed the last bus and had to walk the two miles. Early autumn, this was, the night chilly but not freezing cold. "I was feeling low," he said, "kind of down on myself. As I was passing the monastery—you know, on the hill?—I sensed a . . . a presence. I looked up at the sky, all bright with stars, and I swear I heard a voice say, 'Your father is with you, my son. Be at peace.'"

"'Your father is with you?'"

He nodded, took out his cigarettes. "Two days later, I got a phone call. The first guy hadn't worked out. The sales job was mine if I wanted it." He finished lighting up and shook out his match. "Right away, I thought of that voice."

"And you didn't tell anybody."

"Sounded ridiculous."

"What about your Christian responsibility?"

"I considered the experience private. Between me and God."

Frankie slurped at his coffee.

That evening, from a phone booth, they telephoned his mother in Sainte-Thérèse. His father, who'd phoned earlier, said a few words, then handed him the phone. Frankie hadn't heard his mother's voice in a year. Suddenly she was right next door. Everybody was well. But then: "You're coming home with your father?"

"Mum, I've got work to do here."

"You can get a job in Montreal and help out if you want."

"Mum, I'm not doing that any more. This is the end of the world."

"You were going to be a writer."

"That doesn't mean anything, Mum. Didn't you read *What God Has Done For Me?*"

"I read it, Frankie."

"You've got to believe, Mum. You've got to believe so you'll be saved."

His mother said nothing.

"Mum?" He pressed the receiver tight against his ear. "Are you there?"

"I'm here, Frankie."

"Mum, please don't cry! As long as you believe in Jesus, everything will be all right."

"Frankie, I want you to come home."

"Mum, please!" He too started crying. "You've got to believe so you'll be saved. Tell me you believe, Mum. Tell me you believe."

"I believe in you, Frankie. But I want you to come home."

"Not in me, Mum. Not in—" But he was crying too hard to continue.

"Here, son, take this."

Frankie traded the telephone for a handkerchief.

His father said goodbye for both of them, then led the way to a restaurant across the street. They sat in a booth drinking yet more coffee. Frankie was still having trouble talking. Hearing his mother's voice had upset him far more than he'd expected. His father was saying something about having reserved a second train ticket. "We can pick it up tomorrow. Train leaves next day. That'll give you time to pack, say any good-byes."

"What are you talking about? I'm not going anywhere. I've got work to do."

"What work?"

"My Father's work."

"Frankie, I'm your father. And I think you've been here long enough—too long. You got involved with the wrong bunch, started taking drugs. What you need— "

"This has nothing to do with drugs. I'll never deny the things I've seen. Pretend I didn't see them."

"I'm not asking you to deny anything. But maybe a change of scene—"

"Dad, it's all in the Bible. 'No man, having put his hand to the plow and looking back, is fit for the kingdom of God.'"

"I've made mistakes, Frankie. I know that." His father looked down at the table. When he looked up again, he had tears in his eyes. "All I can say is . . . I love you."

"Jesus said: 'He that loves father or mother more than me is not worthy of me.'"

"Frankie, I'm asking you to come home."

"This is a last temptation. I'm not going any-where. That's final."

Two days later, alone again, Frankie resumed his routine. He went for long walks, spent hours in the religion section of the downtown public library. Only now he had trouble concentrating. His father was gone, but he'd left Frankie awash in memories. He'd colored the old man bad, but now he remembered how, once or twice a year, with Uncle Henry visiting, he'd hang a white sheet in the front room, dig out his projector and show the black-and-white movies he'd made as a young man.

Frankie remembered his masterpiece, a twenty-minute feature called *Retribution*. His father wrote the screenplay and starred as a smooth-talking hoodlum who masterminds a heist, double-crosses his cronies and ends up plunging to his death from a train bridge.

That brought back the old man's love of literature. Frankie remembered how, whenever he complained he had nothing to do, his father would rush off into the front porch, rummage around in his bookcase and return carrying half a dozen dog-eared paperbacks. "Here, you son of a gun! *The Grapes of Wrath!*"

"Maurice, he's just turned fourteen."

"Doesn't matter. You've read *Call of The Wild*? Here's *Martin Eden*. Same author. Here, take it. Or look! *You Can't Go Home Again!*"

He'd flip open the novel and begin reading aloud, waving his arms. When he'd finished he'd snap the book shut: "Here! Read Thomas Wolfe. And don't tell me you've got nothing to do."

All this, during the past year, Frankie had forgotten. Again he recalled the night of the butcher knife. But now he remembered, as well, that next day at lunch, his father tried to apologize. Tried to explain that alcohol makes people say things they don't mean.

Frankie said: "Can I go now?"

Too young to forgive, or even to understand. Was that still the case? Now, as he sat on the steps of the public library in the California sunshine, Frankie

280

wondered: had he judged his father too harshly? And what of his mother? He kept hearing her sob-choked voice saying she wanted him home.

He'd withstood that last temptation.

But the world refused to end and still no new sign. What was he supposed to do? Resume his old job, save like crazy and produce another thousand copies of *What God Has Done For Me*? That didn't sound right. If God wanted more people to read his pamphlet, all He had to do was make *The Chronicle* run it on page one. Maybe he'd finished with San Francisco. Maybe he was supposed to shake the dust off his feet, go elsewhere and do it all again. But where? Los Angeles? New Orleans?

Wait a minute. Maybe his father's visit hadn't been a last temptation, after all. Slowly Frankie rose to his feet. Maybe it was a sign. Maybe God wanted him to return home. Frankie looked up at the blue sky. He'd go to the bank, that was it. See how much money he had. Then he'd visit the bus depot. If he had enough for a bus ticket to Montreal, that would be confirmation. If he didn't, that would mean he wasn't supposed to go—not yet, anyway.

Frankie hurried down the stairs. As he reached the bottom, he broke into a trot. Montreal! Sainte-Thérèse! He was going home to Sainte-Thérèse!

34.

My last morning on Jubilation I awoke strangely early and didn't know why. The light was grey. I huddled deeper into my sleeping bag, determined to re-enter oblivion. Then came a tapping sound, a gentle brushing, at the west window. Incredulous, I thought: Snow? In early September?

On my feet, disbelieving, I looked out. Giant snowflakes were falling like petals, but so thickly that I couldn't see twenty feet. A fragment from James Joyce danced through my mind, something about snowflakes falling faintly through the universe on the living and the dead.

That led me to marvel yet again at Frankie's post-Christian revival, which began in Sainte-Thérèse. Even before leaving California, of course, he'd had doubts. But every time he reviewed his experience, he drew the same conclusion. He'd seen what he'd seen, and what he'd seen proved Jesus was true. He had no choice but to bear witness.

Back home in Sainte-Thérèse, this meant telling and retelling the story of his conversion—how he was baptized, tempted by the devil, saved by the manifesting of Jesus. Old friends and neighbours dropped by when they learned of the prodigal's return, and Frankie felt driven to stand in the living room of his parents' house and tell his story to anybody who'd listen, ending always with his vision of the end of the world, his voice ringing with conviction as he declared, "Give glory to God!"

Some people went silent. Others chuckled. Frankie almost converted his teenage brother, but one old friend left shaking his head: "I can't handle this."

His Uncle Henry managed to change the subject, and later Frankie heard him whisper to his father: "Too much LSD. He'll get over it."

The reaction that hit Frankie hardest came from his ten-year-old sister, whom he overheard: "Mom, what's the matter with Frankie? He's gotten like . . . I don't know, sort of like those Jehovah's Witnesses you hide from."

"Just shush up, Maureen, will you?"

Frankie continued to testify. He strove to give the impression that his conviction was unshakeable. But in truth he was reeling. For months, in San Francisco, he'd lived in silence, working and reading the Bible. Now he couldn't hear himself think over the non-stop blaring of television. Sometimes he'd don an old duffle coat, never mind the weather, and plunge into the winter streets.

But the town itself challenged his faith. Frankie was overwhelmed by its concreteness, its reality—by the continuity it represented. Here was the telephone pole that had served him and his friends as a base for hide and seek; there a shuttered cottage in which he'd stolen his first kiss. The Haight-Ashbury? It didn't exist.

In San Francisco, he'd reasoned that if he could make his father stop drinking, he'd save the family. Suddenly, things didn't look that simple. His mother fretted endlessly about money, but now she worked at home making silkscreen calendars and burlap placemats, and always there was food on the table. His father still had the occasional beer, but never did he come home drunk. He talked mostly about retirement: "You never know. Your mother and I might find each other again."

Christmas came and went. The world showed no sign of ending and Frankie went looking for work. He landed a job installing telephone equipment in office buildings. It was exactly what he wanted—steady work that left him free to think. He moved again into Montreal, renting a room in the McGill Ghetto. There he hoped to spend more time alone, to examine his faith—and his experience—without being called upon continually to proclaim it.

But in the city he came up against other problems. Frankie was part of a crew assigned to run telephone cable from one floor of an office to another, an extended project. Trouble was, the office was teeming with good-looking women. One, in particular, smiled invitingly every time she caught his eye. At night he'd lay awake remembering. Unable to masturbate—what? desecrate the temple of the Holy Ghost?—Frankie began having wet dreams.

He was fretting about this one evening, out walking, when he noticed that a movie by an old favorite director was about to begin: Antonioni's *Blow-Up*. On impulse he bought a ticket and entered. The movie tells the story of a photographer who takes secret photos of a woman in a park. Later, in his studio, he enlarges these pictures and discovers that, in the leafy distance, a man is being murdered. He returns to the park and finds a dead body in the bushes. Only later, when the photographer brings others to see the evidence, the body is gone.

Frankie emerged shaken. The photogapher could be thought to have created a reality out of something that never happened. Had he himself done that? No way. He'd seen what he'd seen with his own eyes: Jesus, the devil, himself as an angel. This was personal experience. He'd seen what he'd seen, and what he'd seen proved Jesus was true.

A few days later, still fretting, Frankie visited St. Joseph's Oratory—the massive domed cathedral that is both a Montreal landmark and a Roman Catholic shrine. Though he wouldn't have put it this way, Frankie was seeking respite from the doubts that had been assailing him since his return from San Francisco. If he could find peace nowhere but in a Catholic shrine, then to a Catholic shrine he'd go.

The Oratory was almost empty, eerily silent—the perfect place to put that unsettling movie behind him. Frankie strolled around the basilica admiring frescoes and statues and stained-glass windows depicting the life of Saint-Joseph, patron saint of laborers, families and the universal church. In a darkened room he watched a short movie about Brother André, the humble door keeper who'd built the Oratory. The man had subsisted for years on flour and water and potatoes. He'd worn hair shirts and iron chains and chastised himself on winter nights by taking ice-cold shower-baths.

In the shrine itself, the heart and soul of the basilica, Frankie stood surrounded by crutches and canes and braces, hundreds of them strung up on the wall and attesting to miracles. He read the testimonials carved in stone—"To dear St. Joseph, Sincere thanks," and *"Reconnaissance à St. Joseph pour faveur obtenue"*—and wondered what it was about Brother André that had inspired people to travel for days to pray to him, and later to draw up petitions to have him beatified, seeking eventually to have him canonized as a saint? Could Frankie really identify with this flummery and nonsense?

A young priest and a middle-aged woman had come into the shrine, and, despite himself, Frankie tuned into their conversation. *"Des fois les experiences religieuses sont des pièges,"* the priest was saying. "Sometimes religious experiences are a trap because as soon as we have them we forget Jesus and build our faith around them. You must separate your faith from your experience. Put your faith not in the things you have seen, but in Jesus himself—Jesus crucified on the cross."

The hair on the back of Frankie's neck started to tingle. The young priest was talking, not solely to the woman, but also to him. Separate his faith from his experience? Believe not in the things he'd seen with his own eyes, but in things he'd only read about? The idea was ludicrous.

Now the priest was warning the woman to beware of the subtle dangers that threaten the spiritual lives of those who trust in their own experience. But Frankie was only half listening. His mind was racing. Separate faith from experience and he'd be left believing only in experience. He didn't believe in Jesus at all—but rather in the things he'd seen. And what, he asked himself, what if there were another way to explain those things? A way that would take into account more nuances and complexities?

The tingling spread down his back. Suddenly, Frankie was trembling with excitement. He laughed aloud and saw the priest and the woman glance over, puzzled. *"Merci, mon père,"* he called to the priest. Then, looking up at the ceiling, he cried, *"Merci, Saint-Joseph!"*

Frankie wheeled and left the shrine at a run. He didn't believe in Jesus at all, but in his own experience.

He trotted through the Oratory and out the front door. Sunshine! At the foot of the stairs he broke into a sprint. Once more he cried, *"Merci, Saint-Joseph!"* Then he raced for the road that would take him around the mountain and back to the heart of the city. Separate faith from experience and Frankie McCracken was born again.

Three months later he met Camille and began falling in love. Meanwhile, intellectually, he retraced his original path at a blazing pace. He again plunged into existentialism and proclaimed that God is dead—though with less conviction. That's where he stood in October of 1969, and on Mount Jubilation I realized that on the night I died—down in St. Petersburg, Florida—Frankie in Montreal was virtually himself again, and he dreamed that he saw me waving to him, signalling, and understood that I wanted him to go back on the road.

Now here we were on the mountain. Alone in the tower, as the morning slowly brightened, I stood shaking my head and watching the snowflakes fall. Cloud-split sunbeams turned the giant, tumbling flakes a million shades of pink and red and in this I recognized my own last sign: a shower of roses from Saint Thérèse de Lisieux.

I pulled on my hiking boots and climbed down the ladder. The snow, soft and powdery, lay two inches thick on the ground. Squirrels and chipmunks had criss-crossed the path to the cabin. Mounting the front steps, I cried, "Frankie!" Thumped on the door. "It's show-time."

"I'm up! Come on in."

I stomped the snow off my feet and entered the cabin. Frankie, fully dressed but bootless, stood hunched over the wood stove lighting matches.

I said, "Have you looked outside?"

He fanned a spark to no avail. "What's to see?"

"Would you believe snow faintly falling?"

Frankie glanced at my wet boots and stepped to the window. "I don't believe it! The warden said it wouldn't snow until Labor Day."

"It's a message from Saint Thérèse."

"Fantastic! Even if it melts, the snow has already reduced the fire hazard to zero. There's no point keeping me here."

"I thought you liked it here."

"I do, I do." Frankie was pacing back and forth, rubbing his hands together. "But I've got places to go, people to see."

"Take your readings," I said. "Talk to the warden. I'll make breakfast."

Frankie pulled on his boots, grabbed his jacket and disappeared out the door. To make breakfast I went into overdrive. Within minutes I had the woodstove crackling and breakfast on the table.

Frankie came through the door stamping his feet and talking: "They weren't expecting this weather so they have no horses at the Crossing. But they'll ride up to collect me and my gear within the next couple of days." He shucked off his jacket and flung it on the bed. "I'll have just enough time to burn the garbage and clean up. Bring some wood inside, cover the rest with plastic sheeting."

"Breakfast is served," I said, whipping paper napkins off the plates.

"Scrambled eggs and bacon?" Frankie sat down at the table. "Where'd you get the bacon?"

I sat down beside him. "Had it in my pack."

"But it must be bad."

I reached over, took half a package of bacon from the counter behind the woodstove and handed it to him.

"Still frozen. How the —"

"Magic is alive." I started to eat. "Dig in. Your breakfast's getting cold."

"You must have brought a special cooler."

After breakfast I packed my rucksack, rearranged the top layer and tightened the straps. Then I made another pot of coffee. When Frankie finished the dishes he sat down with me at the table: "Listen, I'm feeling bad about blowing up yesterday. I've enjoyed your Kerouac fantasy. I just can't get into it, that's all."

"Not to worry, Frankie." From a side pocket of my rucksack, almost as an afterthought, I pulled a dog-eared copy of *Ulysses*. "Here, I want you to have this. Joyce is the father of us all."

Frankie took the book: "I don't know what to say."

"That's professional development." I pulled on my jacket. "Leaves only magic and human relations."

"Come again?"

I dragged my rucksack across the floor: "Help me get this outside."

Frankie held the door while I swung my pack onto the porch. The snow had stopped falling but covered the dark green branches of the trees and lay an inch thick along the rails of the log fence.

We stood a moment, enjoying the transformation. Then I picked up my rucksack and led Frankie down the steps and out the front gate. We had to sit together one last time on the gnarled grey stump. I dropped my rucksack at the foot of the tower while Frankie brushed snow off the stump and sat down. As I joined him, he said, "Magic and human relations?"

"The last shall be first," I said. "Just look at this day!" I waved my arm to take in the sunshine, the sky now cloudless and blue, the whipped-cream mountain peaks. "This calls for champagne."

289

"I'd settle for more applejack."

"Why settle when you can have bubbly?" I reached around behind the stump, produced a bottle of chilled Mumm's and two champagne glasses: "*Voila!*"

Frankie gaped: "How the—"

I wedged the glasses between us on the stump, popped the cork and poured. Handing Frankie a glass, I said, "Be sure there's champagne in it."

Still speechless, he stared at me, hard.

"Emotional honesty," I said.

"Sleight of hand," Frankie said. "Cooled the bottle in the snow. But you're best I've ever seen. Ever work as a magician?"

"Here's to human relations." I picked up the other glass and grinned. "To Camille."

Tentatively, Frankie drank the toast. "What about Camille?"

"Frankie, with women you're sliding. You're back to where you were before your stint as Saint Jack of the Sixteen-Page Pamphlet."

"Don't let's start this again."

"You were rolling down the highway and women were gas stations, remember? 'Check your oil, mister?' In San Francisco, you got spun around and found yourself bouncing through uncharted territory, a desert of dunes and empty roads. You didn't get your bearings until Camille."

"So what about her?"

"Well, we could start with the night you tried to whip off a quickie with Barbara."

"Okay, so you've talked with her."

"She forgave you. Now you—"

"I don't want to discuss it."

"Nobody's perfect, Frankie. If San Francisco taught you nothing else . . . .'"

"I said I don't want to discuss it."

"Prepare to grovel, Frankie." I downed the last of my champagne, stood and carefully set the glass on the stump. "Maybe she'll give you another chance."

"You're not leaving yet?" He stood up.

"Can't ignore the proprieties."

Together we strolled to the tower, but as I bent to retrieve my rucksack, Frankie jumped me from behind, locked me into a half-nelson. "You're not going anywhere," he said, twisting my right arm up behind my back. "Not until you tell me how you know so much about me."

"You sure you want to do this? I was once Black Mask Champeen of my neighborhood."

He twisted my arm higher. "Who the hell are you?"

I gave him an elbow and we fell to the ground in a tangle. Frankie was quicker than I'd expected, stronger than he looked, and we rolled around in the snow at the foot of the tower. Finally, I let him flip me over onto my belly. He straddled me, bent my left arm high and folded a knee over the hold. "All right, who are you?"

"I'm Jack Kerouac."

"I said, who are you!"

"Jean-Louis Francois Alexandre Lebris de Kerouac?"

"Listen, wise guy, how do you know so much about me?"

"Angels are like that."

"You've got an agenda."

"Yes! I want your confession."

"You're holding out on me. Who the hell are you?"

"I'm your brother, your father, your son."

"Cut the crap."

"Your ghost, your shadow, your guardian angel. Frankie, I'm your Doctor Sax."

He twisted my arm higher still.

"You fool! I'm your Self!" In a single impossible motion, I tossed Frankie into the air and sprang to my feet. He landed on his butt, astonished, and I helped him up.

"That was quite a move," he said.

"Black Mask Champeen."

"You're not going to tell me who you are."

I laughed and shook my head and he interpreted this as a "no." I brushed myself off and retrieved my rucksack and this time Frankie insisted on helping me adjust it.

We faced each other and I held out my hand. "Angels can grant wishes, you know."

Frankie shook my hand and grinned. "I don't believe in angels. But I enjoyed our Sinatra duets. Maybe you'll leave me your voice?"

"You've got your own. But if you think you can survive cheap shots, you're welcome to my point of view."

"That should come in handy. Sorry about the rough stuff."

"It's been real, Frankie."

"Be careful going down."

"I'm not going down." I strode over to the tower and started to climb. "I'm going up."

"Want to take a last look around? Why didn't you say so? Leave your pack here."

I kept climbing.

When I reached the platform, I shoved my rucksack through the trap door and clambered after it. Frankie started up the ladder. By the time he joined me in the office, I had my pack on my back and the north window open.

"I didn't want to do this, Frankie, but you've left me no choice." I pulled a red rose out of his shirt pocket and fixed it in his wild black hair, then laughed at the look on his face. "Take care of yourself."

Quickly, then, I climbed onto the chair and stepped out the open window into thin air—or so it would have appeared to Frankie. In truth I stepped onto an invisible dirt road that wound past the tower and rolled away over the mountains, up, up and away.

In my best W. C. Fields voice, I said, "Magic is alive, my boy." Then, in my own voice: "If I am your Self, what are we doing here?"

I turned and strode away up the road.

I hadn't gone twenty paces when Frankie hollered: "Kerouac! Jack Kerouac!"

I turned and did a little jig. "So you do know my full name."

"Wait for me!" Frankie started to climb out the window. "I want to come with you."

"Frankie, no! You've got work to do."

He stopped: "I need you, Jack!"

"I'm with you."

"Jack, don't go! I—I love you."

One last time I drew on Sinatra, broke into song: *S'wonderful / s'marvellous / that you should care for me.*

Frankie laughed despite himself and I watched understanding settle into his face as he perched there on the window sill, my rose glowing red in his wild dark hair. I saw his pride and foolishness fall away and recognized the angel he'd found in the mirror by the ocean, the boy who took his heart into the streets of San Francisco.

I waved once more, and this time, tentatively, Frankie waved back. Finally I turned, hefted my rucksack higher and, madly whistling *When The Saints*, strode away over the mountains.

AUTHOR'S NOTE

KEROUAC'S GHOST is a revised version of a book published in Canada by Pottersfield Press as *Visions of Kerouac: A Novel.* I've changed the point of view; added, deleted and juggled chapters; and wrestled again with the language.

My example is John Fowles. In a foreword to *The Magus: A Revised Version,* the British author reveals that he rewrote his novel not simply because he felt he could improve it, but because he loved it.

Ken McGoogan